"Don't worry. I've got this." Bentley captured her hand and leaned his elbow on the truck's center console.

And he did have this—her truck, her thoughts, *her future*. If he wanted to be with her.

What if Bentley wanted children? She sat up, wanting to get to her doctor's appointment as quickly as possible. "Ow."

"You okay?" Bentley asked, casting her a worried glance.

"Yes." There was ambiguity ahead. Lots of it. In too many parts of her life. Cassie needed answers. She hated change.

"Be careful getting Mia out," Cassie told Bentley when he'd parked in front of the Bent Nickel and was releasing Mia from her child seat.

"Don't worry." Bentley deposited the little girl on the asphalt. "I've got this."

Cassie followed Mia toward the Bent Nickel. Bentley looped an arm around her waist and gently swept her toward the door.

Those small touches. Those words of reassurance. They'd be stopping once she'd fully recuperated. Cassie almost wished she could hold off her recovery a little longer.

Dear Reader,

When I was in middle school, I thought it would be fun to ride bareback *and* double in my sister's forty-acre pasture. I rode behind my niece on her horse and everything was fine until my niece decided to jump a fallen tree. Off I went, landing on the log and severing all but a slim connection of my kneecap to the rest of my leg. Regrets? I had a few. I've been a saddle rider ever since. Which leads me to the kernel of an idea that started *A Cowgirl's Secret*.

Cassie Diaz is in a bind. Money is tight on the Bar D Ranch. But there's hope—if she can last eight seconds on a bull. When things don't go as she'd hoped and she's faced with medical bills, Cassie needs to find an alternate solution to come up with some money. Enter handsome engineer Bentley Monroe. He might be able to fix the family's retired kiddie carnival rides, but in the process of repairing them, he challenges her heart and her dedication to the ranching life.

I had a lot of fun writing Cassie and Bentley's fish-out-of-water romance. I hope you come to love The Mountain Monroes as much as I do. Each book is connected but also stands alone.

Happy reading!

Melinda

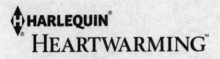

HARLEQUIN®
HEARTWARMING™

ISBN-13: 978-1-335-42642-0

A Cowgirl's Secret

Harlequin Enterprises ULC
22 Adelaide St. West, 40th Floor
Toronto, Ontario M5H 4E3, Canada
www.Harlequin.com

Printed in U.S.A.

Recycling programs
for this product may
not exist in your area.

HEARTWARMING

A Cowgirl's Secret

———

Melinda Curtis

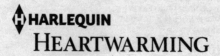

HARLEQUIN
HEARTWARMING

Melinda Curtis, prior to writing romance, was a junior manager for a Fortune 500 company, which meant when she flew on the private jet, she was relegated to the jump seat—otherwise known as the potty (seriously, the commode had a seat belt). After grabbing her pen (and a parachute), she made the jump to full-time writer. Melinda has become a *USA TODAY* bestselling author, and her Harlequin Heartwarming book Dandelion Wishes is now a TV movie—*Love in Harmony Valley*.

Brenda Novak says *Season of Change* "found a place on my keeper shelf."

Jayne Ann Krentz says of *Can't Hurry Love*, "Nobody does emotional, heartwarming small-town romance like Melinda Curtis."

Sheila Roberts says *Can't Hurry Love* is "a page turner filled with wit and charm."

Books by Melinda Curtis

The Mountain Monroes

Rescued by the Perfect Cowboy
Lassoed by the Would-Be Rancher
Enchanted by the Rodeo Queen
Charmed by the Cook's Kids
The Littlest Cowgirls

Return of the Blackwell Brothers

The Rancher's Redemption

The Blackwell Sisters

Montana Welcome

Visit the Author Profile page at Harlequin.com for more titles.

THE MOUNTAIN MONROES FAMILY TREE

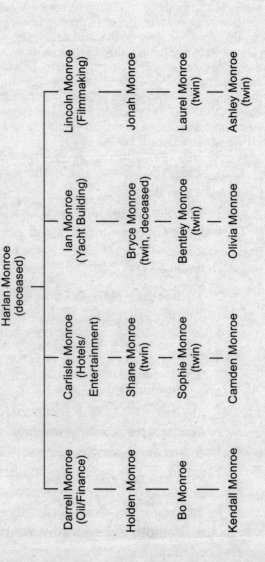

Harlan Monroe
(deceased)

Darrell Monroe
(Oil/Finance)

Holden Monroe

Bo Monroe

Kendall Monroe

Carlisle Monroe
(Hotels/
Entertainment)

Shane Monroe
(twin)

Sophie Monroe
(twin)

Camden Monroe

Ian Monroe
(Yacht Building)

Bryce Monroe
(twin, deceased)

Bentley Monroe
(twin)

Olivia Monroe

Lincoln Monroe
(Filmmaking)

Jonah Monroe

Laurel Monroe
(twin)

Ashley Monroe
(twin)

PROLOGUE

DON'T BE SHY, they said.

They being the Diaz family, encouraging Cassie Diaz to be brave.

Stick to horses, they said.

They being Cassie's brother and grandfather.

Grow up, they said.

Okay, maybe that last one was Cassie's.

Cassie was twenty-nine, and for the first time in her life, she was getting on a bull in a rodeo competition. Her family was going to be very proud of her.

If Cassie survived this ride.

The bull she'd drawn was Tornado Tom, a blue-gray beast that had dumped more cowboys than had lasted eight seconds on his back. This end-of-July rodeo was his first go-round with a cowgirl. History was about to be made by both of them. And hopefully, she'd add to her footnote in history by winning a much-needed purse.

Cassie lowered herself on Tornado Tom's broad, muscular back, and nodded toward the cowboy operating the gate.

CHAPTER ONE

"I TOLD YOU SO, CASSIE." Cassie's brother, Rhett, shook his head.

Cassie dropped her saddle back on the stand, having only lifted it a few inches. She leaned on the horn and cantle, trying to ease the pain that stretched from the top of her hip to her inner thigh. "Don't start."

Don't tell her she shouldn't have tried bull riding.

Don't tell her she should have stuck to horse training.

Don't tell her horse training wasn't going to pay the bills.

There came a point in every young woman's life where she had to accept that some dreams were never coming true—hers being making a decent living training horses. At this point, unless she won the lottery, she needed to set aside girlish dreams and get "a real job," whatever that was.

Cassie wasn't ready. And honestly, she might never be.

Rhett chuckled. "You winning that purse was a long shot, kind of like Grandpa winning the lottery with that ticket he buys every week."

Exactly.

"And here we go," Cassie muttered, glancing at Baby, the quarter horse she'd been trying to saddle when a spasm from her bull-beaten hip sidelined her. "Rhett is on a roll."

"Indeed, I am." Rhett tipped up his black cowboy hat and grinned. "I'm surprised you can walk after that bull stomped on your hip."

The emergency room doctor had been surprised, too. Not that she'd beaten all odds. The orthopedic specialist had given some grim news. News Cassie hadn't shared with her family, because...

"You never should have gotten on that bull, sis."

Because of that. Cassie gritted her teeth and stared at the barn rafters at the Bar D. She hadn't told her family she was considering giving up the ranching life, partly because it was terrifying, and partly because no one in her family had ever given up ranching life— not in five generations.

She continued to stare at the rafters, settling her cowboy hat more firmly on her head. There were cobwebs up there that needed tending to, if one was bothered by such things, which she was, unlike Rhett, who tended to go through life as happy with a tidy environment as a messy one. He preferred to spend his time on extreme experiences, like zip-lining and bungee-jumping off bridges.

Cassie's gaze drifted back down to the photo gallery on the wall behind her brother.

During a streak of good luck and flush bank accounts, her father had insulated the Bar D's barn, which came in handy five or six months out of the year when Second Chance, Idaho, was snowed in. But because the insulation had to be held in with something, he'd installed cheap wood paneling. And because the paneling was so very bare in the breezeway, he'd hung pictures of Rhett and Cassie competing in rodeos when they were kids—Rhett in calf and trick roping, Cassie in barrel racing and trick riding.

Back when I thought that's what I'd do with the rest of my life: cowgirling.

Like horse training or trick riding offered a health plan and retirement benefits. How naive she'd been.

Those pictures had been taken before Cassie's parents decided to take a job managing someone else's ranch in Wyoming and handed back the reins of the Bar D to Grandpa

Diaz. Before Cassie began keeping the Bar D's books and worrying about making ends meet.

Although Rhett looked at the bank balance every month, for some reason he never worried. That made Cassie both annoyed and envious.

"I'm headed into town." Grandpa Diaz walked into the barn, gray felt cowboy hat as dirty as if he'd been tossed in the rodeo arena. He gave her a gap-toothed grin, having had some teeth kicked out the last time he went competitive bronc riding twenty-some years ago. "Want to come with me, Cassie?"

"She sure does." Rhett untied Baby and led him back to his stall, boot heels kicking up dust. "She needs to shake off that injury."

Grandpa gave Cassie an assessing glance. As the only female in two generations of the family, Cassie had always been measured by a cowboy yardstick. "Still?"

"No." Cassie straightened, albeit slowly. "But I'll drive you into town." Grandpa's latest diabetes medicine had given him the shakes. The old man was beginning to need extra care.

A few minutes later, Cassie sat behind the wheel of her pickup, wishing she'd bought a new set of shocks instead of entering that bull riding competition a week ago. She felt every bump on the pine-tree-lined driveway out to the highway. "Should I ask why you're going into town? Is this another coffee date?"

Ever since he'd declared himself semiretired, Grandpa had become very popular with the females of Second Chance.

"Nope. I heard a new Monroe is in town."

Cassie rolled her eyes. Harlan Monroe had bought out Second Chance a decade ago, including the Bar D. He'd turned around and charged everyone he'd bought from who wanted to stay a one-dollar-a-year lease, hoping to give a leg up to citizens and keep his hometown from becoming a ghost town. Earlier this year, Harlan's death meant that ownership of Second Chance passed to his eleven living adult grandchildren plus one. The plus one since two-year-old Poppy inherited in place of her deceased dad. The future of those with leases in town was uncertain, including the Diaz family and the Bar D. It was why Cassie had entered a women's bull riding contest. They needed money in case they were evicted come January 1.

And now she needed money for hip surgery. Talk about out of the frying pan and into the fire.

"This Monroe fella is supposed to be an engine builder." Grandpa sounded enthusiastic.

Cassie couldn't imagine why.

"I've been thinking…"

Here comes another one of Grandpa's wild ideas.

"…we've got all those kiddie carnival rides in the second barn, just sitting there rusting. Maybe this fella can get them working again."

Cassie blew out a breath. "Why?"

"Folks used to pay good money for their kids to ride them."

"But not in the past twenty years, and not in Second Chance." Her parents and grandparents used to take those kiddie rides on the road six or seven months out of the year, providing entertainment at fairs, rodeos and carnivals around the West, keeping the Bar D afloat.

Grandpa tilted his hat at a jaunty angle. "It's time to hedge our bets."

"Fixing up those rides will cost us." Money they couldn't afford to lose. Not to mention the strong backs required to move them from fair to fair every few days.

"Pfft." Grandpa waved a hand. "These Monroes are donating a lot of time and resources to help folks in Second Chance. I bet this Monroe fella will help us for free."

Cassie said nothing. Her luck recently hadn't been betworthy.

SHOULDERS HUNCHED, BENTLEY MONROE sat on the couch in the lobby of the Lodgepole Inn and held on to his tea mug with both hands, trying to make his six-foot-two frame small enough not to get kicked or stepped on.

A preteen girl leaped past, wearing pink ballet slippers, pink tights, a pink leotard and a pink tutu. Classical music filled the room. Bentley thought it was a song from *The Nutcracker*. But he also thought the would-be ballerina danced more like a frozen tin soldier than a delicate sugarplum fairy. Then again, what did he know? Being a bachelor and a man who'd worked on boat construction and marine engines most of his adult life, Bentley was out of his element.

Gabby, the pink preteen, came to a stop near the far wall and then headed back doing slow-motion turns in a wobbly line, strawberry blonde ponytail winging through the air. "Laurel, look at me. Laurel? *Laurel.*"

"This cannot be happening." Instead of looking at her stepdaughter, Bentley's cousin Laurel gave him a dirty look from beneath a lock of loopy red hair in need of a brushing. "Hope is two months old. She's already under your spell, Bentley. And all you're doing is sitting there!"

Bentley nodded. It was true. The tiny baby's

feet pedaled in his direction. Earlier, her twin sister, Hazel, had done the same thing. And all he was doing was sitting, wondering where his sister was, pondering his return to the workforce and drinking tea.

"Laurel." Gabby leaped, shaking the floorboards of the historic inn as she landed. "Watch me."

Laurel wrapped a yellow baby blanket tighter around Hope's stretching toes. "Wyatt's coming for a visit next week, and if the twins prefer you to their biological father, he'll be upset."

Bentley nodded. That was most likely true, too. "I can't help it."

Laurel huffed. "For someone who claims not to like kids and animals—"

"I never said I don't like them." That statement had been made by Bentley's cousin Holden decades ago. Somehow the label had stuck.

Laurel huffed again.

"Laurel." Gabby came to a stop in front of Bentley with a wobble and an unfocused look in her eyes that had Bentley reaching out to steady her until the dizziness subsided. "I'm good." The preteen blushed and flounced backward to sit on the raised stone hearth in

front of a massive, centuries-old cooking fire-place. "Laurel."

From her position next to Bentley on the couch, Laurel glanced up at Gabby with a distracted smile. "I'm sorry, Gabs. Hope was squirming." She adjusted Hope's tiny body, tucking in her arms. "Do it again. I promise to watch this time."

"Again?" Bentley muttered, drawing his heels back against the couch.

"Again," Laurel said firmly.

From the apartment behind the check-in desk, Hope's twin sister, Hazel, let out a cry, followed by a near-shouted plea from Laurel's husband, Mitch. *"Honey?"*

Laurel's brow clouded. She half turned, raising her arms as if about to hand Bentley the baby.

Outside the inn, an engine of some sort chugged, sputtered and died. It was music to Bentley's ears.

"Sounds like trouble." Bentley left his tea mug on the coffee table and bolted for the door, eager to escape upset babies and ballerina-in-training tramplings.

A truck had pulled up to the garage bay attached to Second Chance's general store. Mackenzie, the brunette who ran the place, approached the truck with a pleasant smile.

Before he left the porch, Bentley was waylaid by his cousin Shane, who'd moved to Second Chance when they'd inherited the town in January. He'd encouraged all Monroes in their generation to visit Second Chance. Several had moved to town or created second homes here. Bentley didn't plan to follow suit, intending to stay in town only until his estranged sister made an appearance. He was Philadelphia born, raised and loyal. Go, Flyers. Go, Sixers. Go, Eagles.

Shane looked Bentley up and down. "Why do you look so on edge?"

Bentley backtracked, opened the inn's door a crack so that Shane could hear the classical music and then just as quickly closed it again.

"Say no more." Shane held up his hands. "I heard Gabby was taking ballet lessons online."

Bentley headed down the porch stairs. "She's been dancing around the inn nonstop." Since he'd arrived two days ago. Up the creaky stairs. Down the log-lined hallways. Across the antique-filled lobby and back.

Shane matched Bentley step for step. They were of the same height with the same frame and dark brown hair. They also bore a vague family resemblance in their chins and noses. But they couldn't have dressed more differently. Shane in his business casual—khakis, black polo and leather loafers. Bentley in his everyday wear—blue jeans, navy T-shirt and work boots.

"Gabby is sharp as a tack academically," Shane told him. "It galls her that she isn't a natural at anything physical. She'll be practicing until she becomes a prima ballerina or gives it up altogether."

Bentley watched Mackenzie ask the driver to try starting the truck once more. "If she was my kid—"

"Which she's not." Shane tsked. "Take my advice and stay out of it. Laurel just gave birth to twins, just got married and became a stepmom. Think Mama Grizzly and approach any topic that isn't gushingly complimentary about Gabby or the twins with caution."

The truck engine chugged, coughed and caught, running like a gassed athlete on the last leg of a marathon. Bentley's mind spun through the most likely scenarios—clogged air filter, dirty fuel lines, leaky gasket...

Mackenzie had the man shut the engine off.

"There are a lot of people in town today," Shane noted in a shrewd voice.

Bentley's gaze cut to his cousin. "Meaning?"

"Mackenzie's a one-woman general store and repair garage. She won't have time to fix that man's truck." Shane's smile widened. "You could offer your services."

"If you're pitching me a job as the town mechanic, think again." Bentley designed boats and built marine engines, some of which cost far more than that truck when it was new. Or at least, that's what Bentley had done until the conditions of his grandfather's will had turned his world upside down. Grandpa Harlan had left his assets to his four children, but only if they cut off and fired their kids. The intention was that it would make the grandchildren stand on their own two feet. As compensation, Harlan's grandchildren were given Second Chance in the hopes that they would make something of the town and by extension themselves.

Way to show the love, Grandpa.

"Or you could go back inside the inn," Shane continued in faux innocence. "But since you came here to Second Chance to help out with…"

"That's not why I came." Bentley grew increasingly irritable. "You told me Olivia would be here. When will she be here?"

Shane gave Bentley a searching look. "Why can't you just call your sister and get the details yourself?"

Bentley considered how much he wanted

to tell Shane about the rift between himself and Olivia. *Nothing.* "I stopped calling when she stopped answering my calls or replying to my texts."

"Didn't she spend time with you after her racing sailboat capsized?" Shane continued to study Bentley's face. "Did you argue, or was there too much going on in your head to question Olivia when she said she was fine?"

"Not exactly…" Bentley hedged when in fact Shane was practically spot-on with his last guess. Introverts weren't the best at providing emotional support to extroverts.

"Bentley, someday, a woman's going to need you to step up and get involved, even if her first response is that she can handle everything alone." Shane shook his head. "I know you're the family brainiac and human interaction is difficult for you—"

Bentley saw red.

"—but the fact remains, you need something to fill your days, and it's not just me that could use your help." He nodded toward the truck in need of repairs.

Bentley took another look. "Is that him then?" The man who'd shown up in Second Chance last month claiming to be their long-lost cousin?

"Tanner?" Shane shook his head. "No. Tanner drives an older truck, always wears a cowboy hat and has two kids under the age of six."

Shane had asked Bentley to come to Idaho and help prove that Tanner wasn't a Monroe and wasn't entitled to any of their inheritance, which, besides the small town of Second Chance, included an ancient chest full of gold that Shane and his fiancée, a local rancher, had found back in April.

"I still don't understand how I can help." Bentley's gaze kept drifting to the truck, his mind turning over possible diagnoses.

"You're an engineer," Shane said simply. "You approach problems methodically. Who better to prove Tanner isn't our relation than you?"

"The problem would be a lot easier to tackle if Tanner would make an appearance." Bentley hadn't seen the man since he'd arrived.

"He'll come into town soon. He hasn't been in for groceries in nearly a week." Shane put a hand on Bentley's back and gave him a friendly push toward the truck. "Go on. I know you're itching to take a look at that engine."

AN HOUR LATER, Bentley had fixed the truck engine and was tightening the air filter on the old Dodge pickup. He had to admit, it felt good to lose himself in the quiet and the work.

"Laurel says I need fresh air." Gabby wandered over to the service bay, threatening his peace. She'd changed out of her ballerina costume and into bright purple leggings, a pink T-shirt and red sneakers. She wore earbuds and had tucked her phone in a side pocket of her leggings. Without further ado, she began dancing back and forth across the service bay.

Bentley said nothing. His only acknowledgment of her presence was to glance up if she came too close to a wall or the tool-filled shop bench.

The door that connected the garage and the general store opened, and Mackenzie stuck her head out. "Hey, Gabby. Nice moves."

"Thanks." Gabby didn't break stride. "My uncle Bentley is the best audience."

Bentley contained an eye roll. Not at the honorary title of uncle, but at Gabby's perception of him as being an enthusiastic spectator.

"Bentley's a good mechanic, too." Mackenzie grinned. "Are you still okay out here? I feel bad that you're working on that truck for me."

"I'm almost done." The carburetor had been clogged, which explained why the engine had been cutting out on the climb up the mountains to Second Chance. It wasn't much in the way of a challenge, and, although he wouldn't admit it to Shane, he didn't mind tinkering. Anything to make the time pass quicker until Olivia arrived and he could apologize for being…introverted.

Mackenzie went back into the general store. Gabby continued freestyle dancing. And Bentley gave the engine one last inspection.

Since Grandpa Harlan had passed away and Bentley's father had fired him, he'd been donating his time to various medical equipment start-ups in Philadelphia, working on a range of new mechanical challenges from prosthetics to artificial organs. He enjoyed a technical challenge, more than he enjoyed the company of most people. And he was surprised at how working outside his field had helped lift his spirits.

An old cowboy and a cowgirl entered the service bay, giving a twirling Gabby a wide berth. The old man stopped a few feet away. The late afternoon sun was at his back and created a classic cowboy outline—wiry body, bowlegs, wide-brimmed hat. The cowgirl had a much more intriguing silhouette. The features of both were now in shadow, details inscrutable.

Bentley closed the truck's hood.

"You're the newest Monroe?" The old man

clicked the heel of his boot on the concrete, shifting the way a horse did when idle. "The repairman?"

The cowgirl made an indistinguishable sound.

Bentley's gaze was pulled back to her curves. It was impossible to tell how old she was, how intelligent, how...attractive. "Actually, I'm an engineer," he admitted slowly. To satisfy his curiosity, Bentley took a few steps to the side, wiping his hands on a used blue rag. With each step, the cowgirl's features came into focus.

Bright brown eyes. Long black hair. A delicate face that should have been smiling.

I could make her smile.

Bentley stepped back, startled by the thought. As a child, he'd been a math nerd, solving equations in his head when he was bored and unchallenged, which was often. As an adult, other than the quarterly Monroe family gatherings and Olivia's races, his work had been his life. In the shop, he didn't make small talk. And in his experience, women liked small talk. In fact, they needed it to spark delighted smiles.

Make her smile? Bentley had a better chance of boring her with silence.

"I thought I saw you guys coming in here."

Another cowboy joined the pair. This one carried a toddler girl with dark curly hair and held the hand of a little cowboy of about four or five.

Gabby came to a standstill, staring at the newcomer warily.

Could it be...?

Bentley moved closer to the trio until he could see the fringe of dark hair beneath the man's cowboy hat and his dark eyes. This had to be Tanner, the man claiming to be a Monroe. "I don't think we've met. I'm Bentley Monroe."

The cowboy frowned at him.

"Raymond Diaz." The old man shook Bentley's hand. "My granddaughter, Cassie. And this here's Tanner Paxton. Thought you'd know him seein' as how you might be related."

At long last. The Monroe Pretender. Bentley couldn't look away.

"We haven't had the pleasure," Tanner said in a cold voice. "Since we have business to discuss, Raymond, I'll head over to the Bar D and catch up with you there." The man claiming to be a Monroe stalked off.

If that man was a long-lost Monroe cousin, he wasn't in Second Chance to become a beloved family member.

"I hear you fix things," Raymond said to

Bentley, unfazed by Tanner's cold shoulder. "I was wondering if you'd want to take a look at some carnival rides we've got out at the Bar D. Can't make money off something that doesn't run." Raymond smiled at Gabby but stomped his boot heel impatiently.

He must really want these rides to run.

Before Bentley could respond, Cassie crossed her arms over her chest. A move that told him she was either anti-Monroe, like Tanner, or not happy with her grandfather's request, like Bentley.

I could make her smile.

The geek in Bentley still didn't think that was likely. But that was the thing about probabilities. There was always a chance, slight as that might be, that he could. That was, if he could hold a casual conversation with her without sounding like a tongue-tied engineer.

"You don't have to come," Cassie said in a voice as stiff as Tanner's had been. "These rides are antiques and we can't pay you. The last mechanic to look at them said the engines were so old that they weren't worth repairing."

Ah. She's not happy with her grandfather's request.

"Amateurs," Raymond scoffed. "Bentley, we hear you're a genius when it comes to engines."

A part of Bentley took the compliment at face value. The foolish part, he was sure. But that didn't stop him from accepting Raymond's invitation. "It never hurts to take a look." And while he was at the Bar D, he might be able to learn more about Tanner. The fact that Cassie was breathtaking had no bearing on his decision. None at all. "Admittedly, I work on newer tech. But you never know what might happen if you give something new-to-you a try."

"Oh, she knows." Raymond chuckled, clapping a hand on Cassie's shoulder. "She knows, all right."

Cassie grimaced slightly, her gaze meeting Bentley's.

He imagined he caught a glimpse of emotions in those dark brown eyes—pain, fortitude, strength. And in that glimpse, Bentley felt a connection. There was more to be found at the Bar D than an engine to tinker with and insight into the truth about Tanner. There was this woman.

I could make her smile.

Bentley was annoyed with himself that the thought wouldn't go away.

"You could come now," Raymond said, tottering away.

Gaze shuttering, Cassie turned and followed her grandfather.

Bentley watched her walk off—head high, shoulders back, black hair cascading from beneath a straw cowboy hat. For the first time since coming to Second Chance, Bentley saw something he wanted to focus his complete attention on—*her*. Not the antique engines. *Her*.

This wasn't like him. Not at all.

"Can I go see the carnival rides?" Gabby rushed over, smiling, and said, "My dad says I'm good company."

Bentley rather thought dads were required to say that of their kids.

"And I know how to get to the Bar D," she added with a flash of intelligence in her eyes. "In case you take too long to accept their invitation."

CHAPTER TWO

"It's a mistake bringing Bentley Monroe here," Cassie told her grandfather as they pulled into the ranch yard with Bentley's gray truck close behind them. "Especially when Tanner is here and so clearly doesn't want to be around the Monroes." A fact Cassie didn't pretend to understand since Tanner claimed to be a Monroe himself.

"Monroe business isn't our business," Grandpa said succinctly. "I'll take care of Tanner. You show our Monroe what we're facing."

Our Monroe. Bentley. He had a working-class look to him. He wore a navy T-shirt, faded blue jeans and scuffed work boots, the kind construction workers wore with the steel toes. He was tall with dark brown hair and eyes. And those eyes… They were warm yet watchful, as if he missed nothing but cared about what he noted. And yet, there was something proud about the lift of his chin and ram-rod straight posture that let Cassie know he had hopes and dreams apart from being a car mechanic.

Actually, I'm an engineer, he'd said.

The point stuck with Cassie. No one in the Diaz family had ever gone to college.

"He'll probably turn tail and run the moment he sees the rides," Cassie predicted, subtly stretching muscles from back to hip.

Grandpa shook his finger at her. "Don't you let that happen. We need the support of the Monroes if we want to stay in town. Gloss over the challenges and win him over."

"Stop it. The next thing you'll be doing is offering me up as his bride in exchange for his mechanical services."

"What an idea!" Grandpa rubbed his hands together, flashing her his gap-toothed grin. "You're too picky when it comes to men."

"I prefer to say my dating pool has been shallow." And that Cassie was holding out for head-over-heels love. But had she missed her chance? The older she got, the less she was willing to compromise for any man who was less than her idea of perfect. Not that she had an image in mind. She just had yet to come across someone who she could envision spending the rest of her life with.

Now Bentley and those eyes…

She climbed carefully down from the truck

and glanced around, trying to see the family ranch as Bentley would.

A blue, rambling ranch house sat front and center, half-hidden behind a screen of aspens, leaves glimmering silver in the afternoon breeze. To her left was an arena and a good-sized barn, which was painted the color of redwood bark. Rhett, Tanner and his kids were clustered by the paint-peeling doors. Beyond that was a bit of land with what looked like a run-down obstacle course. A beat-up mannequin sat in a kiddie ride train engine. Nearby, a merry-go-round horse was propped on a wilted hay bale. All targets for Rhett and his roping students. Beyond that was the large, three-sided second barn, which was tall enough and wide enough to park three semitrucks. The interior was packed with Grandpa Diaz's odds and ends, plus small carnival rides, including a small Ferris wheel, the rest of the merry-go-round horses and metal train cars.

From here, Bentley wouldn't see the prettiest parts of the ranch—the small lake on the other side of the rise near the original homestead, the ridge where you could get a good look at the entire valley and the grand Sawtooth Mountains, or the wildflower-filled meadow beyond the tree line that used to feed a hundred head of cattle. The Bar D was the center of her world.

Would Bentley think the Bar D had an air of neglect and that the Diaz family could barely keep up with repairs? She was afraid he would. It wasn't tidy and organized like the nearby Bucking Bull Ranch, the most renowned operation in the area. The Bar D was eclectic and full of character, the same as the three people who lived here.

Stupid pride. It doesn't matter what a Monroe thinks.

When she was a girl, Cassie used to dream about what it would look like when she was in charge—neat hedges, green pastures and an indoor arena where she could ride and train horses year-round. She didn't have spare money to plant flowers in the spring, much less the funds to build a covered arena. She made do with a small training paddock and a pasture the size of a traditional rodeo arena.

Wasn't life supposed to be about more than making do?

Gabby and Bentley joined Cassie just as the Bar D's black-and-tan cattle dog ran up to Bentley, rose up on his hind legs and planted his big feet on Bentley's shoulders.

To his credit, Bentley didn't fall from eighty pounds of canine greeting, although he dropped the large metal toolbox he was carrying to the ground.

"Ajax!" Cassie called the short-haired Australian heeler to her side. When he didn't come, she added, "I'm so sorry," before taking hold of his collar and pulling him off, stifling a cry from the white-hot pain that shot from her hip to her leg. "Ajax never jumps on anyone." He was more likely to get a case of the zoomies and run circles around visitors, particularly new faces.

"My uncle Shane says animals and kids love Uncle Bentley." Gabby rose on her toes and spun around, landing with her arms out as if Bentley were a prize she was featuring on a game show. "I know I love him."

"Go figure." Bentley didn't so much as crack a smile. The word *curmudgeon* came to mind.

Can handsome men be curmudgeons?

"You don't like kids and dogs? Seriously?" Cassie didn't know why she was teasing him. Her hip was on fire, and it was time to take an over-the-counter pain pill because she had a to-do list as long as her arm.

Bentley heaved a put-upon sigh. "I never said I didn't like kids or animals. I love kids and animals. I plan to have some of my own one day."

Despite being curious about that statement, Cassie let it go. The sooner Bentley admitted the carnival rides were a lost cause, the sooner she could get back to horse training and a much-needed paycheck. "Come along then. I'll show you the remains." She led the way to the pasture behind the arena with measured steps that didn't tax her back.

Late, but true to form, Ajax began racing in broad circles around them, an unfocused look in his eyes.

"What's this?" Bentley asked.

"The zoomies, and yes, that's a technical term." Cassie opened the pasture gate. "It's his way of burning off adrenaline and anxiety after meeting new people. He hasn't crashed into anyone on a zoom since he was a puppy. Give him another minute and he'll be fine."

Ajax raced through the gate and began making a wider, slower circle. The afternoon sun made his fur gleam blue-black.

"See?" Cassie closed the gate behind them. "He's petering out."

As if on cue, Ajax dropped down to his stomach, panting. After a moment, his eyes came back into focus.

"Good boy." Cassie gave him a gentle pat on the head. "You've now officially been welcomed to the Bar D."

"Look what's coming." Gabby pointed her hands in two different directions. "It's like Uncle Bentley is Dr. Dolittle. Uncle Shane knows what he's talking about."

A gray tabby stalked out of the second barn toward them, mewing, tail waving smartly in the air. Millie was a fantastic mouser and a consummate flirt. From the far corner of the pasture, Cassie's beloved mare Whistler snorted and began plodding toward them. She was swaybacked and retired, but sweet as sugar.

"They're coming to Cassie," Bentley said curtly, looking away.

Cassie tended to agree with him, but now that she could see the metal skeletons of the carnival rides, reality of a different kind was setting in. "Do me a favor, Bentley, and let my grandfather down easy after you take a look, will you?"

Bentley fell into step next to Cassie. He was a good foot taller than she was, but he kept to her slow pace. "So…uh… You don't think I can get the rides running?"

"No. Nor do I think you should try." She gestured toward the barn. "Just look at them. There's rust on everything." Thick as frost. "You were kind to come out here, but I'm afraid my grandfather has always dreamed bigger than his arms could hold."

Bentley stopped about twenty feet from the barn. Windblown wild grass bent and swayed around his ankles. Ajax sat at his feet. Gabby leaned into his side. Millie rubbed against his calf. And when Whistler joined them, instead of greeting Cassie, the bay mare rubbed her head against Bentley's shoulder.

Bentley turned a put-upon expression skyward.

"You *are* a pied piper, a magnet for kids and animals." Cassie laughed, shaking her head. "I wouldn't have believed it if I hadn't seen it for myself."

"I told you," Gabby said.

Bentley cleared his throat. "Whatever. It's not something I aspire to." And then he gently extricated himself from animals and girl, marching purposefully toward the barn.

Why was he so put out by all that affection?

Bentley surveyed the barn's contents. "Which engine can I easily access?"

"Maybe the Ferris wheel?" Cassie led him over to it. "It has the most space near the engine."

Bentley set his toolbox in front of the Ferris wheel motor and lifted the blue hood over the main engine compartment. "It's electric. Is there power in here?"

"No, but we have a generator somewhere." Cassie headed to the back of the storage barn, moving carefully around boxes and edging between piles of Grandpa's accumulated junk, moving slowly and with care. When she reached the generator, she glanced back. "Found it."

Whistler lingered just outside the barn, looking toward Bentley. Ajax sat near the man's feet. Millie was perched on a stack of boxes behind him. Bentley paid no one any mind.

Gabby knelt in front of the toolbox. "I'll be your assistant. Tell me what you need. Crescent wrench. Phillips-head. Pliers. I do this all the time for Dad." Who ran the Lodgepole Inn.

Bentley grunted, poking around inside the engine. Cassie smiled.

Curmudgeons shouldn't be sexy. Yet, Bentley was. Short hair a dark brown that was nearly black. Strong features, strong arms, strong shoulders. A man of few words, he'd be dependable in a crisis, not that she planned on having any.

Who am I kidding? My entire life is in crisis!

Cassie turned her attention to the generator, peering at the dials to check the oil and fuel levels. Everything looked ready to go. She returned to Bentley's side, as drawn to him as the dog, the cat and Gabby. "If there's any hope of starting this, the generator is ready."

Bentley grunted again, which she took to mean, *Don't bother me. I'm thinking about the problem at hand.*

Curmudgeon.

Cassie bit back another smile.

"Flathead screwdriver." Bentley held out his hand, as cool and demanding as a surgeon.

Gabby dug into his toolbox and handed him the screwdriver without a break in her humming or swaying. She glanced over at Cassie. "I'm taking ballet. Did you ever take ballet?"

"No," Bentley answered grumpily before Cassie could, making both Cassie and Gabby laugh. He hadn't realized the question wasn't directed at him.

"My dad says I can have a ballet barre once they finish remodeling my room." Gabby got to her feet and did a plié.

"You should wait and see if you still want to do ballet next month." Bentley spared Cassie a glance. "She only started last week."

"It's an online class, but I love it." Gabby did another plié, this time extending her arms out and then upward as she rose onto her toes.

"I'll still be doing ballet ten years from now. You've seen me, Uncle Bentley. I'm good."

Another grunt.

Cassie held back a chuckle, leaning on the outer casing of the Ferris wheel engine to ease the pressure on her hip.

Both Tanner's little kids joined them. Mia and Quinn had on cowboy boots. Quinn wore a straw cowboy hat and a superior expression he'd inherited from Tanner. Mia wore a wrinkled yellow sundress and a watchful air. She was a quiet child with an enchanting smile, if one could coax it out of her.

Ajax extended his long, narrow snout toward both children and then settled back against Bentley's leg.

Bentley studied Tanner's kids for a moment before looking up at Cassie. "What's Tanner doing here?"

"Tanner's staying up the road at a cabin you Monroes own. Since he arrived, he stopped by a couple of times. And now, he, my grandpa and my brother are planning to host a rodeo camp for kids. My brother is a former roping champion who teaches and coaches a little. I think Tanner used to organize rodeos for a county fair in Texas. And my grandfather... He chases any carrot that promises profit."

"Chasing carrots isn't such a bad trait.

That's how my grandfather built his fortune."
Bentley's gaze flickered with humor, but only
briefly before his attention returned to the
motor. His hands were deep in the engine
compartment. Metal clanked against metal.

At any moment, he'd realize this was a lost
cause.

"I'm Quinn. My dad says you're working
on a ride." Quinn stuck his thumbs in his belt
loops and rocked back on his heels. "But I
don't see no seats." The Ferris wheel's egg-
shaped cages were stacked against the back
wall.

"Hmm," Bentley murmured.

"He says you should pray it runs," Quinn
continued.

Bentley made no comment, but his eyes
narrowed with determination.

"We used to pray when Mama was alive."
Quinn was on a roll. "We haven't been to
church since. But I could pray for you."

Silently, Mia took Quinn's hand.

"*We* could pray for you," Quinn amended.
"Me and Mia."

"Oh." Gabby ruffled Mia's dark curls. "That
is so sweet."

Cassie echoed Gabby's words. It was sweet
of Quinn to offer prayers. But Quinn's senti-
ments fell upon deaf ears where Bentley was

concerned. He just kept on working. Not that any of the children or Ajax seemed to feel snubbed. They gathered around him contentedly, as if he was Santa Claus, hard at work compiling his "nice" list.

Finally, Bentley withdrew from the engine compartment. His arms were streaked with dirt and grease, not that he seemed to care. In fact, one corner of his mouth tipped up. "Can you start the generator?"

"I'll give it a go." Cassie returned to the back of the barn. Surprisingly, the generator started on the first try. She doubted the Ferris wheel would do the same. Nevertheless, she plugged in a heavy-duty extension cord and carried the end to Bentley. "No offense, but in case something blows, I'm going to get the kids and Ajax a safe distance away."

"Ye of little faith." Bentley waited until she had her charges outside the barn to attach the cord, fiddle a final time with the engine and then hit the on switch.

There was a low, mechanical groan, followed by an ear-popping backfire that sent Whistler galloping away and Millie scampering out of sight. After another grinding complaint, the engine roared to life. Bentley throttled the engine up and back. And then he turned toward Cassie with a big smile and a thumbs-up, and all she could think was: *He could pied piper me right into those strong, capable arms*.

From across the pasture, Grandpa whooped and tossed his cowboy hat in the air. It fell to earth the same way as all his grand plans—without fanfare. But he picked it up and hurried to join them.

Cassie wiped the foolish grin off her face and reminded herself that starting a carnival engine changed nothing.

Her body and bank account were both still a mess.

And curmudgeonly pied pipers with mechanical skills could do nothing about either one.

I MADE HER SMILE.

Irrationally, Bentley wanted to make the cowgirl smile again.

"Can I go for a ride?" A small voice and equally small hand tugged on Bentley's T-shirt as he powered down the Ferris wheel engine. Mia stared up at Bentley with big brown eyes.

"We prayed for you." Holding the side brim of his cowboy hat, her brother hopped around Bentley like an excited bunny rabbit. "We should get a ride."

Bentley hadn't paid much attention to the

youngsters while he was working. But now their cowboy dad was headed Bentley's way.

Shane would be crowing louder than Raymond just had, because here was an in with the Monroe pretender—the Bar D needed someone to work on the carnival ride engines and Tanner was going into business with the Bar D. This gave Bentley a chance to get to the bottom of things where Tanner was concerned.

"Can I go for a ride?" Mia asked again.

Gabby lifted the little girl into her arms. "There aren't any seats on the ride yet, Mia. We have to wait until Uncle Bentley fixes it."

"Fix it, Uncle Bentley," the little girl said, using a finger to twine a dark curl around her ear. She looked like Bentley's sister, Olivia, when she was young, only with darker hair. "Fix it now."

"You can do it, Uncle Bentley." Her brother stopped hopping. When he stood still, he bore a striking resemblance to Shane when he was a kid.

What if they are family? What if they deserved an inheritance?

Bentley washed a hand over his face, trying to reset his perspective. These kids had a similar look to the Monroes was all. Doppelgängers weren't a rarity. Bearing a resemblance didn't mean they were closely related.

Cassie's gaze collided with Bentley's. She stood just outside the barn, leaning over to hold on to Ajax's collar and grimacing. "Can you do it, *Uncle Bentley*?" And then she let go of the dog and gave Bentley a hint of a smile.

A hint of a smile. That's all it took to make Bentley want to forget Tanner's claims and bring the rides back to life, if only to please this cowgirl. It made no sense. No sense.

Still, his heart beat a little faster the longer their gazes held.

Ajax circled Bentley's feet, bumping into kids and nearly knocking Quinn over.

Bentley steadied the boy, noticing a torn seam in the shoulder of his shirt.

"He can do it," Mia said solemnly, faithfully, trustingly. Her dress was faded, as if it had seen too many washings. Her cowboy boots had the scuffed look of hand-me-downs.

If they were Monroes, someone in the family would make sure they had decent clothes.

If they were Monroes...

Bentley ignored the thought. He was a man who stuck to the laws of physics and mechanics. Emotion had no bearing on Tanner's claim. And for all their clothes looked worn, the children looked healthy and well-adjusted.

Ajax finally settled, leaning against Bentley's calf and staring up at him worshipfully.

What had Bentley done to deserve the affection of a dog and three kids? Nothing. Elation over getting the engine to start drained away.

"I told you he could fix 'em, Cassie." Raymond entered the barn. A few feet away from Bentley, he extended his arm over young bodies and clapped a hand on Bentley's shoulder. His grin revealed missing teeth at one corner of his mouth. "You can stop worrying about making ends meet, girl. We're going to take these rides on the road again."

"Hang on. *I'm* not traveling with those rides." Cassie crossed her arms over her chest the way she had back in town.

"Why not?" Her grandfather sniffed. "You get to see new places and meet new people. Not to mention, the pay is better than training a horse or two now and then."

Cassie's arms drew tighter around herself. "Everything still needs the rust taken off and a new coat of paint. We're very far away from operational. And besides, I signed a contract with Ashley Monroe to train horses for that movie she's making here next year."

Cassie was going to work for Bentley's cousin? This was news to him. And impressive. Cousin Ashley was taking the role of movie producer seriously. She wouldn't hire anyone who wasn't highly skilled.

"*Next year*, she says." Raymond shook Bentley's shoulder. "Cassie has work *next year*. You can make all the rides run now, can't you, son? We could be operating in time for the fall carnival season."

"Well…" Bentley hedged, glancing toward the rusted Ferris wheel cages. Cassie was right. It would take more work to restore the ride pieces than it would to make the machinery functional.

"What if Bentley fixes the engines?" Cassie tossed a lock of black hair over one shoulder. "Are you going to pay him for his work?"

"Why should I?" Raymond shot back. "He's a Monroe. They're like our guardian angels."

Bentley was no one's guardian angel. His sister, Olivia, would second that sentiment.

"People deserve to be paid fairly for their work and receive a living wage," Cassie said staunchly.

"Don't get distracted by this project, Grandpa." The slim cowboy who bore a strong resemblance to Cassie introduced himself as her brother, Rhett. "There's more money to be had with Tanner's rodeo school than your rides."

"We can talk business later." Squeezing his way into the barn, Tanner took Mia from Gabby and claimed his son's hand. "Not in front of the Monroe."

Bentley frowned, finding his voice. "My family doesn't care if you hold a rodeo school or not." That might have been an overstatement. Shane would certainly be concerned. He cared about everything the man who claimed a Monroe heritage did.

"Well, *I* care about keeping the Monroes out of my business." Tanner's words were spiteful, even as he walked away. "I know why you're here, and it's not for rides."

"I was invited." Bentley began packing up his tools, creating a racket that had Ajax edging away. "I never said I was something I'm not."

The unspoken accusation—that Tanner had—had Tanner turning back, a dark expression clouding his features. "I know who I am. And I know that sometimes you have to fight with family to get a fair shake." He tipped his hat to Cassie but gave the two Diaz men dark looks. "I won't come back if there are Monroes around."

"You need us, Tanner," Raymond said in a voice just as heated as Tanner's had been. "Same as we need this Monroe. People in hard places have to make hard choices, including swallowing their pride."

"I said my piece." Tanner headed toward the ranch yard and the collection of trucks.

Mia stared over his shoulder, waving goodbye to those in the barn.

Gabby waved back.

But that wasn't the end of the drama. Another argument was brewing.

Cassie stomped her foot a little, a move reminiscent of her grandfather's body language. "I'm not getting into the kiddie ride business."

"Of all the..." Raymond shook his head. "Why not?"

"Because I'm a horse trainer. And maybe I'm not making big bucks now, but I might get more work after next year." There was something in her statement that hinted at vulnerability. But Cassie turned on her heel and walked away.

No one said anything until she went through the gate.

"Grandpa, I'm not keen on running those rides either." Rhett put his hands on his hips, which drew attention to his big belt buckle indicating he was a champion roper. "If Bentley can get the rides running, we should sell them."

"Sell a moneymaker?" Raymond seemed flustered. "I don't understand either one of you."

Bentley latched his toolbox and stood. His job here was done. "Thank you for letting me tinker with a classic. Good luck with whatever you decide to do." He nodded toward Gabby, indicating it was time to go, and then headed the way Cassie had.

"But...but... We need you," Raymond protested.

Bentley kept walking, trailed by a menagerie of humans and animals alike. His odd little superpower had never felt so annoying. "It makes no sense to fix something when your family isn't 100 percent behind it."

"He's got a point," Rhett said.

"Then get in line behind me, boy," Raymond snapped. "I'm doing this for you. You and Cassie."

"You should do it for yourself." Rhett closed the gate after them, leaving the horse on the other side.

At the mare's big-eyed gaze, Bentley relented and returned to the fence to give her a pat, trying to ignore the arguing men. He did the same for Ajax before loading his toolbox in the truck and making sure Gabby was buckled in.

Only then did he give the Bar D one last perusal. The ranch smacked of faded dreams and the faint whiff of desperation. Even the house, where he thought he saw Cassie standing in the front window.

But he'd always been overly sentimental. The Diaz family was probably doing okay and the silhouette in the window was probably just a floor lamp.

CHAPTER THREE

"I'LL BE REHEARSING again after dinner," Gabby told Bentley as he parked in front of the Lodgepole Inn. Up close, its thick, round log walls were imposing. "I need an audience. And since you're not busy, you can come." The preteen spoke as if Bentley had nothing better to do.

And the sad part was, it was true. Bentley wasn't busy. He wasn't…*needed*. At least, his presence wasn't wanted by anyone but animals and children. Things had been different when his twin brother was alive. But now…

Bentley held on to the steering wheel as if the truck was moving, not parked and turned off.

What was wrong with him? He was used to being the man in the corner of the room, the one too preoccupied with his own thoughts about engine mechanics and a boat's hydro-dynamic drag to be bothered with conversation. He was accustomed to being the man who was like a shadow to his more handsome and outgoing twin.

Bryce is dead.

He had been for over two years now. Bentley forced himself to take a deep, calming breath. It had taken the comfort of his workshop at Monroe Machine Works being denied him for Bentley to feel as if he had no place, no purpose that was his and his alone. Since his firing, his volunteer work with start-ups had been fulfilling but it wasn't the same as owning a project and being invested in its success.

I could buy those rides.

He scoffed at the thought. What would he do with them? It was as fleetingly satisfying as making a pretty cowgirl smile.

"Uncle Bentley?" Gabby grabbed the door handle, but instead of getting out, she asked, "Are you coming inside?"

Laurel passed by the inn's front window carrying one of the twins, followed by her husband, Mitch, carrying the other baby.

If Bentley went inside, he'd just be Uncle Bentley, the children's favorite plaything.

Sad sack. That was Bryce's teasing voice in Bentley's head. *You should have asked the cowgirl out to dinner.*

Bentley wasn't that guy. But he was hungry. "I think I'll get something to eat at the Bent Nickel first."

"Wise choice." Gabby opened her door and hopped down. She turned, leaning her elbows on the seat while bouncing up and down on her toes, sending her long, strawberry blond hair swinging. "It's lasagna night here. I read the Bent Nickel's sign outside. Your cousin Cam's special today is beef Burgundy, which is awesome, trust me. I'll do my geometry homework until you get back. It's only summer school, but I pride myself on getting A's."

"You want to be best in class?"

"Yes. Always."

"Math before dance then. Personal priorities." He understood that.

"Personal *standards*," Gabby said with a lift of her chin. "I set myself high benchmarks."

"I do, too." Growing up, Bentley had prided himself on getting better grades than his siblings and cousins. And when he'd realized that they had personalities better suited to sports and to the spotlight, he'd become less competitive with them or more competitive with himself, the way Gabby was. Her hours of ballet practice were suddenly less annoying because he understood why she pushed herself. "Go get that math done."

They amicably parted ways. Gabby ran

up the Lodgepole Inn's porch steps. Bentley headed for the diner as the sun dipped below the pine-covered mountains to the west.

The Bent Nickel was a classic as far as diners went. Checkerboard flooring. Chrome barstools at the counter. Booths flanking each side wall.

Where it veered from being a mere diner was Cam's specials. He'd once been a chef in a five-star Las Vegas restaurant. Now he was a family man who ran the Bent Nickel with his future wife and her two boys. He claimed it was only temporary, but Bentley could see the writing on the diner wall. No more Michelin stars for Cam. He'd have to be content with the stars in the Idaho sky.

"I'll take the special, Cam," Bentley said upon entering the near-empty diner. He'd barely gotten settled in a booth when Shane sat across from him.

"How'd it go at the Bar D?" Shane asked. "Spare no detail."

Bentley wasted no time on pleasantries. He told Shane about the rodeo school and Tanner's standoffish behavior toward Bentley. "His kids seem nice."

"And they look like Monroes." Shane nodded, rubbing his clean-shaven jaw. "Let me ask you this. If you thought you were a long-lost member of a well-off family, how would you act?"

Bentley took a moment to think on it before answering. "First off, my lawyer would probably advise me to keep my distance."

"Tanner doesn't seem the type to have a lawyer," Shane mused, gaze roaming over the yellowed pictures of Old West trappers hanging from the wall above them. Some of the pictures looked like they'd been taken outside the Lodgepole Inn.

Bentley considered Shane. He used to run the Monroe family's chain of luxury hotels with what was rumored to be ruthless efficiency. But lately, his cousin seemed to have found his heart, just not toward Tanner. Bentley shook his head, returning to the question at hand—how he would act if his and Tanner's roles were reversed. "Second, I wouldn't treat the family like the enemy. Unless, of course, someone had made it clear that I was the enemy."

"Like me, you mean?" Shane lifted and lowered one shoulder, guilty as charged. "As the family representative in Second Chance, I asked Tanner for proof. His father's birth certificate should have Grandpa Harlan's brother's name on it—*Hobart Monroe*. That request was met with silence. And when I suggested a DNA test, Tanner told me he didn't trust us not to falsify the results."

"Have you searched for his father's birth records?" That seemed an obvious place to start.

"Tanner hasn't told me his father's first name. I assume his grandmother's name is Ruth Monroe Paxton. After my initial search dead-ended, I thought I needed more to go on, like his father's name or birthplace." Shane drummed his fingers on the tabletop. "You know, my soon-to-be grandmother-in-law is a friend of Ruth's. I might be able to find out Tanner's father's first name and where he was born."

"You tried looking on social media?"

Shane nodded absently, glancing at the old photos once more. "Tanner's not social. On the internet or in person." And then his gaze swung back to Bentley. "Why does Tanner want to hold a rodeo school up here? We're at least an hour from the closest cities in three directions. It wouldn't be convenient for parents to drive their little cowpokes up here. I held a camp for special needs kids this summer and, although everyone was grateful, the camp was criticized for being held in a remote location."

"The only reason to start a venture like a rodeo school is profit." It was Bentley's turn to rub his jaw. "Think about it. Up here, Tanner's operating costs would be low. If he holds the event on Monroe-owned land, he doesn't have to pay a facility fee."

"Money." Shane placed his palms on the scarred Formica. "And if Tanner receives part ownership of the town, he'd never have to pay any rental or usage fees for someone's arena. As it is, we put him up in a house free of charge." There were a lot of empty and abandoned homes in Second Chance. All owned by their generation of Monroes. "What a scam. I mean, if we drag our feet on this, he could live on the cheap for a long time."

"To be fair," Bentley hedged, thinking of Quinn and Mia. "I didn't say Tanner was running a scam."

"If he's unwilling to prove who he is and is out for profit, that is the definition of a scam." Shane slid out of the booth and headed toward the door. A few feet away, he spun around and headed back. "Maybe Tanner doesn't want you out at the Bar D every day because he might let something important slip. Something that would prove he's not a Monroe. But what Tanner doesn't know is that you have a superpower."

Bentley rolled his eyes. "Shane..."

"And don't tell me it's only kids and dogs

that like you on sight. Everybody likes you. You're impassive and nonthreatening. If you get close to Tanner, he might tell you things he refuses to tell me."

Bentley recalled the way Tanner had walked away from him today, not once, but twice. "I don't think we're going to become fast friends, not to mention Cassie and Rhett don't want to travel around running carnival rides. Which means I have no excuse to be at the Bar D."

Shane set his hands on the table edge and leaned over, as if imparting a secret. "Gabby texted me that the rides could be adorable."

An hour ago, the comment would have dumbfounded Bentley. Now he just nodded. Gabby was smart enough to see past the faded paint and rust. "I suppose if people restore Model Ts, they can restore old carnival rides."

"I never thought about it that way," Shane said slowly and in a way that practically had Bentley seeing gears turn in Shane's head. "This community pulls together. There's a painter in town. And someone must know of an auto body shop nearby. I don't mind giving them a leg up if it ultimately benefits Second Chance. And maybe…maybe the Diaz family don't have to run a *traveling* kiddie carnival. There's a flat plot of unused land near the entrance to the Bar D. I drove by it today while you were there." He tilted his head from one shoulder to the other, cracking his neck. "Yes, I was stressing and made a drive-by. But my point is that there's enough room for some rides and a ticket or refreshment booth, and some space for cars to park. The Bar D could market it as a mountain fairyland or Mike Moody's kiddie park."

Mike Moody was the stagecoach bandit of local legend in these parts, the man who'd hidden the chest of gold Shane and Franny had found.

"I'm sure Raymond would love to hear your business pitch." *But Cassie...not so much.*

Shane shook his head. "This idea would be better coming from you. A casual thought tossed out by the quiet, ever likable Bentley Monroe."

Bentley frowned. "I'm likable because I don't meddle or boss people around." Like Shane was wont to do.

"Don't argue with my methods when you don't argue with my results." Shane straightened, looking pleased with himself. "Yeah, I'd put money on you successfully nudging the Bar D in the direction of opening Mike Moodyland in Second Chance and helping me uncover the truth about Tanner."

Cam approached with a steaming plate of beef Burgundy and a proud expression.

"Okay," Bentley murmured in defeat. "If the opportunity presents itself, I'll see what I can do."

But he imagined opportunities, much like Cassie's smiles, would be rare.

THE DAY AFTER meeting Bentley Monroe, Cassie stared at the kitchen's exposed ceiling beams and tried to breathe through the pain in her hip as she followed doctor's orders. He'd told her to lie on a hard, flat surface when she rested and nothing was harder than the linoleum in the kitchen.

Nothing was harder...

Except ignoring the memory of Bentley Monroe's grin and the knowledge that he thought she was courageous. Yesterday, she'd seen him look toward the house right before he left. She'd been unable to stop thinking of him ever since. Did he find her interesting? Attractive? She found him interesting *and* attractive.

"I made water in the potty." Mia appeared at the end of the kitchen peninsula in her bare feet holding the hand of her older brother, Quinn. The hem of her blue gingham dress was coming unraveled. "Watcha doin'?"

"Did you fall?" Quinn's blue jeans and red T-shirt were wrinkled and streaked with dirt. His big toe stuck out of one sock. "Are you hurt? I can run and find my dad." He and Rhett were making a chute for the arena.

"I'm good." Cassie hadn't heard them come in, possibly because she'd been in a painful battle to ease the pressure on her lower vertebrae, and possibly because the kids had left their boots somewhere and weren't tromping around. She rolled over to her hands and knees, took a moment to collect herself and then stood. "Are you hungry? Thirsty?"

"I'll take a cookie, please." Quinn's gaze roamed around the kitchen as if looking for a cookie jar.

"We don't have any cookies." Cassie had banned all processed sweets from the house when Grandpa Diaz was diagnosed with diabetes last year. They rarely indulged in sweets anymore, although a neighbor had dropped off a bowl of peaches that she planned to make cobbler with.

"Chocolate?" Quinn asked with a hopeful smile.

Cassie shook her head and opened the refrigerator, searching for something a child might like. There wasn't much—baby carrots, tomatoes, cheese sticks. Cassie glanced at Mia, who was three. She wasn't certain that toddlers should eat hard foods. "Cheese sticks is the safer choice."

"My dad says you shouldn't play it safe." Quinn scaled a barstool before reaching down to help guide his sister into the seat next to him.

"But I'm not your father." Cassie peeled the plastic from two cheese sticks and placed them on napkins for each child.

"I know that." Quinn frowned. "You're a mama."

"She's a cowboy," Mia said solemnly, pulling the cheese into thin strings. "I'm gonna be a cowboy."

"Cowgirl," Quinn corrected her. "You can't be a cowboy if you aren't a boy. You're gonna be a mama."

A mama...

Cassie had never doubted she'd be one someday. Until now.

Ten years ago, she'd been a starry-eyed nineteen-year-old, thinking that she and Rhett would run the Bar D together and pass it down to their kids and grandkids. And then one day Harlan Monroe had showed up at the ranch, offering to buy them out. At one point, he'd wandered out to the paddock, where she was riding Whistler bareback, wishing the wealthy old man would go away.

There's a skill I haven't seen in a long time, he told her, leaning heavily on a paddock post. He didn't look like a millionaire. His white hair needed a cut, and his tan slacks were as wrinkled as the blue plaid shirt he wore.

She brought Whistler to a stop in front of him. *Generations of Diaz ranchers and horsemen have lived here. If you buy our ranch, I won't be able to pass on the skill.*

The old man tsked. *When I was your age, I didn't know if I was going to have anything to pass on to the next generation of Monroes. I lived hand to mouth, scraping for every dime. But I knew one thing for sure. When life throws up a roadblock, you can either suck on sour lemons or look for greener pastures. It's up to you to decide what you do next.*

At that point, Cassie hadn't decided what her next step would be. Grandpa and her parents had done that. And she'd just gone with the flow, assuming life wouldn't change for her—until Harlan Monroe died, and her parents went to manage someone else's ranch. That's when Cassie had seen the signs of a much-needed reality check. Much as she loved ranching and working with horses, she needed to look for another way to earn a living. But her first foray toward something different— riding a bull—had thrown up one heck of a roadblock. Now everything was harder than before, more painful and less certain, even things she'd assumed would be in her future, like kids.

If the worst turned out to be true and Cassie couldn't have little cowpokes of her own, she needed to pass on her equine knowledge to a younger generation any way she could. Her attention turned back to the two impression-able kids sitting in her kitchen. In the weeks since they'd been coming around, they'd prac-tically become family.

"Mia can be whatever she wants, including a cowgirl. Cowgirls rock." Cassie served Tan-ner's kids water in juice glasses. "Cowgirls can do anything cowboys can do."

Quinn gasped, a horrified look on his face. Cassie made a mental note to talk to Tanner about perpetuating sexist stereotypes.

"It's true, Quinn." Cassie took an old cal-endar out from where it was stored in be-tween two cookbooks. "Cowgirls are tough. You won't see many cowboys riding a horse standing up or hanging upside down from the saddle." She opened the calendar to Jan-uary. "That's me." She flipped to another page. "And that's me." The entire calendar featured Cassie's stunts on horseback. Mom had printed it a few years ago as a gift for Cassie. Although she was proud of her accomplishments, just the memory of the strength it took to perform those stunts made Cassie's back ache.

Quinn put the end of the string cheese in his mouth and tore off a bite, very aggressive-like. "You were in a circus?"

Cassie also needed to talk to Tanner about teaching his kids some basic manners. But first, she had to win an argument with a five-year-old.

"No, Quinn. I was in a trick riding group. We performed at rodeos and fairs." Cassie stopped talking. She sounded like Grandpa Diaz, reminiscing about the past. Looking back, the past ten years had been fun, but had done nothing to prepare her for adulting.

"Did you win trophies? My dad has a bunch of trophies." Quinn tore off another bite of cheese.

"Sure." Cassie nodded. "When I was a kid, I won trophies. And when I got older, I was paid to ride."

Quinn's mouth dropped open. "If I ride, will you pay me?"

"No. You'd have to be in a riding performance troupe to be paid. And the troupe I was in moved down to Ketchum." Cassie took a bowl of cherry tomatoes from the refrigerator and rinsed them off. She set three on Quinn's napkin and one on Mia's. "Nobody around here performs anymore."

Quinn scrunched his nose. "We don't eat red things. Don't you have French fries?"

"No. This isn't a fast-food restaurant. You'll like tomatoes. We grew them in our greenhouse."

Quinn pushed his napkin across the counter toward Cassie, rejecting the tomatoes. After a moment, Mia did the same.

"I need to have a conversation with your dad about vegetables," Cassie muttered.

The back door opened, and three cowboys filled the mudroom, followed by Ajax. Rhett pulled off his cowboy boots and set his hat on a hook, as did Grandpa. The dog trotted inside the kitchen, sniffing everyone present before deciding all was well. He picked up his rabbit squeaker toy and flopped onto his dog bed in the corner.

Squeak-squeak-squeak.

"Another great day for the books." Grandpa disappeared down the hall. "We have a chute."

Rhett began rummaging around in the refrigerator.

Tanner kept his boots on, smiling and nodding toward his kids. "You guys ready to go?"

"Yep." Quinn leaped from his barstool to the floor.

"Yep." Mia held her arms toward her father.

"Where are your boots?" Tanner asked, not moving from the mudroom.

"I'll get 'em." Quinn ran toward the front door.

Now didn't seem the time to bring up vegetables.

"Daddy." Mia's arms were still raised, waiting to be picked up.

Tanner glanced down at his dusty boots. "Cassie, can you bring Mia to me? I don't want to get your kitchen floor dirty."

Without thinking, Cassie moved to help. Too late, she remembered she wasn't supposed to lift more than ten pounds at a time. She bent her knees and picked up the slight little girl anyway triggering a bolt of pain in her hip and pelvis. Despite Cassie's quick intake of breath, Mia settled against her, making Cassie's heart pang.

If I don't get surgery, I'll never have a sweet girl of my own.

The bull had seen to that.

With carefully measured, painful steps,

Cassie carried Mia back to Tanner, stifling a groan when she handed her off.

"Is she wet?" Tanner asked, settling his daughter on his hip.

"No, Daddy," Mia grumped.

"No," Cassie seconded. "She's fine."

"Sorry." Tanner brushed a finger playfully over Mia's nose. "Cassie just carried you so stiffly. Must be because you're a big girl, Mia."

Rhett laughed as he poked around inside the fridge. "Cassie's still sore from giving bull riding a try."

Older brother humor. Cassie wanted to poke him.

Squeak-squeak-squeak!

Without getting up, Ajax gave his toy a good shake, sending the long bunny ears swinging against his face.

"I have a favor to ask you, Cassie." Tanner raised his voice to be heard above the dog toy. He flashed a smile as slick as an icy road.

She supposed some women would fall for that smile. But Cassie had grown up around confident, arrogant cowboys of all ages, shapes and sizes. Tanner's charm and good looks had no effect on her. He was a lot like Rhett, and her feelings toward Tanner fell firmly in the brother camp.

"Tanner," Cassie said gently. "I told you I'm not available for your rodeo school." She could barely saddle a horse much less teach trick riding.

"That's not the favor I had in mind." Tanner's smile widened. "I was hoping I'd be able to leave the kids here with you while Raymond, Rhett and I go drum up business for rodeo school. We plan to drop flyers off at feed stores and a few of the junior rodeos happening within a hundred-mile radius this weekend."

"I don't know…" Cassie reached out and ran a hand absently over Mia's curls. Young children needed caregivers with strong backs and settled laps. And there was a lot to do just to keep the ranch going every day by herself. There would be no lap to sit in until day's end.

"Of course, she'll do it." Rhett closed the refrigerator door. "You're practically family and it's just a few days. Five tops."

"Can we ride horses?" Quinn pleaded. "I'll be good if we can ride horses."

"I'll be good," Mia seconded with that solemn expression of hers.

Tanner's kids were adorable and potentially heart stealing. But the fact remained—Cassie couldn't pick them up or carry them around the way Tanner did. Now was a good time to set aside pride and confess the extent of her injury to her family.

Now was the time…

Now…

"I can't." Cassie kept her tone light. "I'm going to the Ketchum livestock auction Thursday."

"We'll wait to leave until you get back," Tanner promised. "Or you could come along?"

"Don't take her, Tanner." Rhett laughed, giving Cassie a quick side-hug. "You wouldn't just have to watch your kids. You'd also have to keep an eye on Cassie. She has the worst sense of direction."

Cassie couldn't argue with that. She had a habit of getting turned around in unfamiliar places—towns, fairs, large rodeo competitions—which was both frustrating and unnerving. But there was another reason to refuse the trip. She didn't want Tanner to think she was interested in him romantically. "It's best if I stay here."

"And watch the kids?" Tanner asked hopefully.

Cassie hesitated.

"Come on, sis." Rhett gave Cassie a pleading look. "We'll only make good money from this rodeo school if we enroll a lot of kids. You know we need the cash."

Did she ever. "Okay." Cassie relented. "You

make it hard to refuse." Cassie just hoped she hadn't bitten off more than she could chew.

"Thanks. It means a lot to me." Tanner headed for the back door with his kids.

After Tanner left, Rhett studied the contents of the refrigerator once more. "What's for dinner?"

"I don't know." Cassie poked his shoulder. "It's your night to cook."

"It's beanie-weenie night then." Rhett tossed a package of hot dogs on the counter and turned toward the pantry.

"Oh, come on. You're not twelve." Cassie had her hands on her hips, thumbs working the muscles in the small of her back. "Grandpa needs to eat better. There's chicken breast in the fridge and corn ready to be picked in the greenhouse."

"Sounds great if you make it." Rhett waggled his brows teasingly. "I'll move the hay from storage to the hayloft if you make dinner."

"Deal. Just don't forget your end of the bargain." Cassie couldn't have managed lifting hay bales anyway. "And just so you know, the way to a woman's heart isn't paved with beanie-weenies."

"I know. It's paved with kindness and chemistry." Something their mother was fond of saying. Rhett took a sip of his beer. "But make no mistake. The reason I'm single is the same reason you're single. There's no one in Second Chance who strikes your fancy and is as perfect as your hero, Cowboy Campbell."

That wasn't true.

Bentley struck her fancy. And he was perfect so far.

"I think Tanner would make Cassie a good husband." Grandpa trundled into the kitchen. "They have a lot in common."

Cassie shook her head. She couldn't think of a thing.

CHAPTER FOUR

Rhett was restless.

He sat on the top rung of the paddock fence, watching the western horizon turn from blue to orange. He'd come out to close the outbuildings after dinner, but he wanted a moment of peace before he did.

Ajax was doing his own safety check, sniffing around the ranch yard and main barn. Millie sat just inside the barn door, cleaning her paws. The horses were quiet in their stalls. It was the best time of the day, a time to think back on what had been accomplished and look forward to what was ahead. In his case, rodeo school was directly ahead. Despite what Tanner and his grandfather believed, it didn't seem to be a long-term solution to the Diaz money woes. But neither were Rhett's dreams of opening some type of tour business in Second Chance, like river rafting or zip-lining. Not until tourism in the area increased.

"I know that look." Cassie joined Rhett at

the fence, leaning against a post. "That combination of worry and hope."

"Mostly worry with an inkling of impending defeat." Rhett nodded. "I'm wondering how many more sunsets I'll see from the Bar D. And if it's worth fighting to stay or better to start somewhere fresh." He glanced down to Cassie's face. He hated that there was tension around her eyes. It had been there before she'd ridden that bull in Denver though, so he didn't attribute it solely to her recent injury. "You wonder the same thing, don't you?"

"Sometimes." She wrapped an arm around the fence post and then admitted, "All the time, really."

"Rodeo school isn't the answer." Rhett hated to admit it. "It's just a short-term fix."

"Your extreme sport business and Grandpa's kiddie rides aren't the answer either." There was regret in Cassie's voice. "Frankly, I'm not sure that you coaching the next generation of ropers and me training horses is sustainable either."

"And that leaves us…"

"Exactly," Cassie said, about as mournfully as Rhett felt. "We don't know where it leaves us. Maybe I should put away my cowboy boots and hang up my hat. Find a regular job. I hear lots of people are happy working for a steady paycheck."

"I wouldn't be happy. And you wouldn't either." Of that, he was certain. "Maybe Grandpa will win the lottery this time."

The sky tinged a deep orange with hints of purple.

"Don't bet on it. Good night, Rhett." Cassie headed toward the house.

"Night." Rhett hopped off the rail, closed up the main barn and walked around it to ensure the chicken coop was secure for the night. Ajax trotted along with him. Millie had disappeared into the shadows.

Movement up the dirt road caught Rhett's eye. The road led to properties deeper in the woods—the original Bar D homestead sat on the shores of a small lake, and a small cabin the Monroes owned, where Tanner and his kids were staying.

A woman stood about fifty feet away, unmoving, like a deer that didn't want to attract a nearby human's notice.

Ajax noticed. He raced toward her.

"He's harmless," Rhett yelled, rather than trying to call the dog back. Why waste his breath when Ajax was only obedient for Cassie?

The woman wore loose, tan linen pants

and a blue crewneck sweater. She held out her hand like a traffic cop. "Sit!"

Ajax skidded to a stop in front of her.

"Good boy." She patted him on the head.

Ajax accepted the praise and then leaped away, running toward an approaching Rhett, circling behind him and heading back toward the woman, picking up speed.

The woman held out her hand once more, repeating her command. "Sit!"

Rhett could have told her it was a waste of breath. Ajax needed to shed his excitement over meeting someone new. And sure enough, the big dog doubled back behind her and headed toward Rhett for another round.

"Okay, Ajax. Run it off." Rhett stopped a few feet away from the woman. She had sun-kissed, short brown curls and classical features—her nose was just the right length for her face—an observation that gave him the impression that she had good manners. She'd know which fork to use for salad or dessert. "Forgive my dog. He's got new-person anxiety, which gives him the zoomies. Give him a couple more laps to get it out of his system."

Ajax lapped them again.

Her eyes followed the dog's progress. "I've never heard of dogs having anxiety, or zoomies, for that matter."

"It's not just people that get nervous or hold on to memories when things didn't go the way they should have." Rhett rather liked the woman's eyes. They were big and brown, and shone with intelligence.

Ajax came to a stop between them, collapsing to his stomach as if his legs had given out.

"And there you have it. A demonstration of the zoomies." Rhett knelt to give the dog repeated strokes of reassurance. "It's a good coping technique, don't you think?"

The woman laughed.

Almost immediately, she stopped, cocking her head as if listening to the peal of laughter as it died out.

"I haven't laughed in a long time." She gave him a sheepish grin. "Maybe I should run circles, like Ajax."

Rhett stood, returning her grin, and upped the charm ante by tipping his hat, hoping her smile might blossom. "I'll stand still if you want to give it a try, ma'am."

"I'm afraid I didn't wear my zoomie shoes." She wriggled her bare toes in a pair of plastic flip-flops.

They stood staring at each other for a moment as the sky darkened. He felt as if he could stare at her for hours and not get bored. Odd thought, that.

"I've seen you." She gestured toward the land south of the lake. "Riding a horse through the trees like you're chasing the devil himself."

Her admission gave him a little thrill. "I saw you sitting outside the old homestead a time or two." He hadn't wanted to disturb her, so he'd kept to the other side of the lake.

"I like the outdoors, although the weather here has been rather tame." She gazed up at the darkening sky, revealing a graceful, slender throat.

"You should see Second Chance in the winter. No one calls our winter weather tame." Ugh. He was talking about the weather? "Were you headed this way for a reason? Do you need a cup of sugar or to borrow some eggs?"

"I'm not much for the domestic arts." Her gaze came to rest on his face as she shook her head. "I should get back before it gets too dark."

"I'll walk you home."

"No need." She turned and started up the slope.

"I beg to differ." Rhett followed, slapping a hand against his thigh, signaling to Ajax to come. "A cowboy never lets a woman walk home through bear-infested woods." He length-ened his stride until he caught up to her.

"Bears?" Her flip-flop-snapping pace in-creased.

"There's also an occasional wild bull, packs of coyotes and families of raccoons." He could go on, but he didn't want to terrify her.

"Welcome to the wilds of Idaho." She didn't sound afraid. He almost thought he heard her chuckle.

"Yes, ma'am. I'm Rhett Diaz and I'm happy to welcome you to these parts."

She didn't reply, not even with her name.

They didn't say more until they reached the top of the rise and the lake came into view, still as glass in the gathering dusk.

"I hope you're enjoying the lake, Ms. Mon-roe." He may not have known her first name, but his grandfather had mentioned a Monroe was staying at the original family homestead as a favor to Shane. "I'd tell you it's good for swimming or boating, but that would be a lie."

Her gaze cut to him. "A lie?"

"I tipped over my grandfather's canoe when I was sixteen. I thought a canoe date would be romantic." There were just some things a man shouldn't attempt in a canoe. "We nearly sunk the canoe and drowned ourselves. I've hated the water ever since."

Her hand closed around his for a brief squeeze.

The front porch light came on. A large, old man stepped out on the small stoop, splaying his fingers through his bushy white beard. "There you are. And look at that, you've met the neighbors."

Ajax trotted up to him, trembling with excitement. There'd be another round of zoomies in a minute.

The woman wrapped her arms around her waist. In the gathering shadows, she suddenly looked haunted. "Thanks for the company." She hurried inside.

Rhett followed her to the door. "Did I say something wrong?"

"Naw." The old man held out a hand, much the same way the woman had gestured for Ajax to stop and sit. His white T-shirt was imprinted with an odd phrase: Don't Let Fear Define You. "Good night." He closed the door in Rhett's and Ajax's faces.

The sound was like a green light for Ajax. He put himself through his circular paces.

Rhett waited on the stoop until the dog was done, half hoping that the woman would open the door and say something else, maybe invite him inside to talk some more.

But the sky darkened, the wind picked up and the door remained closed.

CHAPTER FIVE

On Thursday, Cassie drove home from the stock auction in Ketchum.

Her sit-bones hurt from sitting too long and she kept muttering, *"A pony?"* over and over again.

That's all she'd been able to afford. A pony.

Ponies were notoriously hard to train and the return would be small. She felt like she was making one mistake after another when what she really needed was to launch a career to sustain her for a decade or so. Pony trainer wouldn't cut it. One trained pony would barely pay for the ranch's monthly electricity bill.

"I shouldn't have bought anything at all." Cassie reached the last mountain pass before the descent toward Second Chance and heard an unusual gasp from the engine. "Oh, no. Hang in there, baby." She couldn't afford repairs or a new truck.

The gasp turned into an all-out engine shudder that wouldn't stop.

Cassie turned out at the overlook, shut off

the engine and gingerly climbed down to check under the hood. "Like I know what I'm looking for." She peered at the engine anyway.

Giving up, she got out her cell phone to call Rhett just as a truck with Pennsylvania plates pulled in next to her.

It was Bentley, looking just as capable as he had the day that he'd gotten the Ferris wheel engine to work. "Need some help?" At her continued look of surprise, he added, "I just made a diaper run to Ketchum for Laurel and the twins."

"I'm so happy Laurel needed diapers." Cassie was gushing. She never gushed.

Yes, Virginia, capable, curmudgeonly pied pipers do exist and they strike my fancy.

"Hold those happy thoughts." Bentley gave her a wry smile. "At least, until I fix something."

"Right." She'd put the cart before the horse.

"What seems to be the problem?"

She tucked her phone back into her jeans pocket. "It sounds like everything in the engine is loose and rattling."

Bentley took her place at the front bumper, peering at the engine. "Can you start it up so I can see what's going on?"

"Could you take a step back?" Cassie made a shooing motion with one hand.

Bentley gave her a blank look. "Why?"

"Just in case a part comes flying at you," she explained, reminded of a similar conversation when he'd been working on the Ferris wheel. "I'm just being cautious." More so than usual given a bull had come flying at her over a week ago.

"I'll be fine." And somehow when Bentley said it, she believed him.

Forty-five minutes later, her truck was running better than it had in a decade.

"What did you do?" Cassie asked him.

Bentley shuffled his feet as if he were unused to compliments. "I tightened up connections loosened by years of you driving over Bar D's potholed driveway. Hoses, wires, clamps, carburetor. You should either fill the potholes or slow down."

It felt like the most words he'd ever spoken to her at one time. She nodded, unable to take her eyes off Bentley, not even to look at the view of the valley and the majestic Sawtooth Mountains.

A gust of wind crested the mountain and rushed between them, reminding her that Bentley was a Monroe, and she was just a tenant of his family's. He could fix her truck and make her heart beat faster, but he couldn't fix the trajectory of the Diaz family.

Unaware of her thoughts, Bentley efficiently put his tools back in his toolbox. "I'll follow you home."

"You don't need to do that." Was she blushing?

"It'd make me feel better."

Her, too. But somehow, she knew he wouldn't be well received by Tanner, who was waiting for her to return before he left to market rodeo school.

"Do you mind giving me some breathing room to…straighten up?" Cassie stumbled over the lie. "I can offer you a big piece of homemade peach cobbler." Because she was certain he'd just saved her hundreds of dollars in repairs, and because a tiny voice inside her head was saying he'd be good company to boot.

Bentley agreed, waiting to leave until she'd gotten her rig back on the road. He followed her down the mountain to Second Chance, turning off at the Lodgepole Inn.

When she pulled into the Bar D's ranch yard, Tanner was waiting for her, along with his kids and Millie, who greeted Cassie with a meow and a swish of her tail before disappearing in the direction of the chicken coop. Ajax sat sunning himself at the main barn door, not troubling to get up.

"I'm going to miss you guys so much." Tanner gave each child a bear hug, a kiss and a declaration of love. "You be good for Cassie." When he turned to Cassie, he looked like he was struggling to hang on to a brave smile. "I put their suitcases and stuff on the front porch and..."

Were those tears in Tanner's eyes?

Cassie wanted to look away.

Sniffing, Tanner lowered the brim of his cowboy hat and said huskily, "This is the first time we've been apart since my wife passed away. I'll call every night." He cleared his throat, got into his old truck and waved as he drove off, leaving his kids clustered around Cassie as if she were a pied piper.

"I'm hungry," Quinn said when Tanner's truck was out of sight. His clothes were clean, for once, although Cassie bet it was only a matter of time until dirt found that spotless shirt.

"Me, too," Mia said, fidgeting with the hem of her red dress.

Normally, Cassie took care of livestock first after an auction. But in this case, she decided to make an exception.

And so it was that when Bentley parked his truck in the ranch yard, Cassie and the kids had just returned to the trailer to unload the pony.

Ajax decided Bentley was worth getting up for, the disloyal beast, thumping his tail at Bentley's touch. Millie appeared, somehow wheedling her way in between Bentley's legs. She rubbed her head against his calf, keeping out of the dog's way.

Bentley had perfect timing. Cassie was beginning to realize she was in something of a bind. The rear gate on the trailer was a drop-down that formed a ramp. Its use required physical leverage. The livestock auction staff had loaded the pony for Cassie, lowering and then raising the gate.

Cassie swallowed her pride. "Can you help me with the trailer ramp?"

"Sure." Thankfully, Bentley didn't wait for her to show him what to do. The cat and dog hung back while he unlatched the trailer's gate and lowered the ramp by himself.

He was good-looking, chivalrous and handy. For the first time in what seemed like forever, Cassie wished she'd cleaned up and put on something fancier than blue jeans and a T-shirt.

The trailer was old and wasn't fancy. It had a webbed net across the back to keep stock from bolting as soon as the ramp was lowered. Not that the pony had designs on escaping, or could. Her lead rope was fastened to the front trailer wall. Still, she moved nervously, shifting her weight on her back legs.

"There's nothing to worry about, girlie." Cassie walked up the ramp and unfastened the netting.

Mia squealed, uncharacteristically demonstrative. "It's a horse for me. It's my size." She clapped her hands and ran toward the trailer.

"Stay back." Cassie pressed a finger to her lips. "And stay quiet. She's in a new place and she's scared."

"What's her name?" Quinn scratched under his cowboy hat.

"Shh." Mia reached for Bentley's hand. "She's scared."

Quinn knelt and slung his arm around Ajax's neck. "We knows what it's like to be scared in a new place. What's her name?"

"She doesn't have a name yet." That wasn't quite true. Her paperwork referred to her as Miss Poppylicious and her hooves were painted a sparkly pink, which said a lot about the pony breeder. Cassie entered the trailer and unhooked the gray pony's lead rope. "Come on, girlie. Let's take a look at your new home."

The little mare moved willingly and daintily until she reached the ramp. And then she just stopped, digging in her hooves the way a mule did when confronted with something unpleasant.

"Come on, girlie," Cassie said in a soothing voice, making a mental note to address the pony's fear in training.

Bentley lifted Mia into his arms and came to stand at the end of the ramp. "Here, horsey-horsey-horsey."

Both Tanner's kids giggled.

Cassie rolled her eyes. "That's not how it works, Bentley."

"Isn't it?" His grin said he'd prove her wrong. "Here, horsey-horsey-horsey."

The pony sniffed the air tentatively but didn't budge. Ajax, on the other hand, sat next to Bentley and stared up at him as if awaiting his next command.

"Here, horsey-horsey-horsey," Bentley said a third time.

The pony pranced in place and tossed her head as if she was working up the courage to obey Bentley's ridiculous summons. Before Cassie could say anything else, the pony launched herself several feet forward and landed sure-footed, quickly trotting the rest of the way down the ramp to nuzzle Bentley.

Startled, both the cat and the dog leaped back. Ajax held his ground, but Millie decided the chickens were more to her liking, trotting off, gray tail snapping.

"What is it with you and your *animal* magnetism?" Cassie stumbled up next to him, hip throbbing in protest. But she couldn't stop smiling. She wanted to nuzzle Bentley, too!

This has got to stop.

"It's nothing." Bentley set the little girl down. "I was experimenting. I didn't think it would work."

Mia, Quinn and Ajax surrounded the pony. Mia and Quinn gave her neck loving pats. Ajax sniffed her from a safe distance before returning to Bentley's side.

"It *is* something. Something about you." Cassie stared into Bentley's brown eyes. "My dog, my cat, my horse and now my pony. They all loved you at first sight."

"That might be an overstatement." Bentley shrugged, looking apologetic.

"I love Uncle Bentley," Mia said. "And my pony."

"See?" Cassie pointed at the sweet child, refusing to correct Mia's impression that the pony was hers.

"What's her name?" Quinn demanded. "Everybody needs a name."

"I suppose her name is Poppy," Cassie said absently, distracted by the thought that she was attracted to Bentley, and had been since they'd first met. "And don't think I've shelved the conversation about pied pipers, Mr. Monroe. There's a story behind this, I bet."

"I'm just an average guy who can't remember the last time someone called him *Mr.* Monroe."

"You're so wrong." Cassie laughed. "You're miles from average."

And probably not perfect, but he seemed perfect to her.

PEOPLE DIDN'T DELVE too deeply into Bentley's past or his personality and he liked it that way.

He'd been close to his twin brother and shattered when he died.

He'd been close to Grandpa Harlan when he was younger and shattered when he died.

Olivia's boating accident had happened just months after losing Grandpa Harlan. Although Bentley and Olivia had never been close, he'd offered her a place to stay after her near drowning. He'd assumed they'd become closer. But Olivia had barely come out of her room. And then one morning, she'd disappeared.

If Bentley's life was a metaphor, there was an empty seat next to him at a table, and as reserved as he was, this year, increasingly, he wanted someone to fill that seat. He'd assumed that person would be his sister. But maybe he was wrong. He studied the delicate lines of Cassie's face. Maybe…

Mia's and Quinn's laughter brought him back to the present, to the Bar D, to Cassie and her probing questions.

She doesn't think I'm average.

Bentley wasn't sure if that was good or bad.

Good, Bryce's voice in his head seemed to say.

And yet, logically, Bentley could not stop thinking that their lives were literally thousands of miles apart. How could a simple attraction turn into a good thing? Good things weren't supposed to be flings.

He studied Cassie's face beneath her cowboy hat.

She had the kind of gentle smile that encouraged conversation. The kind of determined posture that told of hard battles fought. The kind of feminine curves that he appreciated. And yet, despite all that, he knew with certainty that in a crowded room she'd be in the center of the action while he'd be sitting in the back spectating.

"Quinn, can you walk Poppy around the ranch yard? I think she'd like to see her surroundings." Cassie placed the gray pony's lead rope in the little boy's hand.

"What about me?" Mia protested.

"You can help." Quinn stood tall and gave his little sister the end of the rope, while he retained a hold on the middle. Together, they led the pony away.

Cassie turned to face Bentley and said in a quiet voice, "Okay, now give. How did you become the pied piper?"

"I don't know." And that was as much the truth as anything. Bentley glanced around the ranch yard, searching for something that needed doing, any excuse for avoiding conversation. Talk would only make Cassie realize his failings. The horse trailer ramp was still down. The trailer floor was remarkably clean. He lifted the ramp and set the bolt on one side. "Why do you want to know?"

"Because it's a skill. A…a…gift. And you don't seem at all happy with it." Cassie moved to slide the bolt on the other side of the trailer tailgate home. "Can I guess? Are you the oldest of a large family? Did you have a menagerie of pets as a child? Am I warm?"

"No."

Across the ranch yard, Quinn and Mia giggled. Next to him, Cassie said nothing. Did nothing. She was just there, waiting. The way

Bentley was often in a room with others, not actively participating in a conversation but watching everything that went on. Maybe she wouldn't be in the middle of the action.

She could take that seat next to me.

If he spoke. If he told her things about himself he hadn't dared tell others.

Bentley pressed his lips together. Offering information about himself to a relative stranger made him feel vulnerable. And yet, an unusual pressure to speak built inside of him.

He faced Cassie, and when their gazes connected, the vulnerable feeling inside eased enough for him to open up. "As a child, I was always the quiet Monroe. My twin brother could charm the flowers from a beauty queen. My sister could wrestle said beauty queen to the ground." He paused, surprised that so many words had spilled out. "My mother used to say if she didn't hear me, I was most likely out of the way taking apart something to see how it worked."

Cassie chuckled. "I hope you knew enough to put things back together."

He winced. "Not always. My father's laptop was an early fail."

"But none of that explains your pied piperness." Cassie checked on the pony-walking posse. "Surely, you know how your magne-tism works."

"No." Bentley shrugged. "I'm just...*here*. Kids...animals... I don't talk much, which I suppose means I'm a good listener or not much of a threat." He didn't believe his reti-cence explained anything. But whatever it was that drew animals and children to him, Bent-ley was baffled by it himself.

Thankfully, Cassie changed the subject. "I confess, there are so many of you Monroes in town that I've lost track of cousins and sib-lings, family trees and the like. What are your siblings up to now?"

He drew back, wary once more. "My brother died a couple of years ago after a car accident."

"Oh, I'm so sorry." Cassie spoke quickly, and with the utmost sincerity.

"And my sister..." Bentley focused on the pony procession, needing to turn away from the unbearable loss of his siblings. He hadn't known how important they were to him until they were gone. "She used to be a sailboat captain."

Cassie did a double take. "Is there such a thing?"

"Yeah. She raced professionally." He shook his head. "Past tense. She recently capsized a very expensive racing sailboat I designed, and lost all of her sponsorships." The accident alone was enough to break someone's spirit, but without her sponsorships, Olivia couldn't sail again.

Quinn and Mia stopped their procession to hug the tiny pony's neck.

"Poor thing." Cassie touched his arm in a brief show of compassion. "I've heard it said that you have to make your comebacks stronger than your setbacks. But listen to me. I should take my own advice." Her expression became resolute. "Now, I owe you peach cobbler. I'd best get this pony settled or it'll be dinnertime before we eat some."

Thirty minutes later, Poppy was in a stall, fed and watered, and the trailer was backed into its spot behind the barn.

While Cassie led Bentley and the kids to the house, Ajax sprinted ahead and darted in a dog door.

Cassie moved with a stiffness he'd mistaken for pride the other day. Using short, stilted steps, she was clearly in pain as she led them in the kitchen door, took off her boots and then moved slowly to the kitchen sink. "Okay, everybody. Remove your boots and wash the horse off your hands or no cobbler."

Without protest, Quinn and Mia plopped

on the floor and began pulling their boots off with only the barest assists from Bentley. Which was good, since Ajax had appeared with a furry squeaker toy in his mouth.

Squeak-squeak-squeak.

The big dog panted and pranced and teased Bentley to take it, always leaping out of reach when Bentley's hand came toward him.

Squeak-squeak-squeak.

"Don't let Ajax pester you." Cassie transferred dishes from the sink into the dishwasher. Her long black hair fell gently past her shoulder blades. "Ajax plays keep-away, not fetch."

"I'm onto you now, buddy." Dodging the black dog's taunting snout, Bentley unlaced and removed his work boots, and then joined the kids at the sink, which had a drippy faucet. He lifted Quinn and helped him wash his hands.

The kitchen was fairly small, with worn oak cabinets and a green Formica countertop that extended into a peninsula with two barstools. The linoleum on the floor was also a dark green. The appliances were white. A round kitchen table filled one corner, surrounded by sturdy-looking captain's chairs, somewhat nicked and scratched. Like much of the rest of the Bar D, everything showed signs of hard use.

"So you don't have kids?" Cassie's gaze fell to Bentley's ringless left hand. "You're so good with them."

"No. I've never been married." Her direct, conversational approach this afternoon had broken through his usual reticence with strangers and large crowds. So much so, that he kept on babbling as he lifted Mia and helped her wash her hands. "I have a niece. My brother's child. She's two and a half. And my cousins have kids. I'm sure you've seen them around town."

"Yes and…I haven't been married either." Her cheeks pinkened.

Was she uncomfortable sharing details about herself, too? He allowed himself a small smile, directing it at Ajax, who continued to prance about the kitchen making noise.

Squeak-squeak-squeak.

"I'm bored," Quinn piped up, skating around the linoleum and the dog in his holey socks. "Can we watch TV?"

"Yes." Cassie helped them get settled in the living room, which was crowded with two overstuffed brown couches, a recliner and a small nondescript coffee table. One of the Diaz family must have liked green ten or more years ago, because there was outdated green shag in the living room and down the hall.

Shane had told Bentley that the local economy was bad, but here was proof.

Cassie returned to the kitchen.

"You're not so bad with kids yourself," Bentley told her.

"I'll be the first to admit I don't know up from down when it comes to anything outside of cattle and horses. I love training horses and the simplicity of ranch life. But these kids have earned a place in my heart." She stumbled when Ajax leaped around her playfully, bumping into her legs and whipping her with that big happy tail of his.

"I've got you." Bentley steadied Cassie's arm. It was a brief touch, but a lock of her silken hair brushed over his skin and a burst of heat traveled up his arm.

"Ajax," she scolded, eyes closed. "Go to bed."

The dog's tail wag slowed. He ambled over to a large cushion, plopped down on it and gave his toy one last squeak.

"Are you okay?" Bentley forgot about the state of her ranch and her carnival rides. Front and center was her grimace of pain and the color draining from her face. He felt an unexpected impulse to smooth a hand over her back and offer comfort.

Cassie drew a slow breath. "I'm…fine. Ajax took me by surprise, is all."

This fascination with her was taking Bentley by surprise. He wasn't a man who enjoyed surprises. And this attraction… It couldn't lead anywhere. She was close to Tanner and his kids. She'd probably take Tanner's side in his claim for a piece of Second Chance.

Reluctantly, Bentley turned the conversation in a Shane-approved direction. "Did your grandfather give up his dream of resurrecting the carnival rides?"

"No, but we've agreed to disagree." Cassie took the cobbler from the refrigerator and cut portions she placed on small plates. "I need to make money. Honestly, I need more money than I currently make training horses. For a few years now, I've been thinking that I need to find a new line of work. But I love horses, not the carnival ride business. And besides, traveling around and setting up rides…that just isn't for me."

"I was thinking…" Bentley got milk from the refrigerator and poured out the last of it into two small glasses he found in a cabinet, intending to give them to the kids. "There's some flat land down by the highway near the end of your drive. Those rides would make for a good attraction for Second Chance during the spring and summer months. You wouldn't have to take them on the road to make them profitable. I can understand how that would be daunting for...for—" his gaze stroked over her as his mind went over the belabored way she walked "—anyone."

Cassie put a plate of cobbler in the microwave and slammed the door. "You were going to say it would be daunting *for a girl*."

A woman. Cassie was in no way, shape or form a girl.

But her ire had Bentley backpedaling. "That's not what I meant. It's just..." He felt sheepish as he gestured toward her and stated what to him was obvious. "You move like you're in pain."

She froze for a second. "I'm not—"

"My father fell off a horse during a polo game once. He walked like an old man the rest of the summer," Bentley said quietly. "Like you do."

Smooth line, Bentley.

"Oh, you noticed? I... I... Give me a moment." With slow, stiff movements, Cassie delivered plates for the kids to the living room coffee table and then brought a second set of plates to the kitchen table, indicating Bentley should sit across from her.

As soon as Bentley sat down, Ajax moved under the table and began squeaking his toy. Bentley extended his foot and rubbed the dog's tummy. Immediately, the squeaking stopped.

Cassie settled gingerly into her chair and then told him a story about being thrown from a beast called Tornado Tom.

"You rode a bull?" Bentley's opinion of her skyrocketed to a class with adventurous Olivia.

"Only for about three seconds." She crossed her arms on the table, making it wobble. What didn't fluctuate was her gaze on him. It was as steady as her bull riding nerve. "It might have been safer to find a part-time job in town selling quilts and knit scarves at your cousin Laurel's boutique."

"Safer, but it says something about your character that you tried." Bentley stopped rubbing Ajax with his foot only to have the squeaking resume. With a sigh, he kept up with the canine tummy rubs. "My only question is… Why did you feel the need to test yourself that way?"

"Honestly?" Cassie took a bite of peach cobbler, perhaps needing a moment to consider her words. "Besides needing money,

like now, I think you Monroes are going to
sell Second Chance off at the end of the year
when all our leases run out. If bull riding had
been my thing, a few purses would have tided
me over and provided a down payment on the
Bar D. And if your family turned me down, at
least I'd have money to start somewhere else,
doing something else, although I have no idea
what that might be." She paused, stilling in a
way people do when they've said more than
they meant to. "It's not that I want to leave.
I'll miss the sense of history this place has,
that sense of belonging and carrying on family traditions. The Bar D has thrived through
times of feast and survived through times of
famine."

"It's good to think ahead. Clearly, you're a
worst-case scenario thinker, while I…I didn't
even consider the possibility of being made
to start over." Briefly, he explained the odd
terms of his grandfather's will, simultaneously
wondering what it was about this woman that
made him want to learn all about her and have
her learn all about him. "I'm not impulsive. I
thought as a Monroe that I had a job with the
family company for life. And now I'm weigh-
ing my options in Philadelphia." Slowly, as
was his habit.

"Who knew we had that in common."

Cassie was a good listener and easy to talk to. "For all the rug was pulled out from under you, you don't seem very bitter."

He moved crust crumbs around on the plate with his fork. "I think that's because I used to wonder what it would be like to do other things. To work on other projects in other fields. I've always liked a good puzzle." And Cassie was a puzzle to him. Bright, hardworking, courageous. She could be so much more outside Second Chance.

And wasn't that wishful thinking?

He dragged his gaze from her mesmerizing face before he encouraged this fascination they had for each other more than he'd already done. "Look at that. Those kids fell asleep." Bentley pointed toward the living room. "I'll get their dishes before Ajax decides he'd like to finish their cobbler, which was excellent, by the way."

They worked together quietly to clean up the kitchen.

All too soon, Cassie was walking Bentley out to his truck while two kids and a dog slept inside the house. Bentley wanted to stay longer. To listen to Cassie talk about her life. To make note of her tendency to blush when the conversation made wide circles around the fact that they had chemistry.

He stopped to stare toward the open barn with the carnival rides. And then at Whistler as the swayback mare plodded toward the nearest fence separating them. The Bar D was old. The work needed wasn't going to earn Bentley any accolades, except for the gratitude of one intriguing cowgirl. And maybe his cousin Shane.

But whatever attraction he felt toward Cassie, it wasn't anything he should bank on long-term. Her roots were here and his… His were going to be set down in Philadelphia somewhere near his industry. Best keep that in mind and not form any attachments. Besides, once Cassie got to know him, she'd realize that quiet engineers didn't make courageous cowgirls happy.

Bentley turned to face Cassie. "You should talk to Shane about setting up those carnival rides down by the highway. Get his permission to use the land."

"That's only possible if you volunteer to help fix them," Cassie shamelessly pointed out, smiling the way a pretty woman smiles at a man she's interested in.

Me. He could hardly keep a grin from bursting out on his face.

"I could help," he allowed carefully. "I'm

good with engines. But I'm not much good with rust removal or painting."

"If you think I could make decent money running them or that it might help us stay here…I could figure out paint and rust removal."

"Talk to Shane. He's full of…ideas. If he approves your use of that land, I'll come work on the engines."

"You'd better watch out, Bentley." Cassie stared at him as if he regularly hung the moon. "If you continue to rescue me, I might fall under that pied piper spell of yours."

He didn't know what to say to that, so he got into his truck and drove off.

Grinning from ear to ear.

CHAPTER SIX

OLIVIA MONROE WAS LANDLOCKED.

Trapped.

She was used to living where she could smell the salt air, hear waves crashing and feel the ocean wind tug her short hair when she was outside. The ocean used to make her feel alive. She wasn't used to smelling tall pines, hearing them sway in the mountain air, or feeling a crisp breeze on the lakeshore that was more like a cool caress.

She stared out the kitchen window at the small mountain lake. It was calm.

I should feel that calm.

Olivia didn't. She stared at the water and felt fear.

Her mind went back to the day of the sailboat race. It had been the maiden voyage for *Bryce's Heart*, the racing sailboat that her older brother Bentley had designed and built. The craft was everything Olivia had dreamed of in a racing yacht—sleek, lightweight, maneuverable. She was going to win a lot of races helming *Bryce's Heart*. Bentley had looked so proud when Olivia christened the boat, and she'd been so grateful that she'd hugged him.

Lord, how Bentley hated public displays of affection. He'd stiffened and patted her on the back awkwardly. *Go make Bryce proud.*

She'd been so certain that she could.

The ocean had been choppy and the competition fierce. Olivia hadn't cared. *Bryce's Heart* flew over the water. They were going to win the race. Olivia had felt the certainty of it, like a trumpet blast through her veins. They'd approached the first turn marker five boat lengths ahead of the rest of the field. She could be conservative and take the turn at a slower pace, but she'd wanted to make a statement.

Foolish pride.

She'd tried to turn the boat on a dime. The wind had kicked up at just the wrong moment.

She could still hear the sharp slap of sails against the waves as they went over, and the panicked shouts of her crew. She could still feel the cold ocean water envelop her and the crack of the boom against her skull. And then there was darkness.

She'd come to on the deck of a race official's speedboat as a medical crew administered CPR.

Death.

It had come unexpectedly. It had come while she felt like she was on top of the world. And although Olivia had been given a second chance—

There was irony in retreating to Second Chance, Idaho.

—she couldn't get past the fact that she'd been dead. She'd just celebrated her thirtieth birthday. She wasn't supposed to be celebrating a second lease on life.

"You're thinking of the accident again." Sonny's voice cut through her dark thoughts. "If you want to relive the event, you need to talk it through. That's why I'm here." Sonny was a sports psychologist who specialized in treating athletes who had trouble recovering from bad crashes, bone breaks and near death experiences. He came up behind her. With his round girth, white beard and his white hair, he could have been a garden gnome come to life. He had a sense of humor, displayed by his wearing of a red T-shirt that proclaimed: Use Your Words.

She was beginning to think he'd had a month's worth of T-shirts printed up with his motivational messages, all encouraging her to talk and heal.

Talk. That was key to Sonny's recovery plan.

Ask yourself why you're afraid. Confront sadness with your optimism. Apologize to guilt and move on.

Just thinking about having conversations with herself was exhausting. And yet, Sonny's presence was comforting.

"Fear needs a talking-to, Olivia," Sonny was saying. "If you want, you can give fear a name. Why don't we call him Stan? Tell Stan he's like an anchor dragging you down."

It was the wrong metaphor to use. Olivia's gut clenched. "You know I don't want to talk about the accident, not even in role play. If I wanted to talk about it, I have a phone full of people ready to do so. They've left dozens of text messages and voice mails." All of which had gone unanswered. Olivia turned on the tap and rinsed out her tea mug, which was why she'd come into the kitchen in the first place. "There's got to be some other way to move on."

"Oh, sure," Sonny deadpanned. "There's journaling. Writing toxic thoughts on sticky notes. Doodling your feelings. But they all have one thing in common, Olivia, and that's acknowledging the most terrifying thoughts you're trying to hide. You're a smart woman. You can probably figure out ways to hide from your innermost thoughts forever."

"Could I?" She faced him, the untrusty water at her back. "Could I do that and race?"

"No."

She turned back around, staring out the window. On the other side of the lake, no horse and rider galloped through the pine trees. She hadn't seen Rhett ride past today. Thinking about the handsome cowboy she'd met on the road was easier than thinking about having died in the ocean she used to love. But it served no purpose. And Sonny wanted every thought to be purposeful.

Although… Hadn't Rhett mentioned something about an accident he'd had with a canoe on the lake? A near drowning? They had that in common. And commonalities had purpose. They bound people together.

"Olivia, not talking about death won't make the fact that you died and were brought back to life go away. You have to be able to speak about your experience if you want to move past it." Sonny came to stand next to her, stroking his whiskers. "How badly do you want to race again?"

"More than words can express." Olivia set the mug upside down on the draining board, gaze cutting to the small dinghy beached mere feet from where she stood. "I will sail and compete and command a crew again." But her words felt hollow because she was no longer young, naive and invincible.

The deadly power of the ocean had stolen that from her.

CHAPTER SEVEN

AFTER LEAVING THE Bar D, Bentley went straight to the Bucking Bull to see Shane.

He'd barely shut off the engine when Shane hurried down the porch steps to greet him. "This is good news, I hope."

Bentley leaned against the truck bed. "If you're serious about granting Cassie Diaz rights to use that acre of land by the highway, then I think I might be welcome at the Bar D every day, at least until I fix their rides."

Traitor.

Bentley swallowed. Cassie didn't deserve to be used, but he supposed his family didn't deserve to be conned either. Was it too much to ask for Tanner to be true to his word and *not* come to the Bar D while Bentley was working on the rides? It was hard to spy on someone if they weren't around.

"Are you starting tomorrow?" Shane was practically rubbing his palms together with glee.

"No." Bentley frowned. "I told Cassie I'd

wait until you gave her permission to use the land by the highway. Besides, Tanner won't be back for a few days." Bentley explained about the effort to promote their rodeo school.

"Well, when we get the ball rolling, you don't have to fix those rides at warp speed." Shane checked something on his phone. "In fact, when Tanner returns, make sure you take breaks and talk to him."

Bentley thought about subdued Mia and staunch Quinn. Again, he felt a sour label being applied to himself: *traitor.* "You make it sound so underhanded."

"It would be underhanded if you worked on the Bar D under an assumed name. People *like* you. Heaven only knows why. You hardly say a word."

Oh, he'd said plenty to Cassie today, talking as easily as if she was a member of the Monroe family. "I'm not cut out for this spy stuff. Why don't you just ask Tanner out for coffee?"

"You think I haven't?" Shane scoffed. "If he'd just meet with me and tell me how much money he wants to leave Second Chance, I'd be able to sleep at night."

"I assume you've calculated the value of his share of Second Chance and the gold."

"Of course." Shane frowned.

"And you consulted with Cousin Holden

about making him a fair offer to leave town?" Presumably one that wouldn't be the equivalent to a full share.

"Of course." Shane's frown deepened.

"Uncle Bentley! Uncle Bentley!" Three young cowboys pounded down the front steps. They were Shane's soon-to-be-adopted sons, as he was marrying their widowed mother. Each carried something.

"Papa Shane said you could fix my video game." Davey, the oldest, thrust a game console toward Bentley. "It freezes."

"What's this?" Bentley scowled at Shane.

"Papa Shane said you could fix anything." Charlie, the middle boy, cut in front of his older brother and placed a tablet on top of the console. "This is slow."

Little Adam wormed his way between his older brothers. "Papa Shane said you're like one of Santa's elves." He grinned as sweet as a Christmas angel and handed Bentley a truck and its remote control. "We've been waiting for you to visit. And now it's just like Christmas."

"You're a card-carrying member of Santa's workshop, Bentley. Don't deny it," Shane teased. "Someday we'll get you to sing Christmas carols with us."

"You're such a comedian, Shane." From an

early age, the Monroes had assumed Bentley could fix things and didn't mind being shoved away somewhere to do so. Although the advantage of that was sometimes Grandpa Harlan had sat with him.

You have talent for knowing how things work, he'd told Bentley one sunny summer day. *And a sense of humor you keep locked inside.*

Everybody wants to make a joke. Bentley shrugged his shoulders, which were bent over a clock radio he was fixing while his siblings and cousins were swimming in the pool. *And they enjoy the spotlight telling a punch line gives them.*

Grandpa Harlan had ruffled his hair. *Spotlights are wide enough to shine on all Monroes. You'll remember that when I'm gone, won't you?*

Bentley hadn't believed the part about the spotlights at the time. But eventually, he'd found his own place to shine. And now, he needed to find another.

"Adam, hold the door for Uncle Bentley." In the here and now, Shane inclined his head toward the farmhouse, while Bentley juggled electronics and memories. "Now, don't argue. Stay. Dinner will be ready in a couple of hours. You'll have this stuff fixed in no time."

Bentley would have liked to prove his cousin wrong. But he had everything repaired and in good working order before Franny, his future cousin-in-law, had dinner out of the oven. Which meant, he had nothing to occupy his thoughts at dinner, other than Cassie, who he shouldn't be thinking about, and Tanner, who he didn't want to think about.

"Pass the green beans, Bentley." In exchange, Shane handed Bentley the plate of biscuits. "Gertie, have you heard anything from your good friend Ruth?" Also known as Tanner's grandmother.

The entire table seemed to groan—Franny, her three boys, Franny's sister-in-law, Emily, even Bentley. Apparently, Bentley wasn't the only one tired of Shane's dogged campaign to trace Tanner's family history.

Gertie was Franny's grandmother-in-law. She had short, flyaway white hair and piercing eyes that seemed to drill a hole in Shane's meddling head. "I haven't talked to her since June. Did you invite another Monroe to my table to press me for information?" She leaned toward Adam, her youngest great-grandson. "I feel like I'm being interrogated."

Adam giggled. "I don't know what that means, Granny Gertie."

"She's making a joke," Shane grumbled. He set the green bean platter in the middle of the table. "Where did Ruth settle when she left Second Chance? Some small town in Texas?"

Gertie picked up her knife and fork, tapping their ends with finality on the wooden table. "I'm sure I don't remember. She left town decades ago."

"Wow, this meat loaf is delicious," Bentley told Franny, shifting in his antique wooden chair.

"Thank you." Franny gave her fiancé a significant look, which Shane ignored.

"And whatever you've got in the oven for dessert smells delicious," Bentley added before Shane could continue the third degree.

"And to think the Monroes call Bentley the quiet one." Emily nudged her nephew Charlie, earning a frown from Shane.

Bentley considered taking his plate out to the front porch, but he was afraid the three boys might follow him. He glanced down at the family Labrador, whose gray muzzle was practically in his lap, big brown eyes staring up at him adoringly. Or perhaps he was hopeful that Bentley would slip him something from his dinner plate.

"Is it so hard to give me one little thing?" Shane held up a hand, thumb and forefinger touching.

"Ruth is family," Gertie said with finality. "Like a sister to me. And don't forget that she's your great-aunt. You don't investigate family."

"Oh, so you know for a fact that Tanner, Ruth's grandson, is a blood relation of mine?"

Gertie narrowed her eyes. "I've lost my appetite." She scooted her chair back and stood. "Harlan wouldn't have wanted proof. He'd take Tanner—*and Ruth*—at their word." Contrary to her statement, Gertie must have been hungry. She carried her plate, utensils and water glass to a room just off the kitchen and closed the door.

Shane half turned to face Bentley, who had just put some very creamy mashed potatoes in his mouth.

He swallowed. "What?"

The table gave a collective laugh, as if the joke was on Bentley.

Adam picked up a green bean with his fingers. "Papa Shane wants you to talk to Granny Gertie."

"Yeah." Davey squirted ketchup on his slice of meat loaf. "He gave you *The Look.*"

"We all know what *The Look* means." Charlie took a big bite of biscuit, causing a squirt of jelly on his cheek.

Still staring at Bentley, Shane raised his eyebrows.

"The Look means I'm supposed to talk to her?" Bentley sought confirmation from Franny and Emily, but the women had their heads bent over their plates.

"Everybody likes you," Shane reminded him softly.

"You can fix anything," Adam added, before stuffing a green bean in his mouth.

"You're not going to let me eat in peace until I do this, are you?" Bentley asked Shane.

"Nope." Shane's answer was echoed by those three boys. "Nope. Nope. Nope."

"Fine." Bentley crumpled his paper napkin and placed it next to his plate. "Nobody touch my mashed potatoes." Because they were fabulous and that serving dish was cleaned out.

He got up and left the dining room for the kitchen, pausing to knock on the door. "Gertie?"

"Not interested!"

Bentley turned back toward the dining room, arms extended in supplication.

Everyone at the large dining table was grinning at him, even the women.

Shane made a shooing motion with one hand. "Do it for the family."

Of all the things Shane could have said to Bentley, that was the one statement that had the power to move him.

"Okay, but I mean it, don't touch my mashed potatoes." Bentley faced Gertie's door again and knocked. "Gertie, I hope you're decent because my food is getting cold and I'm coming in." He opened the door.

Gertie perched on the edge of her bed. Her dinner sat on a nearby TV tray. Her bedroom was stuffed with heavy dark wood furniture, crocheted doilies, framed photographs and several miniature stagecoaches. The old woman dabbed at her mouth with her paper napkin. "If you've come on Shane's behalf, you aren't wanted."

"No Monroe ever admits to doing Shane's bidding." But Bentley pretty much figured that everyone did so at one point or another. He closed the door, careful not to dislodge a dark brown cowboy hat hanging on the back. "Will you humor me so I can finish eating?" He picked up a small ceramic stagecoach. "Reminiscent of the infamous Mike Moody?" The man who locals claimed had robbed a stagecoach and then hidden a fortune in gold.

"And his sister, Letty." Gertie nodded,

scooping up a bite of mashed potatoes dripping with butter. "She was the brains of the gang, you know."

"So Ashley and Jonah tell me." At least, that's the way his Monroe cousins had written their script. "Have you met Tanner?"

Gertie shook her head. "He hasn't come by to pay his respects. And I don't drive anymore. Have you met him?"

Bentley nodded. "Prickly man. His kids must take after their mother." He allowed himself a small smile.

"She's dead, I heard," Gertie said matter-of-factly. "It's tough being widowed. You should make allowances for Tanner's hard edges."

Bentley was grateful for the opening. "It's tough leading a family, as you well know. Shane doesn't have it out for Tanner."

In the dining room, the rest of the family laughed uproariously.

Gertie harrumphed. "Blood doesn't bind family, hearts do. And Shane knows that. He's now as much Clark to us as he is Monroe. But there's something about Tanner that brings out the worst in Shane."

"Agreed." Bentley moved closer to the door. After all, this was going nowhere, and his food was getting cold. Still, he hesitated, hand on the knob. "I know why Shane's being a pain about Tanner, but I don't know why Tanner's being a pain about anything. Do you?"

Frowning, Gertie shook her head.

"Ruth might know," Bentley said gently. "And if she doesn't, at least Shane will know that you consider his feelings as important as Ruth's." He left her, returning to his seat. He took inventory of his dinner and then fixed each of the assembled with a hard stare. "All right. Who ate my mashed potatoes?"

CHAPTER EIGHT

AFTER A NIGHT of babysitting, Cassie herded Quinn and Mia into the Bent Nickel Diner the way Ajax would have guided lost sheep toward safer pastures, except stiffly and without any power or grace.

She felt like the Tin Man in the Land of Oz when he'd been in need of an oil can. She was getting worse instead of better. So much for hoping she wouldn't need that surgery she couldn't afford or that she could put it off for several months or a year.

"Uncle Bentley!" Quinn spotted Cassie's favorite Monroe in a booth toward the back and ran over, followed by his sister. "We're here for breakfast." They climbed in the booth.

"Two hot chocolates to start them out, please." Cassie trailed along at a slower pace, still working the morning kinks out of her back, hip and legs. The stiffness was spreading.

Bentley turned warm brown eyes her way, but his gaze quickly morphed into one of concern. "If you're looking for Dr. Carlisle, you just missed her."

She waved him off.

"If you're looking for Shane, he hasn't come to town yet this morning." Bentley frowned.

Cassie shook her head, hobbling past his booth. She reached the community coffee cistern and claimed a mug from a stack there. "We're out of coffee at the Bar D." She poured herself a generous cup. Black. "We're also out of milk for the children and hay for the horses." Cassie held the hot mug of coffee beneath her nose and drank in the rich smell. "Well, technically, we're not out of alfalfa. It's in the storage barn." Her gaze lifted to Bentley's. "I just need someone with a strong back to move it to the main barn's hayloft."

He studied her face, murmuring a contemplative "Oh."

Cam topped two hot chocolates with whipped cream. "She means you, cousin."

"Oh." Bentley looked like he was processing Cassie's poorly articulated request and leaning toward refusal. "Cam, can you take the kids over to the counter and wipe their hands?"

Quinn stared at his palms. "My hands aren't dirty."

"His hands aren't dirty," Cassie echoed. "We washed up before we left."

"Apparently, their hands aren't dirty." Cam carried the hot chocolate mugs around the counter toward Bentley's booth.

"Cam." Bentley gave his cousin a put-upon look.

The chef glanced up at him. "Oh, message received, 'cuz." He set the mugs on the lunch counter and tapped the vinyl cushion on an empty barstool. "Your hot chocolates need to cool, guys. Let's practice good hygiene and get those hands good and superclean while we wait. I've got wipes."

Cassie couldn't imagine the need for such a production. What did Bentley have to say that the kids couldn't hear?

While Mia and Quinn rushed from the booth to their hot drinks, Bentley motioned for Cassie to come closer.

She took a few self-conscious steps toward him. "What? Did I ask too great a favor?"

"To move hay? No." Bentley raised his eyebrows. "I'm concerned for you, because you look… How did it go with the kids last night?"

"Fine. After you left, we made cookies." Cassie wanted to sound like it had all been hunky-dory, but it hadn't been. "After eating a dozen cookies, they wouldn't eat dinner. And at about eight o'clock they ate the last of the peach cobbler while I did the last rounds, closing up in the outbuildings." She took a generous sip of coffee. It was so hot that it nearly burned her tongue.

"In other words, they were all sugared up," he surmised.

She nodded. "And they were still bouncing off the walls at ten, while I..." This would have been embarrassing to admit if it were the only embarrassing thing to happen last night. "I was flat on my back in the living room, trying to ease the pressure in my hip while they used me as the infield of a racetrack...circling and circling until...*crash*." She glanced over her shoulder to make sure the kids weren't listening. They hadn't meant to hurt her.

Cam was wiping their hands with wet wipes.

Bentley leaned forward. "And then..."

Cassie lowered her voice. "There were tears when they landed on me." Not hers, although Quinn had landed on her hard enough to push the air from her lungs.

"Oh." Grimacing, Bentley drank some of his tea.

"Mia's scratched knee wasn't the worst of it. She was really upset. Kind of like Poppy when confronting the hinges of a horse trailer ramp. Only louder."

"That's rough."

"And then I learned they don't sleep alone. They need an adult in the room."

Bentley nodded slowly. "This might explain why Tanner is so cranky."

Cassie raised her mug to that, taking time to drink more much-needed, superhot caffeine. "So I slept on the guest room floor." Which wasn't as bad as it sounded since her orthopedist had recommended sleeping on her back on a hard surface. "But after about twenty minutes, Mia lay across my chest like a possessive barn cat, and later—I lost track of when—Quinn snuggled on one side of me and Ajax on the other side, so—"

"You got no sleep," Bentley surmised.

"Absolutely none." Cassie gulped the mug dry. "How did you know?"

Bentley ran a hand in a circle around his face, and then made the same motion in the general direction of Cassie. "Everything about you today looks...worn-out."

Cassie had enough pride to be offended, even though she knew it was true. She finger-combed her hair over one shoulder, realizing she'd forgotten to put on her cowboy hat this morning. She glanced down. At least, her boots were on.

"I'm concerned about your health," Bentley continued. "You look—"

"The kids want to drink their hot chocolate with *Uncle* Bentley," Cam interrupted, placing their mugs back on the booth's table.

Quinn and Mia scrambled onto the bench seat just as Shane pulled up outside in a new black Suburban.

"Can you keep an eye on the kids while I talk to Shane?" Cassie set her empty coffee mug on Bentley's table. "I need to ask about using that land." She didn't wait for Bentley's answer, because she knew it would take her a bit of time to get to the door on her stiff legs and there was no telling if Shane was coming in the Bent Nickel or the general store. She didn't want to have to chase after him.

To his credit, Shane took one look at Cassie coming out the diner's door and held up his hands as if passing her a gift. "Whatever you're asking, the answer is yes."

Cassie didn't think twice. "I need someone to help Bentley move hay at the Bar D this morning." Because her forgetful brother hadn't shifted the alfalfa as promised. He also hadn't told her that he'd used the last of their coffee yesterday.

Shane's jaw dropped. "Somehow... I thought you were going to ask me something else."

Cassie's slow steps finally brought her in front of Shane. "I also need to ask if our family can use your land to set up some kiddie carnival rides. Bentley mentioned the pasture on the highway at the turn to the Bar D might work. I know the rides are in bad shape, but I want to fix them up. I need to make some extra money." Rather desperately.

"That was the question I was expecting." Shane looked relieved. "And if you have a plan about signage, safety, hours of operation and staffing, I think we can work something out. As you know, I've been trying to increase Second Chance as a stop along the highway, not a stop sign on the highway." He gestured toward the one stop *sign* in town on the far side of the Lodgepole Inn.

Everything Shane mentioned about running the rides...

Signage, safety, operating hours, staffing. Cassie felt as if the burden of opening such a place was too much for her.

Shane grabbed her arms. "Are you okay?"

"I just... I didn't think through all the implications of operating the rides." She'd foolishly assumed that Grandpa Diaz would handle all that. How was she supposed to train horses *and* hang out all day at the highway waiting for business? "I'm sorry. Maybe I jumped the gun."

Shane slowly released her. "I have experience running a business. Let's talk after my cousin and I move hay."

"I'd like that." It was a big step and potentially life changing, and Cassie suddenly felt overwhelmed.

"Excuse me." A blond pregnant woman wearing glasses approached Cassie. "We haven't officially met, but I'm Dr. Carlisle, the town doctor."

Shane introduced Cassie. "I'll talk to Bentley about this hay business. See you, Doc."

Dr. Carlisle waited until Shane was inside the Bent Nickel to say more. "I couldn't help but notice your gait." She pointed across the highway at the medical clinic. "And now that I know your name, I'm remembering something about a rodeo accident?"

Cassie nodded. "Bull trampling, my brother would say." She held a hand over her hip. "It put a hitch in my getup, my grandfather would say."

"I'd say you look like a woman in need of some pain relief." Despite the unvarnished truth of her words, Dr. Carlisle had a gentle air about her. "I'd love to talk to you about your care and pain management."

Cassie took a step back. "That's very kind, but I have a doctor in Boise." One she owed money to.

Dr. Carlisle's blue eyes were large and knowing behind her thick, black-framed glasses. "I don't charge for consults. And I'm trained in all sorts of pain management techniques, from holistic to herbal to traditional medicine. That's a benefit of having treated pregnant women for years."

"I wish I could accept, but…" Cassie lowered her voice. "Honestly, I can't afford any more medical bills."

Dr. Carlisle brushed a lock of Cassie's hair over her shoulder. "But that's a benefit of living in Second Chance. The Monroes pay for my time. And currently, I don't have any patients. What have you got to lose?"

Cassie blinked back unexpected tears. "I guess…nothing?"

"Look at that. What a relief," Bentley told Shane as Cassie limped over to the clinic with Dr. Carlisle. "It hurts me just to watch Cassie walk today."

"I have nothing to compare it to." Shane

stood while filling a coffee mug at the cistern. "But she didn't look so good."

With a clatter of an overturned mug, a wave of hot chocolate crossed the table toward Bentley. He quickly slid out of the booth and out of harm's way before it cascaded over the edge.

Mia's face drained of color. She held up chocolaty hands and gave one of those wind-up wails that promised more and louder upset.

"Nope. None of that." Bentley swung her into his arms and headed for the restroom. "Cam, you've got a cleanup in aisle two," he joked, relieved that Mia had fallen silent when he'd picked her up. "And when you're through, can you bring us another hot chocolate? Only this time with a lid and a straw? Hands aren't meant for drinks, Mia." He might have noticed she was playing with her drink if he hadn't been watching Cassie.

"It's okay, Mia." Quinn trotted at Bentley's side. "Daddy says everybody spills." He stopped at the kitchen door. "Wowzer."

Bentley backtracked to see what the little guy had found so awe-inspiring.

Ivy, who ran the diner with Cam, was prepping a tray of cinnamon rolls. Her older son, RJ, was standing on a stool and whisking what looked like eggs in a bowl. Her younger son,

Nick, sat on the floor in a back room and was building a tower with colorful blocks.

Cam joined them at the door. He took one look at Quinn and said, "Hey, Nick, can you use help on your tower?"

Nick leaped to his feet and thrust a fist in the air. "Always!" He ran over to Quinn. "Want to make a castle?"

Nick's energy appeared to have overwhelmed Quinn. He clung to Bentley's leg.

"Go on." Bentley gave Quinn an encouraging nudge.

"Yeah, go on," Cam seconded. "I just need you to stay in the back room, okay? No hanging out in the kitchen with the chefs."

"We're cooks," RJ insisted, lifting his whisk and letting eggs drizzle from it into the bowl. "A diner needs cooks."

"Yeah, yeah, whatever." Cam returned to the dining room and new customers coming through the door.

"Come on." Nick grabbed Quinn's hand and together they ran over to his blocks.

"We need to get your hands clean, little girl." Bentley carried Mia to the restrooms, but then stopped, staring at the two doors. He probably shouldn't take Mia into the men's room, but the alternative... He knocked on the women's room door. "Hello?" When he received no answer, he opened the door and held it ajar with one leg while he held Mia close to the sink. Thankfully, it was a small restroom. "You're going to have to turn on the water."

"I'm a big girl. I can do it." Mia sounded as plucky as her words, nothing like the little siren who'd been upset after spilling hot chocolate.

A few minutes later and they were back in the main dining room, settling into a clean booth with Shane.

"Cam!" Bentley waved down his cousin. "I'm going to need two breakfast specials and two kids' plates of pancakes."

Cam looked at Bentley, and then at Mia, who was sucking down her hot chocolate through a straw like nobody's business. "I'm going to recommend the sausage and eggs for the little ones. Take it from a pro. You don't want to overly sugar kids."

"Good point." Bentley nodded. "Why didn't you stop me, Shane? You live with three youngsters."

"Do you know how much energy those boys burn off running around the ranch?" Shane tsked. "I say, let them eat pancakes."

Mia grinned at Shane. "I like you."

Shane tugged one of her delicate curls. "I wish your daddy would say that to me."

She smiled and slurped her hot chocolate.

Shane sat back in the booth. "I heard we're going to move hay for Cassie."

"That's what I heard, too." Bentley glanced across the road to the medical clinic. "This has been a year of new experiences."

"And it's not over yet." Shane lifted his coffee mug in a toast.

Time passed. Bentley worried about Cassie. Their food came. They dug in. Bentley worried some more.

"Bentley Monroe!" Suddenly, Cassie stood in the doorway of the Bent Nickel. She looked looser than Bentley had ever seen her before, and her cheeks were flushed. "I need you."

"Now that's an entrance," Shane said half under his breath.

Dr. Carlisle was at Cassie's side. She held on to the cowgirl's arm and escorted her to their booth.

"Only one?" Cassie blinked an unfocused gaze at the occupants. "I left you in charge of two kids, Bentley. Did you lose one?"

"I'm over here." Quinn waved from the counter where he'd been eating next to Nick. An array of green plastic army men were staging a battle between them.

Cassie stumbled slightly as she turned to look their way. Dr. Carlisle kept her fairly steady, even when Cassie spun back around and grabbed a slice of Bentley's toast.

"What's going on here?" Bentley asked. And he didn't mean toast theft. He looked to the doctor.

"I gave Cassie a pain pill." Dr. Carlisle set a small prescription bottle on the table. "This happens sometimes."

"I can't hold my liquor either." Cassie swiped Shane's coffee cup and slurped some down. Her brown eyes were dilated.

"Obviously, she can't drive home like this or supervise children." Dr. Carlisle gave Bentley a stern look.

Bentley's mouth went dry. "What?"

"She means you need to drive Cassie home and supervise the kids," Shane said, unable to prevent a smile.

"And someone needs to stay with Cassie until the effects of the prescription medication wear off." Dr. Carlisle continued to stare at Bentley. "She needs bed rest for two days. And she designated you as the adult she wanted in charge."

"Two days?" Bentley was still in shock. "No. I'm not nursemaid or nanny material. Just ask any of my family." Ask his sister, Olivia.

"This is like being called into the principal's

office." Cassie perched on the edge of Bentley's bench seat. "Detention, here I come." She slumped against him.

"She's going to be like this for two days?" Bentley tried to hold Cassie upright without pushing her off the edge of the seat.

"No. I'm halving her dose from this point forward. But Cassie needs rest. She hasn't been getting any because she refused prescription pain pills after her injury." Dr. Carlisle bent down to look Cassie in the eyes. "We agreed. You're going to try two full days of bed rest, then come back to see me."

"Agreed." Cassie wiped her mouth with the back of her hand.

Dr. Carlisle stood, straightening her thick black glasses. "She isn't to walk on her own for the next four hours. Got it?"

Bentley nodded, because it was expected that he would agree.

Dr. Carlisle left.

Always the more capable Monroe, Shane pulled out his phone. "You've got to move hay, play nurse and watch kids. I'm calling in reinforcements."

"Reinforcements," Bentley murmured. "How long is Tanner going to be gone?"

"Until Monday." Cassie surveyed the dishes on the table, took Bentley's fork and stabbed a bite of sausage from Mia's plate. "It's Friday, you know."

"I know." Bentley's gaze cut to Shane. "Quinn and Mia should stay with you."

"Me?" Shane shook his head. "I've already got a houseful of kids."

"Three boys. What's two more kids in the scheme of things?"

"I'm a girl," Mia piped up.

Shane ignored him, explaining the situation to Franny before hanging up. "Okay, Franny says we can take the kids tonight to give Cassie a good night's sleep. But they're back in your care tomorrow."

"I was just supposed to fix rides," Bentley grumbled, still shell-shocked.

"But dogs and kids love you," Cassie crooned, stabbing another bite of sausage.

While Cassie finished eating under Cam's watchful eye, Shane drove Quinn and Mia to the Bucking Bull. Meanwhile, Bentley bought food, milk and coffee to take to the Bar D and shoved some necessities from his room at the inn into a backpack. And then he drove Cassie home.

Cassie was a puddle in the seat. If not for the seat belt, she might have slid to the floorboards. "I'm a mess."

Bentley knew better than to agree. They rode in silence for several more minutes.

"You're not going to like this left turn," she told him.

"Why not?"

"Hairpin." She sighed. "My truck always groans when I make a sharp left."

Bentley made the turn, complete with unhealthy mechanical sound effects. He hoped her truck only needed power steering fluid. He came out of the hairpin curve and made the turn onto the Bar D's drive, trying to avoid the potholes. "Why haven't you had Mackenzie look at your truck?"

"Costs money. We need money to feed stock. But now maybe I need money for surgery?" Her head lolled toward him. "Stupid Tornado Tom cost me more than my entry fee. I can't lift a hay bale. I can barely lift my own saddle. I can't earn my keep. And without surgery, I won't be able to have children."

Bentley didn't have to ask if Cassie wanted children someday. She looked mournful.

"That Dr. Killjoy Simon." She wagged her finger back and forth. "He advised me not to have babies unless I pay for an op to fix me."

"What?"

"Dr. Carlisle said that's only one opinion. But Dr. Killjoy Simon is a specialist and he told me not to hope." She wagged her finger once more, slumping farther into her seat. "Now you…you wouldn't listen to a killjoy. You'd look up all the big words and have hope and babies. You'd make beautiful babies. You should find someone to make babies with. I mean, babies are important. I've seen all kinds of babies. Puppies, kittens, bulls. I always thought someday I'd have a litter of my own." She giggled. "I mean a bunch of kids, not a litter. And I wouldn't expect them to clean toilets unless it was their turn." She tsked and then mumbled something about beanie-weenies.

A car barreled past the ranch yard and headed toward the back of the property.

"Who's that?" Bentley craned his neck but couldn't make out who'd been at the wheel.

Cassie was occupied with trying to release her seat belt. "Someone staying at the old homestead."

Bentley pressed the catch for her and made sure the belt didn't smack her in the face upon its release. "Don't get out. I'm going to help you down." He hurried around to her door, hindered by Ajax prancing in his way. "Really, dog?" He gave him a cursory pat.

The truck's passenger door popped open. Cassie's boots slid toward the ground and the rest of her might have ended up there, too, if not for Bentley catching hold of her, and sliding an arm around the small of her back.

"I got you." She felt right in his arms, as if she belonged there.

"You don't have to help me," Cassie said into his chest. "I'm self-sufficient."

"Right." Bentley gritted his teeth and hoped he wasn't hurting her in some way. He repositioned Cassie so they were hip to hip. And then, half carrying her, Bentley made it inside the mudroom, where he had her sit while he removed her boots.

Eyes closed, Cassie placed her hands on Bentley's shoulders. "This is nice. Nobody ever takes care of me."

"They should," Bentley said gruffly, fighting an impulse to kiss her.

Happy as a clam, Ajax pranced around them with his squeaker—*squeak-squeak-squeak*—wriggling up against Bentley, swatting them both with his enthusiastic tail wags.

"Go to bed," Bentley told the dog.

"All right, all right." Cassie's eyes cracked open. "I'll go to bed. You are by far the most demanding man I ever met."

He wasn't. He couldn't be. But Bentley hurriedly removed his boots. And then he got her back on her feet and moving down the hallway.

"Where are you taking me?" Cassie lolled her head around. "We passed my room."

"Why didn't you say something?" Bentley got them turned around and into a pretty room with yellow walls and a turquoise quilted bedspread. It was a tidy room, accented with childhood memories. Horse-themed medals and trophies, faded postcards of national parks tacked to a flowery bulletin board, a bookcase with a top shelf devoted to novels for young readers, including a collection of Cowboy Campbell stories that he wouldn't have recognized if they hadn't been a favorite series of his grandfather's.

He helped her into bed and positioned pillows on either side of her so she wouldn't roll off.

"Bentley." Her soft palm rested against his cheek. "Has anyone ever told you that you talk too much?"

His eyes widened. *Never.*

Her hand slid to the coverlet and her eyes drifted closed. Her hair was in disarray.

He tried to straighten the black locks without touching all that soft smooth skin of her face and neck. Impossible. He stopped trying and stared down at her.

This woman.

She'd tried to ride a bull. She'd tried to push

through the pain of her injury without pain medication. She was facing a distressing decision—push through the pain to help her family or save her future by seeking expensive medical care. It made Bentley's decisions regarding where to work next feel inconsequential. But he could help Cassie in small ways—take care of the ranch while she rested, fix the engines on those rides, give her a strong shoulder to lean on.

"I'm worried about you." Impulsively, Bentley leaned over and pressed a kiss to her forehead. "For luck."

She stirred but didn't waken.

There was a small armless chair in the corner covered with purple flowered upholstery and adorned with a white faux fur pillow. He'd never have chosen a chair like that for Cassie. It was too feminine, too dainty. And yet, it complemented the teal bedspread beautifully.

He pulled the chair next to the bed and sat down. Ajax curled beside him, resting his head on Bentley's foot.

After a moment, Bentley took Cassie's hand. He sat like that until Shane showed up with the promised reinforcements to move hay.

CHAPTER NINE

"How much more do we have?" Shane stood in the bed of Cassie's truck after hefting a bale of hay toward a stack near the cab. He removed his gloves and stared at his palms. "My blisters are getting blisters."

Bentley wasn't faring much better, but they weren't going to get done any sooner by pausing and comparing blister sizes.

While he and Shane did the literal heavy lifting and made sure the stock was cared for, Franny was lifting her fair share in the house with the kids and Cassie.

"Bentley? Bentley? *Ben*." Shane blew out a breath. "Did you hear me? How much more do we have?"

"Bentley," he said his own name with more than a trace of annoyance. Shane knew he wasn't one for nicknames. "Franny said we had to stack hay three bales high and fill the truck twice. Do the math. That's about twenty-four more bales." Grabbing the binding wires, Bentley hoisted another bale onto the tailgate.

Thankfully, this was their second load. Bentley hefted another next to the first, thinking of Cassie doing the same. She was so small, so slight. Even without an injury, moving hay bales was serious business. Her back needed time off from ranch work to heal. More than two days.

"Twenty-three." Shane put his gloves back on and swung a bale onto the top of two others. "I took a look at those carnival rides when we got here. You've got your work cut out for you. They're in horrible shape."

Bentley lifted a bale, resting it on his thighs as he walked to the truck. "I'm not worried about getting the engines to work. I'm more concerned with restoring the parts kids sit on." He tossed the bale onto the tailgate.

"Twenty-two." Shane heaved a bale toward the cab. "Have you seen the lake at the back of the ranch?"

"No. Why would I have? Focus, will you?"

Childish laughter drifted to them from the house.

Kids. Bentley hadn't given serious thought to having any of his own yet. His work was fulfilling, or at least, his work had been fulfilling. He needed to find something to fulfill him once more. Long-term. But kids… The thought of Cassie unable to have them saddened him in a way that felt personal, as if he couldn't have them either.

Despite Shane's protests, he and Bentley made short work of the second hay bale transfer. They drove to the main barn, packed the hay onto the lift and unloaded it into the loft. And then they fed the horses and pony, which were loud and restless since it was approaching noon.

While Shane swept the barn floor clean, Bentley took a moment before refilling each stall's watering trough to look at the pictures in the breezeway. His attention had been caught by a picture of Cassie standing on a saddle atop a galloping horse that looked like Whistler. He couldn't imagine wanting to try anything she'd done when it came to riding horses or bulls. They had nothing in common. Logically, his attraction to her made no sense.

Quinn and Adam skipped into the barn, giggling. They were about the same age with hair the same dark brown color. By the sly smiles on their faces, they were also similar in their intent to make mischief.

Adam tugged on Shane's shirt. "We want to go riding."

"You can go riding when we get back to the Bucking Bull." Shane swept hay into a small pile. "Quinn is spending the night. He can go, too."

"But Quinn has a new pony here," Adam protested.

"Her name is Poppy and when she first got here, she was scared." Quinn stood by the stall at the end where the pony was stabled. It was also where Bentley was filling a water trough from a hose.

Adam galloped to the stall. "I gotta ride her, Papa Shane."

"Not happening, buddy." Shane finished sweeping hay out the door. "I promised your mom we'd be back to the Bucking Bull in time for you to do your chores before dinner, chores you didn't do this morning."

"Mucking stalls." Adam kicked a booted foot at a stalk of hay Shane had missed.

"You get to muck stalls?" Quinn blinked his wide brown eyes.

"Get to?" Adam put his hands on his hips, and then his little brow furrowed. "Haven't you ever mucked stalls?"

"Nope." Quinn grabbed onto Bentley's arm, and then hung on, lifting his booted feet in the air. He grinned.

For the life of him, Bentley couldn't understand why Quinn had developed such a fondness for him.

"All the big boys muck stalls at my house," Adam said in a tentative voice that tried not to hope for too much.

"*Adam.*" Shane pointed two fingers at his eyes and then at Adam's. "I see you, and I know what you're doing."

"But, Papa Shane…" Adam held his hands out as if confused. "If Quinn's a big boy, he should be *allowed* to do big boy stuff. Like cleaning out stalls."

"Stop." Shane put the broom away. "Go get Mia, your brothers and your mom. We're ready to head back to the Bucking Bull."

"All right. Come on, Quinn." Adam dragged his feet toward the door. And when he was out of the barn, he could be heard to say, "Quinn, if you really want to be a big boy, you can help me muck out stalls."

"*Adam!*"

CASSIE CRACKED HER eyes open.

She was in her room, which was dark, and she wasn't alone, which was unusual.

Bentley sat in a chair next to her bed. He was looking at something on his phone. She must have made some sound or movement because he glanced up. He didn't speak but it was as if she heard his voice in her head, telling her he was worried about her, telling her she could use some good luck.

Right. The next thing she'd be telling herself was that he'd gotten down on one knee and proposed while she slept.

"I am no Sleeping Beauty," Cassie mumbled.

"What did you say?" he asked, leaning closer.

"I'm thirsty." She scrubbed a hand over her face, trying to cool her cheeks before they gave away her slip. Her brain felt foggy.

Bentley set his phone down and helped her sip some water.

She tried to remember why he was in her bedroom. And, oh... Then she wished she hadn't.

"I made a fool of myself today, didn't I?" Was it still the same day? Cassie remembered entering the Bent Nickel and calling Bentley's name, but recalled only snatches of conversation since then. "Besides the accident, the last time I took pain meds was when I had my wisdom teeth pulled. I remember trying to text Miles Hendrix to pledge my complete love and utter devotion. Thankfully, I only sent him GIFs. After the medication wore off, I realized he wasn't the guy for me." Miles had wanted to cheat off her homework, something

Bentley would never do. "Honestly, if I behaved inappropriately today with you, I apologize." And yet, she wasn't sorry he'd been there for her.

"No apology necessary. You slept," he said simply, shrugging those broad shoulders. "You needed it. How do you feel?"

"I feel…" Cassie did a mental inventory of her injuries. "I feel achy, not like a tightly strung guitar string that's being plucked every time I breathe. That means I feel better."

"The doctor said you need a half dose every six hours." He shook out a pill from the bottle on the nightstand next to her bed.

Cassie disagreed. "I'm fine. I need to get up soon and take care of some things around the ranch. Feed and water the stock. Lock up."

"Shane and I took care of everything." He held a half pill out to her.

"I'm fine."

Bentley gave her a look that told her not to mess around.

"What?"

"On the advice of Shane…" He swore softly before starting again. "I can't believe I just said that. Look. The last time you told me you were fine, you fell out of the truck and into my arms."

She wished she remembered that. Heat

crept up her throat and into her cheeks. "It's Miles Hendrix all over again."

"You didn't make a pass at me if that's what you're afraid of." His hand and that pill came closer.

"What a relief." Her cheeks continued to burn though. "I mean, you and me… It shouldn't… I don't…" She was digging a hole. "Where are the kids?"

"At the Bucking Bull. They're spending the night. Franny and Shane were here earlier."

Franny owned and managed one of the best run ranches in the valley. And now she knew that Cassie couldn't do the same. She turned her head away from Bentley. "I need to move hay."

"Done." His warm fingers turned her chin back toward him, and those steady brown eyes captured her imagination. "My grandfather used to say that you can't take care of others unless you take care of yourself. You're taking two days off. Doctor's orders." He placed the cut pill in her hand and picked up her water glass.

Cassie relented. It was a half dose, after all. It was when she was handing the empty glass back to Bentley that she realized something. She was wearing her pajamas. "Where are my clothes?"

And then she spotted the clothes she'd worn earlier. They were piled on top of a full hamper. A purple bra cup thrust past her green T-shirt.

"Oh." Cassie placed her hands over her hot cheeks.

"Franny helped you change." Bentley got to his feet, turning his back to her clothes hamper. His cheeks were as red as Cassie imagined hers were. "She said you'd be more comfortable in…" He trailed off, licking his lips.

Those lips… Cassie imagined them pressing lightly to her forehead, her cheek, her mouth.

She covered her mouth with both hands to prevent her from saying anything she'd regret later.

She felt vulnerable lying in bed in her pj's with her unmentionables on display.

Bentley held up his hands in mock surrender. "You can blame Franny for everything."

If that were true, then why was he still blushing furiously?

"I'd much rather blame myself." The choices and risks she'd made had put her in this predicament. But the odd thing was how the idea of kissing him wouldn't subside.

"Don't be so hard on yourself," he said

gruffly. "I'm going to go make some tea, and then I'll check on you again. Dr. Carlisle wanted me to make sure you could handle half a dose."

Cassie hoped the effects would be minimal. Because she couldn't quite convince herself that it would be wrong to ask him for a kiss.

"KNOCK-KNOCK." SHANE came in the front door of the Bar D shortly after 10:00 p.m. "Surprise."

Two kids ran around Shane's legs and into the house, and were immediately greeted by Ajax.

"We're back, Uncle Bentley." Quinn ran into the kitchen. "Watcha doin'?"

Mia crashed into Bentley and hugged his leg. "I missed you."

"I just finished fixing the kitchen sink." Bentley had already repaired the kitchen table so that it didn't rock anymore. He patted Mia's curls before returning a wrench to a toolbox he'd found underneath the sink. "Shouldn't you guys be in bed and asleep at the Bucking Bull?"

"About that…" Shane set down the bag with the kids' clothes and toothbrushes on the kitchen table. "Mia refused to sleep at the ranch. And Quinn won't sleep without her."

"I want you, Uncle Bentley." Mia raised her arms to be picked up.

With a sigh, Bentley obliged. She nestled against his shoulder.

It's going to be awful if Tanner isn't a Monroe.

Quinn leaned against his leg and yawned. "Can we have cookies?"

"Granny Gertie gave you enough cookies." Shane headed toward the door. "I'm out. See you in a couple of days."

"Wait. You're not coming tomorrow?" But Shane was gone, leaving Bentley to take stock of his two charges.

They both yawned. Given what had happened to Cassie the night before, Bentley knew he needed a strategy for bedtime. But first, he had to get them ready for bed.

"I tell you what," Bentley said a few minutes later when the kids had brushed their teeth and changed into their pajamas. "I'll make you a fort to sleep in and tell you a bedtime story, but only if you promise to *sleep* in the fort." That was one of his grandfather's bedtime ploys—blanket forts and bedtime stories.

Without waiting for their complete agreement, Bentley went into the living room and used the couch cushions for fort walls. He reinforced the structure with throw pillows and blankets he'd found in the hall closet. He stepped back to admire his work. "All we need now is a roof."

"I got a blanket." Quinn dragged a bedspread into the living room.

"Great." Bentley looked more closely at the bedspread. It was teal. "Hey. This came off Cassie's bed."

Quinn shrugged. "She didn't wake up when I took it."

"Fine." It was a relatively warm summer night. Cassie should be fine without it. Bentley draped the bedspread over the fort walls. His work had turned out halfway decent. Of course, the big test was whether or not it was still standing in the morning. He glanced around. "Where's your sister?"

Quinn pointed down the hall. "Sleeping with Cassie."

"Get in the fort." Bentley went down the hall to retrieve the little girl.

Mia was lying across Cassie's chest. Both had their eyes closed. As Bentley picked Mia up, she began to wail.

"Shush now. Your daddy would want you to be a big girl, wouldn't he?" Bentley carried a now-quiet Mia down the hall and deposited her inside the fort. "Look how cool this is. And now it's story time."

Mia crawled into the fort, which was now occupied by Quinn and the dog. Luckily, Ajax hadn't brought his squeaker toy.

Bentley settled down on the floor and rubbed the dog's ears. "Once upon a time…" He struggled for a moment, unable to remember any fairy tales. "There was a boat captain who won many races sailing a boat her brother built."

"What's a boat captain?" Mia yawned.

"Someone who…*drives*…a boat across the water." Bentley got out his cell phone and pulled up a picture of his sister, Olivia, standing at the wheel of her sailboat. Brown curls blowing in the wind. Her face glowing with confidence. She was meant for great things. He hoped she knew that.

"Oh." Mia snuggled deeper in the blankets.

"A girl." Quinn pouted.

"There are girl and boy sailors," Bentley told him.

"Just like there are cowboys and cowgirls." Mia nodded.

"Get on with the story," Quinn grumbled.

Right. His story. Bentley put his cell phone down. "There once was a boat captain who could navigate her boat anywhere, just by knowing the ocean currents and by looking at the stars. And she knew how to harness the wind with her sails to go through the water fast. She didn't need anyone."

The kids fidgeted.

His story needed some pizazz. "One night, while she was sailing by the light of the moon, something flew overhead."

"A chicken?" Mia yawned once more.

"A bat?" Quinn guessed, wide-awake.

"No." Bentley shook his head, searching for an idea that would intrigue the children. He couldn't tell them about the boat capsizing and Olivia nearly drowning. "It was…Santa Claus."

"What?" Quinn sat up.

Mia's eyes fluttered heavily.

"We lie down for bedtime stories." That had been something Bentley's Grandpa Harlan insisted upon.

Smart old man.

Quinn lay back down.

Bentley went on with his story. "It was Santa. Rudolph had thrown a horseshoe." That was a stretch. "And Santa needed a lift to deliver presents in time for Christmas."

"Was this on a lake?" Quinn drew the blanket up to his chin. "The one out back? Can we go look for Santa tomorrow? I bet he's staying at the house. There's a boat, too."

Bentley shook his head. "No. This story happened on the ocean."

He proceeded to weave a story about how Captain Olivia had helped save Christmas. Gradually, Quinn's interruptions grew less frequent. Until Bentley's voice was a whisper and the kids seemed fast asleep.

A sound had him glancing up.

Cassie leaned on a wall in the hallway, smiling at Bentley in a way that had him rising to his feet and going to her side.

CHAPTER TEN

"THAT WAS AWESOME," whispered Cassie. She leaned against the door frame, eyes glued to Bentley.

He was awesome.

Bentley's dark gaze was warm as he got to his feet and approached her.

The house was quiet. The dog and kids were quiet. By rights, Cassie's body should have been quiet. But blood pounded in her ears and her mind wove happily-ever-afters that started with *if we were married* and ended with *this is how every day would close.*

"You should be in bed." Bentley's voice was as tender as his touch. His fingers circled her upper arm. He smelled of alfalfa. He led her back to the bedroom, straightened her covers and made sure she was tucked into bed.

"Am I dreaming?" Cassie asked, still lost in the foggy impression that they were a couple. "Or is my quilt missing?"

He chuckled.

The deep sound quickened her pulse all over again.

"Quinn took your quilt for the blanket fort," Bentley whispered.

Cassie wanted Bentley to whisper in her ear all the time. That deep voice. That sweet tone. But she also wanted…

Cassie sucked in a breath as reality dawned. "I took a pain pill."

"Half. Hours ago." Bentley's gaze sharpened. "Are you feeling okay? Concerned about something?"

"No," she lied, when in fact Cassie *was* concerned. Very concerned. Her fingers curled around the sheet and blanket near her neck.

"If there's something bothering you—" Bentley smoothed a lock of hair away from her face "—you can tell me."

Oh, she was bothered, all right. The pain pill had loosened her filter. It made her want. It made her want Bentley to take her in his strong arms and reassure her that everything was going to be fine. Her back. Her bank balance. Her… Her *life*.

"Stay," she blurted in a tone she might have used on Ajax. Almost immediately, she wished she hadn't said anything. "I mean…don't leave just yet." *Or ever.* She gritted her teeth. "I'm never taking another pain pill again."

The corners of Bentley's mouth twitched, as if he were fighting a smile. "I think Dr. Carlisle would disagree. According to her, you're taking half a pill every six hours."

"I can't." She had no filter, no pause button. "If I do, I'm going to say something to you that I'll regret."

He chuckled again, and it had the same effect on her. "I doubt *I'll* regret it."

She hid her face and how silly she felt. "Where's the sympathy?" She peeked at him from between her fingers. "I fed you cobbler."

"And I fixed your wobbly kitchen table and your leaky faucet." He drew Cassie's hands down. Their gazes connected. His brown eyes had little black flecks. And why wouldn't they have? His eyes were as unique as he was. "I'm not going to judge you by what you say when you're on medication."

"Really?" She could love this man.

"Really." He held up the covers, presumably so she could tuck her hands beneath them. "It might ease your mind to talk about something else. Tell me something about your childhood. Living here in the mountains you must have picnicked a lot. Hiked some trails. Taken a lot of trail rides."

Cassie shook her head slowly. "There aren't many marked trails around here. And working ranches don't have much time for recreational rides." And she'd never ridden anywhere alone for fear of getting turned around in the trees and lost.

"Oh." Bentley's brow furrowed slightly. "I somehow had the idea that you'd be this great explorer, being a courageous bull riding cowgirl and all."

He thinks I'm brave.

"I want to make a pass at you right now." Cassie stiffened. "I mean… *See?* I have no willpower. None!"

Bentley's laughter filled the room.

If Cassie's back hadn't been a mess, she'd have rolled over and turned away to save some of her pride. Instead, she was left lying there, horrified. Stuck.

"Uncle Bentley." Mia stumbled into the room and rested her torso on the mattress. "Can I sleep in here?"

"No." And without another word, Bentley turned off the bedroom light and escorted Mia back to the living room.

Leaving Cassie alone with her want and embarrassment.

AT DAWN, THERE was a human dog pile in the living room.

Mia was nestled in Bentley's arms. Quinn

hemmed the man in on one side and Ajax on the other.

Cassie could relate to being at the bottom of the pile, but she was also glad. Seeing Bentley corralled took some of the sting out of her behavior the night before. If he made reference to her words, she could redirect things to his current situation on the floor.

"Help," came a soft plea from Bentley. He extended a hand in Cassie's direction.

"The pied piper has met his match." Cassie padded into the living room. She'd dressed for ranch work in blue jeans and a T-shirt, moving carefully but with more ease than the day before. "I'm not supposed to lift more than ten pounds." She called softly to Ajax, who got up, stretched and then trotted over to her.

Partially freed, Bentley set Mia down on the carpet where Ajax had been and stood, shaking and stretching out the kinks as he walked past Cassie and into the kitchen. "Come on, boy. Outside. Cassie needs to sit at the table and be pampered."

Cassie was no fool. The effects of the pain pill had worn off. Her head was clear. And yet, she still harbored the warm fuzzies for Bentley. It wasn't like her brother or grandfather ever encouraged her to sit down while they made the morning coffee.

Cassie lowered herself tentatively into a chair at the kitchen table, marveling that it didn't rock. What else had Bentley told her he'd done? That he'd fixed the leaky faucet? Oh, man. For a woman living on an old ranch, he was definitely a keeper.

But he was also a Monroe and had no plans to live in Second Chance permanently. She assumed. That was a conversation she was too timid to broach.

A few minutes later, the dog was back in and Bentley had the coffee brewing. He faced her and leaned against the counter. Even rumpled from sleeping in his clothes, he was easy on the eyes.

"How are you feeling?" he asked.

"Better." *Still slightly embarrassed about last night.* "I'll feed the livestock after I get some coffee in me."

"No, you won't. Dr. Carlisle said two days in bed." Bentley went to a high cupboard and took out the bottle with her pain meds. "It's time for a dose."

Elbow on table, chin on palm, she presented her case. "I'm so much better than yesterday that I don't need another dose of truth serum. Work on a ranch doesn't stop just because a rancher has a few aches and pains."

"If you don't follow doctor's orders, you're

going to be like that truck of yours." He rattled the pill bottle and stared at her, dark eyes so intense she couldn't look away. "Held together by a wish and hay bale wire. Go back to bed, Cassie."

She might have reframed his last sentence as a sexy invitation if Bentley hadn't shaken her pain pills like a small maraca. As it was, she had to dig herself out of the hole her conversation last night had created. And the only way to do so, the only way to regain her pride and self-respect, was to drag herself back to work. "I have chores to do. Thank you for helping me yesterday, but I can't slack another day or I won't have earned my draw."

"Your paycheck?"

"Yes."

"Take a sick day and go back to bed, Cassie. This pied piper can feed grumpy cowgirls, sleepy kids and hungry livestock." Bentley smirked, daring her to contradict him. "Besides, I gave Dr. Carlisle my word that I'd watch over you. I'd hate for it to get out that I couldn't handle one patient."

He wasn't encouraging her to suck it up? The coffee machine sputtered and gasped the way Cassie wanted to.

Bentley poured a cup of coffee and brought

it to her. "Why do you look confused at the thought of spending another day in bed?"

Did she? "Because…I want to soldier on, to pull my weight, to…to…to not be a *burden to my family*."

Bentley crossed his arms over his chest. "What's that supposed to mean?"

She rushed to explain. "If my brother and grandfather knew I was more seriously injured, they'd want to use the money meant to pay the bills to pay for my medical expenses. The cost of my surgery is going to be astronomical. It'll put this place under." Although it frustrated her to think it, she might better serve the family working elsewhere and devoting a portion of her pay to keeping the ranch afloat.

"Hang on." Bentley shook his head slowly. "Didn't Dr. Carlisle tell you that she wanted to see you again tomorrow? And that she wasn't sure you needed surgery?"

"Did she?" Cassie muttered more to herself than to Bentley, "I thought that was wishful thinking on my part."

"It's what you told me." He frowned. "Listen, if you feel better after one day of bed rest, think how great you'll feel after two. Your family isn't due back until Monday. Take this pill and go back to bed." He held a hand over his heart. "I solemnly swear not to wreck the place today while you recuperate."

"I'm hungry." Yawning, Quinn climbed onto a barstool. "What's for breakfast?"

"Compromise," Bentley said with a smile that was suddenly disarmingly gentle.

"IF WE CAN'T ride Mia's pony, I wanna go see if Santa's in the house by the lake." Quinn balanced on his boot heels and swiveled his toes back and forth like windshield wipers.

They were in the barn's breezeway in front of all those pictures of Cassie doing amazing things on horseback. Bentley had just finished feeding and watering the stock and refusing Quinn's and Mia's repeated pleas to ride Poppy. Having spent several weeks each summer at a family ranch in Texas, Bentley knew how to saddle a horse. What he didn't know was the pony's temperament. And he wasn't going to risk Quinn's and Mia's safety by letting them ride.

"Will Santa have candy canes, Uncle Bentley?" Mia twirled one of her dark curls with one finger.

Bentley gave the pair his full attention. "Why are you convinced Santa lives at a lake?"

"You said Captain Olivia saved Christmas."

The soles of Quinn's feet hit the ground. "You said she had a boat." He pointed beyond the ranch house. "It's back there. And so is Santa."

Bentley rubbed a hand over his face. "I think you fell asleep while I was telling that story. Santa found Captain Olivia on the ocean."

"I'll show you." Quinn took Bentley's hand and led him out of the barn.

Mia caught up and grabbed onto Bentley's other hand. "To the lake. To the lake."

They were heading toward the road someone had used yesterday when Bentley had arrived with Cassie. She'd mentioned something about someone staying at the old homestead. "How do you know where the lake is?"

"We live in a house on the other side." Quinn bent to pick up a rock and threw it.

Out of nowhere, Ajax bolted past and ran for the rock as if it were a thrown ball. He sniffed around the ground before returning to the trio and performing his semicircles around them, herding them along.

"That dog needs a ball," Bentley noted.

"He has a noisy rabbit." Quinn threw another rock, which Ajax chased down, again finding nothing to put in his mouth and bring back.

Like the main driveway, this road was lined

with tall pine trees. On the far side, an empty pasture languished. The dirt road ascended a small rise.

Mia gave up on walking, stood in front of Bentley and raised her hands in a silent request to be picked up.

Bentley swung her to his hip. "And here I thought our hike was going to tire you out." And result in a nap later.

She snuggled against him, placing her head in the crook of his neck.

"Choo-choo." Quinn hurried ahead, shuffling his feet as he made train sounds and kicked up a swirl of dust in his wake.

Ajax and Bentley gave the dust cloud a wide birth.

Finally, they reached the rise.

A lake filled most of the valley ahead, its shores spreading close to the door of a small cabin. Sunlight glinted off its smooth surface. A small dinghy sat in the middle of the lake, drifting aimlessly. Two people lay on the little boat's bench seats, faceup, although they were too far away to make out more than the fact that it was a thin woman and a rather large man.

"Hey!" Quinn waved for all he was worth. "Captain Olivia! Santa!" And then he ran down the road toward the water's edge.

Two heads popped up on deck. The man had a mantle of white hair and beard. The woman had a ruffle of short brown curls.

A seaworthy knot formed in Bentley's stomach.

It can't be.

Bentley hurried after Quinn.

"Captain! Santa!" Quinn had reached the shore and was shouting enthusiastically.

The woman sat on the bench in the back. She started an outboard motor. Her features gradually became clearer the closer the boat came to shore.

Bentley's gaze connected with the woman and his mouth went dry.

He set Mia down, needing both feet on solid ground without additional ballast to tip him over.

"Hello, Bentley." Capable as always, his sister, Olivia, had the engine blades up and out of the water before the boat came to rest on the muddy shore.

There had to have been noise. Birds singing. Wind ruffling tree branches. Water lapping against the shoreline. Bentley heard nothing. Instead, he saw his sister entertaining his family with stories of a boat race when they were kids. He felt the stiff back of a wooden rocker in the corner of his grandfather's living room.

He tasted the bitterness of being cast aside, overlooked, ignored. That was the fate of the lone Monroe who considered every word before speaking, who didn't tell jokes with any skill and was content to be part of the crowd rather than compete to be a leader of it.

"How?" Bentley asked Olivia in the present. There were multiple questions implied in that one word. How had she gotten here? How long had she been here? How long was she going to wait before letting him know she was in town?

"Hello, Santa." Quinn held on to the bow of the boat and hopped up and down, splashing a little in the shallows.

"Ho, ho, ho." The older man with Santa whiskers humored Quinn. "Would you like a boat ride?"

"Yes." Quinn didn't wait for permission. He scrambled on board.

Not one to be left out, Mia came forward, although she said not a word.

Bentley found his voice. "They need life jackets."

"And we've got them." The older man reached under a seat. His T-shirt had a big ear printed on it, and the words: I'm All Ears. "I'll take them out, Captain."

Bentley lifted Mia into the boat, then held

it steady while the kids were helped into their
flotation devices. When they were seated, Olivia slid off the back into waist-deep water.
She wore tan utility shorts and an orange tank
top. It didn't bother her that her clothes got
wet. Why would it? She'd practically been
born in the water, born to lead, born to command attention and affection and loyalty.
Whereas Bentley…

Let's hear what Bentley thinks. Bryce had
often created opportunities for his twin to
shine when the family was together. And
those opportunities had more often than not
been squandered. It was only now, as an adult,
that Bentley was more comfortable convers-
ing or sharing his opinion.

Had the situation between Bentley and Olivia been reversed, he would have told her he
was in town. He would have texted that he
was alive and well. In fact, he'd texted her
as much when he'd arrived a few days ago.
They'd never been close, but this… This hurt.

When the old man was settled at the outboard motor and the kids arranged on the center seat, Bentley pushed them offshore, and
Olivia pushed them toward the center of the
lake.

And then the siblings stared at each other.
And all Bentley's good intentions to apolo-

gize for whatever had happened in Philadelphia fell away like dry needles from a tall pine.

"YOU'RE BACK." CASSIE was pouring herself a glass of water in the kitchen when Bentley and the kids returned to the Bar D.

Earlier, she'd changed out of her clothes after breakfast because Franny was right—bed rest felt much more restful when in your pj's. Just now, she'd thrown on the blue chenille bathrobe she'd rarely worn before and was feeling rather regal for a woman hosting others in her flannel men's pajamas.

Ajax rushed in and rushed past, nose to the ground, searching the house for his squeaker toy.

"We saw Santa," Mia said solemnly, removing her cowboy boots in the mudroom.

"We went for a boat ride." Quinn stood tall and rubbed his hands across his ribs. "I'm hungry. Cookies?"

Cassie shook her head. "You ate all the cookies the other night." Her attention was caught by Bentley, who was unusually silent, even for Bentley.

"I saw my sister," he said thickly.

"The Monroe staying in the old homestead is your sister?" Cassie murmured. Then, as understanding dawned, "I'm sorry. I didn't put two and two together. Did you two talk?"

"They yelled," Quinn reported, searching the countertops, presumably for food.

"But not at us." Mia beamed up at her beloved "Uncle" Bentley.

Ajax pranced into the kitchen, squeaking his toy bunny in front of every human present. *Squeak-squeak-squeak.* And then he returned to his dog bed and flopped down without another squeak or squawk of his toy, clearly exhausted.

The kids looked beat, too. A little sweaty, a little droopy.

Bentley hadn't moved since closing the mudroom door, hadn't acknowledged Mia's adulation or Ajax's adoration. His lips were pressed together, his shoulders up by his ears and his hands shoved into his pockets. He looked in desperate need of a hug.

"A hike like you guys just made calls for cartoons." Cassie got the kids glasses of water, string cheese and crackers, and settled them in the living room with the television on. When she returned to the kitchen, Bentley had moved and was staring out the window toward the lake. "You want to talk about it?"

"No." His posture remained rigid and closed

off. "You should take your pill and go back to bed."

Cassie wanted to retort that she felt better, and he shouldn't have yelled at his sister. She and Rhett weren't siblings who argued much. But if voices were raised, feelings invariably got hurt no matter how much you loved someone. She handed Bentley her glass of water. "Drink up. It's easy to get dehydrated at this elevation. That's often draining."

Bentley accepted the glass with a murmur of thanks and then frowned into its depths. "My sister… She's been here with a…therapist for…" He lifted a pained gaze to Cassie. "Well, you probably know how long she's been here."

"A good while." Six weeks or more. It was interesting to know that the old man with Olivia was a therapist. She couldn't imagine needing a personal counselor, much less going on a retreat with one. Cassie knotted her robe's belt about her waist. "I just thought of her as one of many Monroes who've come to town. If Grandpa told me her name, I've since forgotten it."

"Shane knew. And he didn't tell me." Bentley looked as if the rug had been swept out from under him.

If their roles had been reversed and it had been Cassie kept in the dark from Rhett, she'd be fighting tears and the heavy weight that came from a lack of family honesty.

Cassie took a step closer to Bentley. "Are you feeling betrayed because you were left out of the loop?"

His nod was ever so brief, but he stared at her with barely contained pain. This man needed a sympathetic ear. And because he carefully measured out words the way she measured sugar for the cobbler recipe, she waited until he was ready to talk.

A television cartoon ended. A commercial about squirt guns began. Quinn slurped his water. Ajax sighed in his bed.

Before the pill kicked in, Cassie needed to return Tanner's phone call. He'd left her a message checking up on the kids while she dozed this morning. She also needed to check in with Rhett and Grandpa. Her phone was in the bedroom. But she stayed in the kitchen, waiting for Bentley to say something. Anything.

And then finally, when Cassie was beginning to doubt that she'd ever hear a confidence from Bentley, he spoke. "I know I should feel relieved that Olivia's seeking help. But I just keep thinking that she came to me after the accident, and I couldn't give her what she needed. Her brother let her down."

"You shouldn't be so harsh on yourself. She came to you first."

"And left hurting." He shook his head. "You know what they say about engineers. *There is no math equation for love.*"

"Don't say you're incapable of emotion or compassion. You couldn't be the pied piper if you didn't empathize with others." Cassie couldn't help herself. She marched right up to Bentley and wrapped her arms around his waist. She wanted to give him the forgiveness he so obviously sought, but she couldn't. She didn't have the right. Instead, she rose up on her toes, intending to press a single kiss to his cheek. Instead, her lips landed on his.

And before she realized what was happening, Bentley was returning that kiss.

Only not so gently and in a quantity that numbered more than one.

BENTLEY HADN'T DATED much in his life.

Relationships required the right words—something Bentley had never excelled at—and a significant chunk of time—something Bentley had never made room for, what with his challenging career and lofty invention goals.

He blamed inexperience for letting one glorious kiss with Cassie lead to another. First kisses were supposed to be brief with a check-in regarding mutual agreement, the acknowledgment of chemistry, if any, and respect given by taking a step back so that such assessments could be made.

Therefore, it made no sense that his arms encircled Cassie like the fragile flower she was, and that his brain had no immediate plans to release her to measure her reaction or his. Her kiss held promise. Her kiss promised belonging. And his lips… They were operating as if the full stop button didn't exist. In short, he was a train that hadn't left the station in what seemed like forever, and now that he was on the rails, he was a runaway.

Did he mind? Not one iota.

Kissing Cassie felt as vital to his equilibrium as his next breath.

His sister had laughed when he'd told her he'd been worried sick about her. She'd smirked when he'd told her he wanted to help her return to the sport she loved by building her a new racing sailboat. He'd been flattened by Olivia's retort to his claim that he could be her rock.

Your boat killed me.

Something inside Bentley's chest clenched. Such bitterness toward him. He'd had no idea his sister felt that way.

Cassie murmured something against Bentley's lips.

Instinctively, his hold on her loosened, and Bentley would have stepped back if not for her arms refusing to yield. Instead, they stared at each other, a hairbreadth apart, both breathing heavily, mouths close enough for a second round of mind-numbing kisses... If only there weren't those darn rules of engagement that were coming back to him now.

Yes, reason had returned, shoving aside his pain and grief over the confrontation with Olivia. Opening the door to embarrassment and awkwardness over taking the comfort this woman had offered him and turning it into a kissfest.

"I should..." Bentley said at the same time that Cassie said, "That was..."

They both stopped talking. They both dropped their gazes to each other's kissing apparatus.

Kissing apparatus—the term used by nerds to distance themselves from an overly enthusiastic kissing binge.

They both tried to fill the ever-widening gap of awkwardness once more.

"Should I..." Cassie said at the same time that Bentley began, "Can we..."

Smiles dissolved the uneasiness but not the connection of arms circled around each other.

"And here I thought today was shaping up to be one of those worst days ever," he said, meaning it.

"And to think last night I told you I wanted to make a pass." Her smile extended into a grin that made him want to use his kissing apparatus to start a second round of kissfesting.

"You think that I made the first move? As I recall, your lips touched down first." He almost didn't recognize his own voice. It was low and husky and he loved that she blushed when he used it.

"Are you guys getting married?" Quinn appeared at their side with his empty water glass.

"No." Cassie lurched free, grimacing and reaching for her back.

In a blink, Bentley had his arm around her, stabilizing, supportive. "It's a pain pill and back to bed with you."

"For a man I just met, you want me in bed an awful lot," Cassie joked.

But the spark between them was no jest. In fact, it was more powerful knowing that she felt it, too.

And rather than revel in that knowledge, Bentley's brain began to leap ahead, testing possibilities and outcomes of future kissfests, relationship directions and what forever might look like.

He was incredibly disappointed with the dead end all his conclusions led him to.

CHAPTER ELEVEN

"You owe that man an apology," Sonny said crisply, following Olivia into the run-down little house. "What have we discussed about fear and blame?"

"Blame is related to fear." Olivia sat on the old brown couch, not caring that her clothes were still wet. "Funny that you should mention relations. That was my brother."

Sonny took a seat on an orange club chair. "You blamed your brother for *your* boating accident." He didn't state it as a question.

She answered it anyway. "Yes."

Sonny fluffed his white beard. It had grown an inch since they'd arrived in Second Chance. "Last year, you lost a race. Did you blame your brother?"

"Of course not." A weight seemed to drop on her chest, making her breath come in short, shallow gasps.

"But you blame him for this accident." Each syllable was sliced with angry disbelief.

"Yes." Olivia clung to her opinion, bitter as it tasted on the back of her tongue.

"Was he on the boat with you?" Sonny didn't shout. He didn't emphasize his words with hand gestures. And that cold calm made his anger that much more apparent. "Was he?"

"No." She was panting now and certain that Sonny could see it. He saw everything.

"And yet you blame him for the boat capsizing?"

"Yes. Why are you mad at me?" He was never mad at her.

"I'll answer your question if you answer mine." Sonny rested his elbows on his knees and steepled his hands. "*Why* do you blame your brother for a boat capsizing? A boat he wasn't on? A boat you were captaining?"

"You don't get it," she gasped audibly. "Bentley built the boat. He was months behind."

"And…"

Olivia's fingers curled around the wet hems of her shorts. "And when we finally christened it, it was race day. I had no time to familiarize myself with the boat. Every boat has a feel. Each rudder's response is different. Every hull has a distinct ride on the water."

His fingers went from steepled to clasped.

"Knowing this, you could have raced an existing sailboat."

"I could have, but this boat… It was marvelous. Unique. Fast. Even in the harbor. Faster than anything I'd ever sailed before. If only Bentley wasn't such a perfectionist. I could have had it a day or a week early. Practice makes perfect." And that's what she'd always striven to be. "After Bryce died, Bentley and I put our heads together. I told him everything that slowed my pace in a race. He sat down and designed a boat to solve every flaw. *Bryce's Heart* was supposed to bring us closer. Instead, that boat killed me."

Not nearly. It had killed her. Bentley had killed her.

"Your brother made the perfect boat for the perfect captain," Sonny murmured, straightening in his chair. "But no one is perfect. Not even you. You were impatient. You were greedy. You craved the power that comes from winning."

Olivia slapped her hands on her thighs. "That's what they say when women compete. They assign unpleasant terms to us, like we're competing because of greed and a lust for power. I wanted to win, just like any other man or crew out there. That's not greed. As part of my team, Bentley knew I needed that boat days before the race started in order to have a perfect win. *He* let me down."

"Do you hear yourself? You hired me to help you defeat your fear, but all you want me to do is wave a magic wand and make everything better. *You* made the decision to take that boat out without test runs or practice. *You* made the decision to overcanvas around that buoy. *You* put everyone's life at risk, including your own." He stood, joints popping. "You made those decisions because you refuse to control your emotions. Impatience, desire for power, greed. I'm trying to teach you how to be a more perfect captain than you were before. But you continue to let your feelings rule you. You continue to place the blame at everyone's door but your own. There's no point in my staying here if you can't embrace the process. You have to talk. You have to admit weakness and fear. You have to apologize when *you* are in the wrong. To your sponsors. To your crew. To your brother." His tone softened. "Even to those young children who witnessed you yelling cruel, cruel things."

You killed me.

It was a nasty thing to say. The weight pressed harder on her chest.

"Go to your room, Olivia." Sonny went toward his.

"To meditate?" She sucked at meditation.

"No." He paused in the bedroom doorway, half glancing at her over his shoulder. "I want you, Olivia Monroe, to stand in front of you, Captain Olivia Monroe, and state your case in the mirror. Defend your actions on the day of the accident."

"And if I can't," she said in a small voice that didn't sound like her own.

"Then maybe you'll finally realize the truth about yourself. And then maybe you can start to heal." He entered his bedroom and closed the door.

Leaving Olivia with nothing but her own ugliness.

CHAPTER TWELVE

CASSIE DIDN'T MIND bed rest.

Not when it meant she could listen to Bentley interacting with Tanner's kids. His patience, his dry humor, his good nature. She admired it all. Cassie drifted in and out of sleep alternately picturing the pained look on Bentley's face when confronted with one of Quinn's outlandish statements and remembering the heated look in Bentley's eyes after he'd thoroughly kissed her.

Ah, yes. Bed rest. A time for romantic tomfoolery.

That's what Grandpa Diaz would have said had she told him during their earlier phone call. And if he could see the dreamy look in her eye, the one caused by Bentley, not a dose of pain medicine, he'd shake his head.

Dwelling on romantic notions was ten times better than wrestling with the uncertainty of her future.

Bentley made cold cut sandwiches for lunch and barbecued chicken legs and skewers of vegetables for dinner. He served Cassie her meals in bed and made sure she had a glass of water on her bedside table to take her dose of pain medicine. At sunset, he fed the stock and closed up the barn for the night.

While he was out, Tanner called, asking to speak to his kids, apologizing for missing her afternoon call. For whatever reason, Mia and Quinn didn't mention Bentley, which was probably for the best, given Tanner's obstinance about the Monroes.

Once Bentley was back, he supervised bath time and bedtime, again with the blanket fort in the living room. And although he'd been in the house most of the day, when he came into her room, she got the distinct impression that he was regretting those kisses. But it was an impression, and she couldn't imagine why he had regrets.

Finally, the house was quiet. Finally, Bentley came into Cassie's room and pulled up a chair.

They stared at each other without speaking. Cassie plucked at her blanket. Bentley's knee bounced. Cassie swallowed thickly, certain she was about to be friend-zoned.

He cleared his throat. "About what happened in the kitchen…"

Cassie hurried to fill the void. "You think

it was a mistake." She wouldn't say the same. "Why?"

He continued to sit and watch her, as if waiting.

Waiting for what?

And just when she was about to ask him to say something, there was a knock on a door.

BENTLEY TOOK A cue from Ajax to locate the door knocker.

The big black-and-tan dog stood in the mudroom and growled at the back door.

Bentley turned on the porch light, took hold of Ajax's collar and opened the door.

"You?" Olivia stood there, clearly shocked. "What are you doing here?"

Ajax stopped growling and surged forward with a tremendous amount of tail-wagging, probably remembering Olivia from earlier today or…having made friends with her weeks ago.

"I might ask you the same thing." Bentley released Ajax's collar and stepped onto the porch, closing the door behind him. "Why are you here?"

Olivia stopped petting the dog and retreated a step. "I wanted to apologize for the kids hearing us argue."

"The kids are asleep."

"Can I speak to their dad? Um... Rhett?" She wore black Keds, blue jeans and a yellow zippered hoodie. In this light, she looked too thin. Her mop of short brown curls seemed as if it hadn't seen a comb all day. And there were circles under her eyes that had been hidden earlier by her sunglasses.

His worry for her returned, trying to break through the protective guard he'd erected after their earlier argument. He resisted softening. She'd blamed him for the accident, and he'd spent most of the summer agonizing over where she was and how she was doing.

Ajax sat at Bentley's feet and leaned against his leg, bumping Bentley's hand with his snout, demanding to be petted. And perhaps giving him sibling advice.

The dog knows better than to hold grudges.

Bentley forced out a breath. "Look. It doesn't matter who you're here to see." Other than the sting that it wasn't him. "They're all in bed."

His sister nodded. "I...uh...I should apologize." Her tone was at odds with her statement. Very unrepenting, that tone. *"To you."*

Something akin to a growl welled up in his throat. "Did Santa..." He corrected himself. "Did your therapist tell you that?"

She nodded again, scuffing her feet in a

way that she never would have done before
the accident. As if she was uncertain, as if her
confidence had been shaken and she was no
longer the tough-talking captain of a nearly
all-male racing crew. And then she straightened, a determined look crossing her gaunt
features. "I hit rock bottom after the accident. Rock. Bottom," she repeated, making
the statement sound life-affirming. "I couldn't
shut my brain off. I couldn't sleep. Every time
I closed my eyes…I…I relived the accident. I
relived dying… I still do."

Bentley swore and all his defenses failed
him because he knew that she'd been trapped
underwater and had to be resuscitated.
"Olivia—"

"No. Let me finish." She raised a hand that
was also too thin, practically skeletal. "I have
to say the words out loud. It's part of my healing plan." Again, there was sarcasm in her
tone. "Today was the first day I got into a
boat and went onto the water. I couldn't before. There are just too many *what-ifs* floating
around in my head. Everything that happened
that day was…my fault, not yours." Those last
words came out in a rush. "And now, boats
represent failure and—" her posture deflated
once more, along with the timbre of her voice
"—water represents death. My death."

Bentley said nothing, obeying his sister's command. He rubbed Ajax's velvety ears and considered how Olivia had never faced her own mortality before.

"Everything that's happened between us since the accident is my fault, too." Olivia grimaced. "I shouldn't have gone to you for help. I know that you hate emotions and being emotional."

Bentley was beginning to believe his family had a much different opinion of him than he had of himself.

"I wanted something you couldn't give." Olivia hung her head. "After I left, I went home to Mom and Dad. I didn't last there more than a day. They had questions I couldn't answer. Judgment I couldn't handle. Doubts about my future." She added in a mumble, "I have enough doubts of my own."

Their parents had always expected them to be high achievers. It was the Monroe way.

"The silence of your apartment was almost preferable." Olivia ran a hand through her short curls. "I know now that you couldn't give me what I needed. And when I left, I should have texted you that I was alive and not exactly well, but well enough. That was cruel. But I was just... *I am still* in a bad place. A toxic place."

So she'd come here instead. A part of Bentley still raged about that.

"What was it you wanted, Olivia?" Bentley asked in a hoarse voice. "From me, I mean." Maybe if he knew, he could help her the next time something like this happened.

His sister gestured toward Ajax. "To be held while I broke down. To pretend you weren't freaked out that I'd lost my nerve. To make small talk beyond asking me if I was okay." She kept talking. Apparently, there was a long list of things she'd needed.

But Bentley didn't hear another word she said because he was thinking. What Olivia was describing was needing someone to be the person she relied on. An ally, a trusted friend. Why hadn't he been able to do that for Olivia?

He knew the answer to that question. He and Olivia were very different people and it made it hard for them to relate to each other. Bentley was a thinker. She was a doer. She didn't understand him at all. But she was family, and Bentley would never turn his back on family, because life—as Olivia was learning—was a fragile thing.

"I'm sorry, too," Bentley said when she'd stopped listing his failings. "But now that I know, I think if Bryce were here, he'd want us to hug it out and promise to do better next time."

"Next time?" Olivia recoiled.

"Next time we argue. You know we will," Bentley said with certainty. "Because you're going to climb the ladder out of rock bottom. And whatever you decide to tackle next, you'll do it with all the swagger and confidence you had before the accident."

"How can you be so sure?" she whispered.

"Because you're too stubborn to give up on yourself, although you've given up on the rest of us." He meant himself and his parents. He came forward and hugged Olivia, consumed with guilt because he hadn't been able to do for his sister what he was doing for an Idaho cowgirl he'd only just met.

But that was going to change, whether Olivia liked it or not. Somehow, he was going to help her, even if it was only by giving her the space she wanted.

"DOES MY SISTER often come calling in the middle of the night?" Bentley sat down heavily in the chair next to Cassie's bed. "Asking for your brother?"

"No. That's who knocked? Are you okay?" Cassie reached for his hand. "Wait. Did you say she asked for Rhett?" *Whoa*. Cassie stored that tidbit away for another day. One where her brother was home.

Bentley closed his cold fingers around Cassie's. "I'm…enlightened. We had a little family kumbaya. And now, I suppose, you and I should have ours."

He thought she was upset about those kisses? "We don't need to patch anything up."

"We need to talk," Bentley said firmly, placing her hand back on top of the blanket. "I don't want to leave you in the lurch. But I came to Second Chance to repair the rift with my sister and—"

Oh, no, he's leaving!

"—I've done that."

"You can't leave town," Cassie blurted, wishing she could blame this feeling of impending heartbreak on half a dose of pain medicine and not a tenuous connection with a man she barely knew.

I know him. That was a certainty. She knew his character, if not his life story.

"Cassie…" he began again.

"Don't." She blinked back a sudden well of tears. "What about the carnival ride engines? You promised me you'd get them to run if I talked to Shane about using the land."

"Do you really want me to fix them? You want to spend your days selling ride tickets and buckling kids in?" His gaze was level. His eyes saw the truth.

But the truth… The truth was that she dreaded the idea of running a small carnival. But if she admitted it, he'd leave.

And so, she lied.

CHAPTER THIRTEEN

"You look more like yourself." Bentley was making breakfast when Cassie entered the kitchen the next morning.

He'd taken over household operations as if he belonged in the house. And he looked like he belonged in his blue jeans and black T-shirt, standing there in his bare feet and yawning. It was all Cassie could do not to sidle up next to him and rest her head on his shoulder. If only he didn't want to leave.

"Cassie?" A bit of mischief flashed in his dark eyes. "Earth to Cassie."

"Was she a spaceman, too?" Quinn sat next to Mia at the counter. They both crunched on crisp bacon.

"I'm a cowgirl, not an astronaut." Cassie rolled her shoulders. "And today is by far the best I've felt since a bull stepped on me."

Quinn stopped chewing to stare at Cassie. "You survived a stampede?"

"I survived something," Cassie agreed.

"You've got a doctor's appointment this

morning." Bentley dished out scrambled eggs for Cassie and the kids. "I'll drive you into town and treat the kids to hot chocolate."

He was kind and considerate, and she was going to miss being coddled when he was gone. Because Cassie knew Bentley wouldn't stay after he fixed those engines.

"Hot chocolate!" Quinn threw up his hands and wiggled on the barstool. "Yay!"

"Yay!" Mia echoed, grinning at her brother.

Cassie's time with Bentley was coming to an end. And tomorrow, Tanner would return and his two little charmers would be gone, as well. Without those distractions, she could figure out her future. She smoothed one of Mia's wayward dark curls, choosing her words carefully. "Are you going to spend time with Olivia later?"

"No. She doesn't need me," Bentley said simply in that Bentley way of his, as if no one needed him.

Cassie wanted to tell him that she needed him, but she knew that he wouldn't believe her once Grandpa and Rhett were home.

"Olivia might have told you that because she doesn't want to be a burden." Cassie picked up her plate, intending to eat standing up, which kept her near him. "I bet she'd appreciate your support and your...your...sensitivity."

Bentley choked a little on his coffee. "Kids, go brush your teeth." He shooed them from the kitchen. And then he turned to Cassie, a wicked look in his eyes. "Supportive? Sensitive? No guy wants to hear that."

"What are you saying? That you aren't supportive or sensitive? That you don't want to be?"

"Trust me on this. No woman wants a supportive and sensitive man. I should know. I've been one all my life."

Refusing to back down, Cassie lifted her chin, excited to see another side of this reserved, complex guy. "I guess city women don't know a good thing when it's standing right in front of them." The way Bentley was standing right in front of her.

"Cassie…" He began to speak, low and resolved.

The skin on her arms pebbled.

"I told myself I wasn't going to do this again." Bentley closed the gap between them and kissed her. His hand came to rest ever so gently on her hip. And his mouth—it connected with hers. And as before, he took.

And she was so ready to be taken—into his arms, into his life, away from here.

All too soon, the kids came running back. *Away from here.* Her heart panged. Was that what life had been coaxing her to do? To make a decision that had her leaving the ranch?

"We're lucky we're chaperoned," Bentley murmured, drawing back. And then he was all business, as if that kiss had never happened. "Come on, kids. Bring your dishes and load the dishwasher."

They complied, the way all kids complied with the pied piper.

She complied with the pied piper and she was glad that she did.

Because that man can kiss.

Cassie moved slowly, stretching out their time together, finishing her eggs, slipping into her boots and hat, grabbing a denim jacket on the way out the door. All the while thinking about that kiss and the feeling she had of being swept away.

I'm just an Idaho cowgirl.

Until I'm not.

Every time she glanced at Bentley, her heart pounded. And not in a bad way. And every time her gaze connected with his, she knew he was considering what to do about the sizzle between them and wondering if it was real. When they'd first met, he'd been standoffish. But now—today—he was reaching for her. Something was building between them. Wasn't that worth swallowing her pride and running carnival rides? Or perhaps hanging up her hat and becoming a city girl?

Her mind spun with possibilities that made her quiet.

When they walked out to the ranch yard, Bentley insisted upon driving her truck.

He was a capable driver. Even so, she told him, "Watch out for the next pothole. It's deceptively deep." *Like you.*

"Don't worry. I've got this." Bentley captured her hand and leaned his elbow on the truck's center console.

And he did have this—her truck, her thoughts, *her future.* If that's what he really wanted.

Uncertainty tangled inside her. What if Bentley wanted children? She sat up, wanting to get to her doctor's appointment as quickly as possible. Instead she gave herself a back spasm. "Ow."

"You okay?" Bentley asked, casting her a worried glance.

"Yes." There was ambiguity ahead. Lots of it. In too many parts of her life. Cassie needed answers. From a doctor. A guidance counselor. And maybe even a relationship guru. She hated change.

"Be careful getting Mia out," Cassie told Bentley when he'd parked in front of the

Bent Nickel and was releasing Mia from her child seat.

"Don't worry." Bentley deposited the little girl on the asphalt. "I've got this." And he did. His gaze connected with Cassie's, warm and a bit challenging.

She followed Mia toward the Bent Nickel, stepping up on the sidewalk. For just a moment, she felt off-balance.

"Don't worry. I've got you." And Bentley did. He looped an arm around her waist and gently swept her toward the door.

Those small touches. Those few words of reassurance. They'd be stopping now when she was released from bed rest. Cassie almost wished she could extend her recuperation.

Dr. Carlisle came out the diner door, baby bump first. "Look at you, Cassie. Moving so easily."

"Thank you," Cassie murmured, stealing a quick glance at Bentley.

Quinn and Mia darted past the doctor and rushed toward the booth where Shane sat with little Adam. Nick was playing with a set of green army men at a back table.

Kids. Bentley wanted them. He was a natural with them.

And Cassie might not be able to have them.

"I'd better get in there to watch those two."

Bentley removed his arm from around Cassie and went inside.

She missed his warmth and strength almost immediately.

"Those Monroe men." Dr. Carlisle tsked. "Charmers, the lot of them. I have one at home." She pointed toward the medical clinic across the road. "Shall we?"

THE GLOW OF Cassie's presence faded as Bentley sat down across from Shane and gave his cousin a dirty look.

"Hey, kids." For once, Shane seemed to take a hint. "Why don't you all take seats at the counter?"

Miraculously, Bentley huffed and puffed and kept the angry words inside until the kids were ten feet away. And then he leaned forward to whisper, "You didn't tell me Olivia was here."

Shane mirrored his body language, leaning over the Formica and whispering, "She swore me to secrecy. *No one* knows she's here. I deliver her groceries once a week and—"

Bentley swiped a hand across the air between them. "*You knew.* And you didn't tell me. I asked you when she was coming. You asked me if I'd seen the lake out there. You knew I was worried. You knew she was a wreck."

"And now you've seen her." Shane sat back and shrugged. "I'm sorry, but…now you know."

"That's all you've got to say?" Bentley was afraid he might lose his temper. "Don't talk to me as if this is okay. It's not okay. You lied to me."

"Hey, fellas." Their cousin Cam appeared at their table. "Do you need to step outside? You're scaring my customers." He pointed toward the lunch counter, where four kids stared at them with wide eyes.

"We aren't taking our conversation outside," Shane said evenly. "I'm apologizing to my cousin and in about thirty seconds, he's going to accept my apology."

"Hardly. I might harbor bad feelings toward Shane for several months, if not years," Bentley said through gritted teeth.

Cam shrugged. "You know, a lot of people feel that way about Shane."

"I should leave town," Bentley said.

"Wrong answer." For the first time, Shane dropped the repentant act. "I need you to discredit Tanner."

The tension Bentley had been feeling about staying just to appease Cassie eased. Here was an excuse that didn't involve his heart and impossible forevers. His cousin expected him to stay.

"All right." Bentley jumped at the excuse. "But you owe me."

"Shane owes lots of people." Cam grinned. "Good luck on claiming that debt."

Shane scoffed. "It's a debt of gratitude."

"We prefer cash," Cam quipped.

A FEW MINUTES after leaving Bentley's company, Cassie sat in an exam bay.

Dr. Carlisle was peppering her with questions while performing a gentle exam. "How's the hip? What kind of back pain have you been having? Did you really stay in bed the majority of every day? Did you catch up on sleep? What do you think of Bentley?"

"What?" Cassie blinked at the last question. "Why would you ask about Bentley?"

"Because everyone in town, including the Monroes, are curious about you two, including my fiancé, Holden *Monroe*." Dr. Carlisle chuckled. "According to the family, Bentley isn't the kind of guy who goes out of his way to help people."

"He doesn't?"

"He stays in the background. They say he's brilliant, but a good-natured follower."

A follower? No way. He'd stepped up for her back when they'd been relative strangers. How could his family be so wrong about him?

Cassie shook her head. "The Bentley who took care of me the last few days went above and beyond, and he did the same for Tanner's kids. He never sat back, and he never complained." Except when she'd called him supportive and sensitive.

If I shower him with compliments about his sensitivity, will he kiss me again?

Cassie allowed herself a private smile.

Dr. Carlisle put down her tablet. "You've responded nicely to rest. But you've still got a way to go. I'd like you to get an MRI in Ketchum next week. You mentioned fractures in your hip, but because it's the weekend, I have yet to receive copies of your X-rays and files."

"And surgery?" Cassie couldn't stop herself from asking.

"Let's tackle rest before we talk surgery."

"But Dr. Killjoy... I mean, Dr. Simon said I'd need surgery." She'd need that surgery if she was going to have a fighting chance to spend the rest of her life with Bentley.

"Bear with me. I'm operating in the dark without your case history, but..." Dr. Carlisle's brow furrowed. "Dr. Simon said you needed surgery?"

"Yes. I only spent the one night in the hospital but that's what I remember."

"Ah." Dr. Carlisle put her hands on her baby bump. "Do you know what my mother liked to do?"

"Um… No?" Was this a trick question?

"My mother liked to feed people. But she was only good at cooking two things—eggs and chicken. So, if you came to our house, you had eggs or chicken."

"Oh?" Cassie was confused.

"You don't follow?" Dr. Carlisle gave a brisk nod. "We're all good at something. We all play to our own strengths. Just like my mother. What's your strength?"

"Horse training?" Cassie wasn't sure why she'd answered in question form.

"Interesting. Me? I'm good with women's health issues. Women are all so very different that I have to have a big bag of tricks to help all my patients thrive." Dr. Carlisle crossed her arms. "Now, the orthopedist you saw might have been a brilliant surgeon."

"I get it." Cassie nodded. "As a surgeon, he's probably good at surgery, which means that's what he recommends most often."

"Yes." Dr. Carlisle nodded. "Although, there's a chance he's not that kind of surgeon, not to mention he talked to you after you'd been given strong pain medication?" She raised her brows.

"I might not have understood him," Cassie allowed, but she had a recollection of the word *surgery* being spoken often and with seriousness.

Dr. Carlisle nodded again. "I need to see your file. But based on the way you responded to rest, there's a good chance that you won't need surgery. We just need to make sure of it after you've had a chance to rest a bit more."

Cassie would have collapsed back on the exam table if she wasn't sure it would hurt like heck. "What about kids? Dr. Simon told me the weight of a baby would wreak havoc on my spine. And maybe cause paralysis, which was also a risk of the surgery?"

For once, Dr. Carlisle didn't immediately reassure her, not even with a smile. "First things first. Let's get your mobility back and schedule the MRI. And while you're healing, I'll touch base with Dr. Simon."

"Sure. Right. Of course." But Cassie knew that she had many sleepless nights ahead of her, counting sheep and wondering if kids were in her future. "I want kids. It's important."

"IT'S KILLING YOU, isn't it?" Bentley asked Cassie an hour later when they'd returned to the Bar D. He was giving midday supplements to the older horses. "You can't stand not helping with the ranch work."

Actually, I was enjoying the view.

She had been memorizing the image of handsome Bentley working in the barn.

Cassie sat on a bench padded with a saddle blanket. Tanner's kids played checkers at her feet. "Actually, I was thinking I could take one of the horses out to the paddock for some training." That didn't require lifting more than a crop or a horse treat. Easily manageable. And it would help pass the time.

"You should wait another few days." Bentley's voice was even, neutral. The voice of reason.

"Don't you want to see me do something I'm good at?" She wanted to show Bentley more than her weaknesses.

"I have." He pointed to the wall of pictures in the breezeway.

It wasn't the same as having him watch her work.

The sound of vehicles approaching put a hold on that conversation and had them all moving outside to the ranch yard.

Shane pulled up in his black Suburban, followed by someone in a blue truck who parked out of Cassie's line of sight. There were at least three people in the Suburban, but glare on the window prevented Cassie from making out faces.

Shane popped out of his vehicle first. "Sorry about the impromptu visit." He smiled cheerfully. "Everything just fell into place, so we decided to stop by."

"Really." Bentley frowned. "Are you sure this wasn't planned, and you just didn't tell us when we were in town earlier?"

"I'm sure." Shane came around to open the rear passenger door, helping Adam down. The little cowboy ran straight to Quinn. And then Shane opened the front passenger door and helped an old woman out.

Cassie's jaw dropped. "Flip? What are you doing here?" The old woman had a reputation for staying close to home. Her home, that is.

"Shane just hijacked me," Flip said, almost good-naturedly.

"I thought she could paint the rides for you." Shane went to the rear of the Suburban, waiting for whoever got out of the truck.

"I'll need creative license." Flip had short, grayish-brown hair that was longer on one side than the other. She gave Cassie a sharp once-over. "That means I'm the boss."

"Versus Shane?" Bentley made a sound suspiciously like a laugh, earning a dark look from Flip.

A man came around the rear of the Suburban. He and Shane approached Cassie. And as the man came closer...

"Cassie, you probably know Miles Hendrix." Shane introduced Miles to Bentley. "He grew up here, but now runs an auto body shop on the outskirts of Ketchum."

Miles Hendrix? My Miles Hendrix?

Sure enough. Miles wore a black Rolling Stones T-shirt, blue jeans and work boots. One might say he'd drawn from the same wardrobe as Bentley. But it was there that the similarities ended. Miles had long, shaggy brown hair and the beginnings of a beer belly.

"Miles Hendrix." Bentley gave Cassie a knowing smile, as if he knew about her high school crush.

That can't be.

But Bentley's smile offered to share a private joke with her.

How in the world does he know about Miles?

After the full dose of pain medication, Bentley probably knew all her secrets, including that she didn't own a single boring white bra. This was no joke. Her cheeks began to heat. Thankfully, Ajax had developed a case of the zoomies after meeting Flip and Miles. He raced around and distracted everyone.

"Cassie, I think your rides can use some sanding down of the rust and body filler for all those dents and holes," Shane said when Ajax collapsed near his feet.

"Bringing classic cars back to life is my passion." Miles grinned, possibly directing what remained of his youthful charisma toward Cassie. "Haven't seen you in a while, Cassie."

Holy moly. Cassie couldn't tell if that grin was because Miles was remembering her emoji-filled text messages from high school or if he was pleased as punch to have work. Her arm shot out, finger pointing toward the second barn. "The rides are in the lower pasture." Cassie escaped in that direction.

"Papa Shane, can we stay at the barn?" Adam asked. "We promise to be good."

"Do you remember how we talked about what a promise means?" Shane was clearly dubious about the boy's intentions.

"It means I am what I say?" If Adam had received a lecture on good behavior and the value of his word, he didn't sound as if he fully understood the concept.

"We'll be good," Quinn said.

Shane relented.

Cassie admitted the remaining group through the pasture gate, closing it after them. The late morning sun was warm on her face as she walked ahead. Whistler ambled toward them from the other end of the pasture.

Bentley caught up to her. "Miles emphasized his *passion*, Cassie. I bet he remembers those texts you sent in the aftermath of your wisdom teeth being pulled."

"I can't believe I told you that." She frowned, wanting to take back the confession. "It may have been the first time I made a fool of myself with a man, but it wasn't the last time. Or the most recent."

"So the past few days…" Now Bentley was frowning. "You think it was all foolish?"

"No. I…" Cassie glanced back at their audience, who were following at Flip's slower pace and falling behind. "Can we talk about this later?"

"I'm not much good at this, am I?" Bentley said softly. "It's probably for the best if we just forget everything that's happened between us."

Such logic. He was probably right. But everything inside Cassie rejected reason and common sense.

Impulsively, Cassie grabbed his arm and

whispered, "I can't forget. And you won't either."

Bentley's frown deepened. "I'm adding things up and realizing there are too many obstacles in our path. I know this is shiny and new and exciting, but I don't want either of us to get hurt."

Why did he have to make so much sense? If only she wasn't twenty-nine, staring down thirty and realizing that it was time to be sensible. She feared that sensible was incompatible with romantic.

"Tanner would say something about not playing it safe," Cassie told him. But now wasn't the time to argue. She turned and faced the rest of the group but kept her gaze on Bentley. "This is where your passion is tested. If you agree to proceed, it's going to be tough but possibly worth it."

Bentley didn't say a word, not even to validate that he knew she was talking on two levels—their relationship and the restoration of the carnival rides.

Flip leaned on Shane's arm, staring at Bentley and Cassie rather than the rides behind them. And then she set her sights on Miles. "I haven't seen you in years," she said in a busybody tone of voice. "How many times have you been married? I've forgotten."

"Twice." Miles grinned unabashedly. "Doesn't

mean I don't believe in love. It just means I'm not a very good husband because I get lost in my work. It's my passion, you know."

"We know," Bentley said tightly, as though through gritted teeth, staring down at Ajax, who'd taken up a position at his feet.

"I'm looking for someone who isn't looking for a wedding ring." Miles turned his grin toward Cassie.

And Cassie was caught. If she said he was wrong, Bentley might assume she wanted him to marry her. And if she said she wasn't, Bentley might assume something else entirely.

"What woman isn't interested in a wedding ring?" Flip laughed, winking at Cassie. "Even I can see the advantages of permanent companionship. Take Raymond Diaz…"

"I'd rather not get involved in someone else's idea of romance," Shane said, half under his breath.

Whistler joined the group, making her way straight to Bentley. Millie trotted over from the main barn, greeting Bentley with a full body rub and a loud purr.

"The pied piper is in fine form," Cassie noted softly, before saying in a louder voice, "Does anyone want to get a closer look at the rides?"

"Sure." Miles bravely headed inside.

"No, thanks." Flip peered at the barn's contents. "I see rust. Lots of rust. And no room to get creative." She turned around and waved at Shane, as if giving up. "Good luck."

"Hang on." Shane caught the old woman by the shoulders and carefully turned her around. "It's not like those are your working conditions. Bentley's going to haul everything you need out here."

"I am?" Bentley seemed as surprised by this as Cassie was.

"No, Shane." Flip dug in her heels. Literally. "You can't just drag my projects out here in the sun and wind. Do you know what sticks to wet paint?" She brushed off Shane's hold.

"Everything?" Bentley sounded like that was a guess.

"Exactly right." Flip nodded. "Everything. Dirt, leaves, cobwebs, bugs. I could go on."

"No need." Shane stared at the mess inside the barn.

"Uh-oh." Bentley leaned closer to Cassie. "You see that look in his eyes? He's not giving up."

"Well, I am," Flip said firmly, obviously having heard Bentley.

A bolt of apprehension struck Cassie. What if Grandpa was right and the rides were a legitimate way to make ends meet? She had a week ahead without progress on a horse she was being paid to train and a pony she'd invested in. Should she embrace this idea?

Before she could commit, Miles emerged from the barn. "The good news is that I've restored worse. The bad news is that you'll have to transport them down to my shop. What Flip said applies to me, too. Whatever bonding agent I use to fill the dents and rusted out pieces needs to be protected."

"I'm afraid that goes for me, too," Bentley said. "It's one thing to start the engines, but another to take apart and refurbish them to run another fifty years or so. I don't see them being done in less than two months, and that's with a crew working full-time."

So much for the rides helping Cassie make ends meet in the short term. This was just another reason why working for someone else would be smart. Paid sick days seemed like a luxury.

"You know what I think?" Shane said as if no one had spoken. He rubbed his hands together. "I think transporting them is too much work. And—"

"Here it comes," Bentley murmured.

"The answer is simpler than we think." Shane pointed to the three tall bays. "In order to remove the rides to transport them, we'd need to haul most of that junk out. We'd have to empty out one bay, maybe two. But what if at that point we make the bays a workshop? I'm sure we can order sheets of plastic as temporary doors. That way, the team can work on everything here. I could organize a group of volunteers to help us clean things out."

"Yee-haw!"

As one, the adults turned to face the main barn.

Poppy burst out of the breezeway with Mia, Quinn and Adam on her little back. She had a bridle on but no saddle.

"Yee—" Adam tumbled off the back and into the dirt.

"Adam?" Quinn glanced over his shoulder and then fell to the ground.

Mia clung to Poppy's mane as the little gray mare came to a stop by the pasture's fence. "Look at me, Uncle Bentley. I'm a cowgirl!"

In a dress, no less. Cassie needed to urge Tanner to get his daughter some blue jeans.

The two boys sat in the dirt and laughed gleefully, none the worse for wear.

Shane and Bentley ran to the rescue. Shane took hold of Poppy's reins while Bentley lifted Mia into his arms.

"Are you okay, sweetie?" Bentley asked her.

Mia nodded. "I'm a cowgirl."

Bentley helped Quinn get to his feet. "Are you okay?"

"Yep." The little boy dusted off his jeans with his cowboy hat.

"I hope you're okay, Adam." Shane gave his soon-to-be son a dark look. "You promised not to get in trouble."

"But, Papa Shane." Adam rubbed his dusty backside. "We didn't mean to. We weren't going to ride Poppy. We were just gonna sit on her."

Shane rolled his eyes, handing off Poppy's reins to Cassie. The pony looked none the worse for wear either, including her sparkly hooves. She nuzzled Cassie's pockets, as if searching for treats.

Shane marched over to Adam. "What do you think your mother is going to say when I tell her about this?"

"You don't have to tell her." Adam was still rubbing his backside.

Shane nodded. "You're right."

"I am?" Adam brightened.

"*I'm* not going to tell her." Shane nodded again. "*You're* going to tell her."

"But…but…I'm gonna be mucking out stalls until I'm fifty!" Adam wailed.

CHAPTER FOURTEEN

BY MIDAFTEROON OF another day of watching Tanner's kids and Cassie, Bentley was beat.

He'd played four games of checkers, three games of I Spy, two games of War, and one game of Yahtzee. He'd fed the kids, cleaned up after the kids and fed them again. He'd laughed at their joy and their innocent outlook on life. He'd relished Mia's hugs. And through it all, he was aware of Cassie watching them, smiling at them, laughing with them.

If he tried hard enough, he'd be able to frame Cassie as part of a group he associated with the Bar D—Raymond, Rhett, Tanner—not the woman he wouldn't mind kissing again. His reframing tactic might have worked if he wasn't acutely aware of Cassie's every move, her every wince of pain, her every glance that dropped to his lips.

Yeah, it was time to go.

And time for Cassie to admit she didn't want to run those rides. If she bailed on the idea, he wouldn't have to fulfill his promise and continue to come around. He wouldn't be reminded that Olivia was a stone's throw away. As it was, Shane was arranging a bevy of volunteers to help clean out the barn tomorrow. There was still time to recruit a decent mechanic to replace Bentley.

But the truth was, he didn't want to be replaced in any capacity that involved Cassie. Sadly, he was too responsible to let what he wanted guide his actions.

"Cassie?" From the kitchen peninsula, Bentley caught her eye from where she rested on the couch. "You don't really want Miles, Flip and I to go through all that trouble on the carnival rides, do you?"

Cassie lifted her chin. Oh, she knew what he was trying to do, and she was having none of it. "My grandfather expects me to follow through on this."

"But are you going to be happy operating the rides?"

"I need to do my part to keep the family ranch afloat."

Bentley knew all about family obligations. But he also knew about family resentments. He'd give Cassie a few more days to think about it. And during those days, he'd keep his distance. Now was the time to put that idea into practice. To get the kids' attention, Bentley did a drumroll with his hands on the counter. "Do you know what time it is?"

"Time for cookies?" Quinn asked hopefully. He sat on a barstool eating a cheese stick.

"Better than that. It's time for milk shakes in town at the Bent Nickel." Bentley smiled at Cassie. "And once we're in town, I think I should stay. My job here is done."

After a moment, Cassie got to her feet. She came into the kitchen, passing close by Bentley on her way to the sink to deposit her empty water glass. "I'll drive us into town."

Or you could kiss me again.

Bentley kept still to avoid reaching for her or stepping into her path. Now that she was in close proximity, he was torn. On the one hand, he wanted her to put into words what he was feeling—that he'd never felt this way about someone before. The thrill of her being near. The way his heart pounded when they kissed. The way she simultaneously felt familiar *and* new. On the other hand, they wanted different things out of life. Since they knew they faced obstacles up front, why pursue anything? Why form attachments that would eventually be broken?

When Cassie had rinsed out her glass and put it in the dishwasher, Bentley took her by the arm before she could walk past. "You'll be fine tonight? Alone with the kids?" He could make another blanket fort before he left.

"We'll be fine," she reassured him. She placed a warm palm on his cheek. "You've given me a good jump start on recovery. And now the kids know the ranch routine."

"And you promise not to lift anything heavy?" He was torn between putting a little distance between them and drawing her closer.

"Cross my heart." Cassie made an X over her heart with one finger and went into the mudroom. "Don't give me those sad eyes, Bentley. You'll be back to work on the ride engines tomorrow. And then, you can get a status report as to how we managed to get through the night. Come on, kids. Get your boots on."

Bentley gathered his backpack and put his boots on, feeling a bit melancholy. The Bar D had been a home of sorts over the last few days. And now it would just be a place he showed up to. And when he returned, he'd have no excuse to kiss Cassie.

When they got to the ranch yard, Bentley strapped Mia into her car seat and made sure Quinn's seat belt was secure, and then he took one last look around the ranch. Ajax plopped down at the barn door, ready to keep watch until Cassie's return. Whistler whinnied from the pasture gate. The pines on the rise behind the house seemed still in the breezeless afternoon. He could imagine Olivia sitting in the small dinghy on the lake just beyond the trees, face lifted toward the sun as she tried to rebuild her confidence on the water. He could imagine Cassie working with the horses under the watchful gaze of Millie, the barn cat.

But what Bentley couldn't imagine was Cassie running a carnival down by the highway.

"You're not going to run those rides on your own, are you?" Bentley found himself asking as he climbed into the front passenger seat.

"I hope my grandfather and Rhett will rotate shifts with me." But Cassie put more hope than certainty into her words. "As it stands now, I won't be contributing income unless I operate those rides. And they won't be ready to run in time for the last of the summer tourist season. It's all rather demoralizing."

Bentley wanted so much more for Cassie. A happy life free from worry. A fulfilling life full of joy. She'd told him that horse training was her passion, not strapping kids in a small Ferris wheel and standing around giving them their money's worth. "What is the career progression of a horse trainer?"

"Progression?" She chuckled, but rather mirthlessly. "There is no CEO position, if that's what you mean."

He watched the ranch disappear in the side mirror. "In many careers, the more experience and skill you have, the more money you make."

"But it's not as if I'm based in the horse-riding capital of the country." Cassie gave a cheerless laugh. "And I don't have a reputation past Boise. It's why I was thrilled when your cousin hired me to train horses for her Western film next year. It could open doors for me… If we can make ends meet until my first paycheck. And Rhett's. He's going to be on the crew, too."

Bentley had no idea what it felt like to live paycheck to paycheck. He made a mental note to ask Ashley when Cassie's work would begin.

"I'm gonna be a train driver when I grow up," Quinn announced. *"Choo-choo."*

"Me, too," Mia said. "Or a fireman. What are you, Uncle Bentley?"

"I invent things. And I improve things."

"Like rocket ships?" Quinn asked.

"No." Bentley turned in his seat so that he could see the kids. "Like lighter, faster boat engines that use less gasoline. Or sail rigging that is more efficient for adjustments by the crew. Or boat hulls that minimize drag through the water but resist capsizing." To keep loved ones safe. That should be his next project.

No one said anything.

"Did I just speak French?" Bentley asked, eliciting a polite laugh from Cassie. "What I meant is that for the past ten years, I've been making faster boats for Captain Olivia."

"Oh," they all said, drawing out the word.

"I like the captain," Mia said.

"She's cool," Quinn agreed. "When she's not yelling at Uncle Bentley."

"I can't wait to tell my brother the captain came calling." Grinning, Cassie turned onto the highway. And although they only sat next to each other, the distance between them seemed to widen. "In the dark of night, no less."

"I'd forgotten about that." Bentley frowned. His sister wasn't in a good emotional place to start a relationship. But she'd be furious if he told Rhett that.

They rode in silence into town. It felt like this was goodbye.

Shane was coming out of the general store when Cassie parked in front of the Bent

Nickel Diner. He waved. "Bentley, can I have a word?"

"After I get the kids inside," Bentley told him.

Cassie dismissed Bentley's excuse. "We'll be fine." She led them into the diner.

This is what it'll be like when I'm gone and she's healthy. Cassie being independent and capable, able to get along without him.

Bentley wondered if he could get along without her.

Shane drew him to an empty corner of the parking lot and handed him a padded envelope. "Open it."

There was a DNA kit inside. "What's this?"

"If the opportunity presents itself, we can settle this thing with Tanner," Shane explained quietly. "Mind if I join you for a cup of coffee? Or in your case, tea."

"We're having milk shakes." Something inside Bentley soured. He shoved the DNA test kit inside his backpack but stayed put. "Shane, I can't get a DNA sample from Tanner. I'm not staying at the ranch anymore." Not to mention it felt underhanded to collect it without Tanner's permission. It probably wasn't even legal. "If Gertie knew you're doing this—"

"That test isn't for Tanner." Shane grabbed Bentley's arm and tugged him toward the diner. "I think we can take a sample from one of the kids."

Bentley recoiled, shaking his cousin off. "No. First, you don't tell me Olivia's here and now this? What's happened to your moral compass?"

"When did you start talking so much?"

"I grew up." Bentley was having a hard time not shouting. "I assumed you did, too."

"Ha, ha. Give the kit back to me." Shane held out his hand. "I'll do it. I'll swab a straw or something."

"No. These kids…" Bentley was fond of them. If they weren't Monroes… He set his jaw. He was their uncle Bentley. He wanted them to be family. "Leave them out of it."

Shane kept his hand outstretched. "Quinn and Mia will be cared for either way, either with a payoff to their father or with a proper share. My search for Tanner's father's birth certificate is hitting dead ends. And yes, this is a little bit shady," Shane allowed, lowering his hand. "But it achieves closure. We have to think of the family. *Our* family."

Bentley glanced into the diner.

Mia and Quinn were perched on barstools on their knees. Cassie looked like she was telling them to sit their booties down. *Cassie.* Bentley knew she wouldn't approve of anyone stealing their DNA. But Shane was right. They had cousins and siblings to think about. And Tanner was being a pain in the butt when it came to proving his claim.

"I get it," Shane was saying. "I'm fond of those kids, too. But they deserve to settle somewhere. And no matter the outcome of this DNA test, Tanner will have the funds to put a down payment on a ranch of his own. Maybe one large enough that he can hold his rodeo school there."

Bentley swallowed thickly. "I know you management types have to frame the hard decisions in a way that allows you to sleep at night, but I just want you to know that I don't buy into that—"

"I wouldn't expect you to." Shane opened the Bent Nickel's door. "Think of the family. Our family."

Bentley went inside, carrying his backpack carefully, as if it held the crown jewels. He joined Cassie and the kids, taking a seat on a barstool next to Quinn, putting the backpack at his feet.

Cam set two milk shakes on the counter. "I've got your tea coming right up, Bentley."

"What's that red thing?" Quinn pointed at the cherry, looking aghast. "It's ruined."

Bentley plucked the cherry by the stem and

ate it. "There. Problem solved." He unwrapped a straw for Quinn and handed it to him.

"No. That red thing touched the milk shake." Quinn crossed his arms over his skinny chest, refusing the straw, the drink and open-mindedness.

Shane sat in a booth, watching. In fact, everyone in the diner was watching. When the DNA results came back, they'd all know that Bentley had been the one close enough—often enough—to collect the sample.

It won't matter. By then I'll be gone.

That was optimism talking, trying to protect his heart and assuming Cassie would give up on the rides in the next few days. But hot on the heels of optimism, pessimism weighed in. Cassie would never quit on those rides or go back on her word to her grandfather. And when the DNA results came back, everyone would know who'd done the deed.

I'm not usually the dirty deed doer.

Bentley started to sweat. He put the straw in Quinn's milk shake. "Here. Drink from the bottom. The cherry didn't touch the bottom."

"No." Quinn was adamant. "Red things are bad."

Maybe the boy's obstinance was for the best. Bentley couldn't collect a DNA sample if the kid refused to drink through the straw.

He wasn't even sure how to collect the sample when the swab was still in its package at his feet. If he opened it, Cassie would see. Logistically, this was a fail.

Mia stuck her fingers in the whipped cream on her chocolate shake, trying to grab hold of the cherry stem. Once she did, she put it in her mouth and chewed it. "I like it. It's good. It's goodie good." She took the straw that Cassie offered and used it like a spoon to eat the whipped cream. It wasn't the right tool for the task. Whipped cream dripped on the counter and on her dress.

"Your sister ate hers." Cam put another one on top of Quinn's. "Go on. Give it a try."

"Drink up," Bentley said instead. Who cared about a cherry?

Quinn's frown deepened. He pushed his milk shake away.

"I have to make water," Mia announced, placing the middle of her straw in her mouth. The ends jutted out the corners. "I want Uncle Bentley to take me." That's what Bentley assumed she'd said. It had sounded more like, "I-wa-Unk-Benly-to-take-me."

Bentley was now well versed in kiddie speak.

Cassie stood. "Oh, but, honey—"

"It's okay." Bentley got to his feet, as well.

"I'll take her. I've done it before. We have a system." He was running at the mouth. Nervous. So nervous. "You can…um…help solve the milk shake crisis with Quinn." He slung his backpack onto his shoulder and escorted Mia.

The straw was still in her mouth. It glistened with her saliva.

All Bentley needed to do was hold her straw while she went into the bathroom. Open the test kit and swab it. And then give it to Shane to mail in.

Bentley knocked on the ladies' room door to make sure it was empty, swallowing back doubt and self-loathing.

If I do this, Cassie will never speak to me again.

"WHAT'S GOING ON HERE?" Tanner stood in the diner's doorway. He tipped his cowboy hat back and glared at everyone.

Conversation in the diner dimmed and died away. Quinn snatched the cherry on his milk shake and ate it, which was ironic since he'd been telling Cassie repeatedly that everything about his milk shake was ruined by the red thing. And she'd been thinking that the only thing ruined in Second Chance were her chances of a relationship with Bentley.

"Where's Mia?" Tanner demanded, marching across the dining room.

"Daddy!" Mia ran from the back of the diner, followed by Bentley, who looked decidedly uncomfortable at seeing Tanner.

Tanner swept Mia into his arms and then did a three-hundred-sixty-degree turn, glaring at anyone and everyone, but especially at Shane and Bentley. "Somebody better tell me what's going on."

"We're having milk shakes," Cassie said simply.

"Because you can never feed a child too much sugar," Shane murmured impassively.

"Unless, of course, you want them to sleep at night." Bentley sat down, swinging his backpack to the ground.

"I meant," Tanner ground out, "why are my kids in town with the likes of *you*?"

"I love Uncle Bentley," Mia said, all innocence right when the room needed it. Although her word choice…

"Uncle…" Tanner's face turned beet red. He opened his mouth, but before he could say anything, Bentley cut him off.

"Think carefully about your audience before you say anything you might regret later," he cautioned.

"In case we really are family," Shane added.

Tanner pressed his lips into a thin line, shifting his ire to Cassie. But he held his tongue. And then he held out his hand to Quinn. "Let's go, son."

"But…" Quinn stared at the milk shake. "I didn't get to drink my milk shake."

"And I love Uncle Bentley." Mia reached for him over Tanner's shoulder. "I wanna stay."

"No." Tanner took hold of Quinn. Both his kids were crying as they left.

The door swung shut behind him amid a silence that was unusual for the Bent Nickel.

And then Gabby glided in, spotted Bentley and twirled in his direction. "Look, Uncle Bentley. Look at me!"

The pied piper sighed, apparently put out.

He always makes it seem as if he doesn't deserve anyone's affection, when in reality he's so good, so caring.

Cassie was falling head over heels for him. In love. Her heart swelled with the emotion, with the beauty of it, with the beauty of him. It had come at an inconvenient time for her, and Bentley would say it was impossible for him. But… Love… She tried to back up into a sweet and safe crush, blinking back unexpected tears.

Cassie needed a moment. Blindly, she turned and followed Tanner out. She had a practical excuse. He needed Mia's car seat. "Tanner, wait."

Quinn and Mia were pleading their milk shake case to no avail.

Tanner opened his dusty truck and placed them on the front bench seat, one after the other. And then he faced Cassie. "I left them in your care. I trusted you wouldn't go against my wishes and cozy up to those Monroes."

Oh, she'd cozied up to one Monroe, all right. That fact made her freeze on the spot.

Tanner's gaze was piercing. "Oh, I see how it is." He nodded toward the diner. "You and *Uncle* Bentley."

"That's not… We aren't…" Why couldn't she find the words to say there was nothing between them?

Because I wish there was!

"You told them I was leaving, and the Monroes swooped in, trying to turn you and my own kids against me." He gestured toward his truck, where both kids were still protesting being taken from the diner. "I thought I could trust you. We're in business together."

"We're friends, Tanner." Cassie stuck her hands in her pockets and gave the children what she hoped was a reassuring smile. "You're in the rodeo school business with my grandfather and brother, not me. And I'd expect a man who claims to be a Monroe to want to form stronger ties with his family."

"Family? My wife was family." Tanner removed his hat and ran a hand through his dark hair before putting it back on. He cleared his throat. "My grandmother is all the family I have left and she means nothing to the Monroes." He turned and embraced his children. "I'm sorry I lost my temper. I love you. Both of you. You know that, right?"

The pair nodded, clinging to their father.

"We'll get milk shakes another day," Tanner promised, his voice husky with emotion.

Bentley opened the diner door. He caught Cassie's eye, asking a silent question—*Are you okay?* Her heart swelled with love for him once more. She gave Bentley a grateful smile and waved him off.

Cassie was determined to make peace with Tanner, not only for Quinn's and Mia's sakes, but for her grandfather and Rhett. "You're back a day early, Tanner. How did your trip go? Well, I hope."

Tanner released the kids, turning slowly to face her. His smile was feeble, but at least it was there. "I signed up over fifty kids. We're going to have a rodeo school."

"That's great. I'm happy for you." And Rhett and Grandpa.

"We're going to need your help." Tanner's smile grew a little warmer. "We'll need someone to check in students and run the snack bar. And…I may have promised a couple of young girls that there'd be a trick riding seminar. We need something to attract more cowgirls."

Cold anger shot through Cassie, and not just because she wasn't physically ready to teach. "I hope you're not saying that girls can't sign up to learn bronc or bull riding."

"Girls can participate in any event. Any event." Some of her resentment must have lingered on her face because Tanner hurriedly added, "I'm not asking you to perform or demonstrate trick riding. I know it can take weeks, sometimes longer, for injuries like yours to fully heal. All I'm asking is that you think about how you'd teach without demonstrating."

"I can't." Cassie went to her truck and retrieved the bulky child seat, carrying it over to him, trying to achieve leverage so as not to strain her back.

"Just think about it," Tanner said, taking it from her.

Sighing, she shook her head and returned to the Bent Nickel. But it didn't feel the same as before.

Shane and Bentley sat at the lunch counter

where the milk shakes were. Shane had that bubble wrap envelope he'd given to Bentley when they'd arrived. Their heads were bent together, and they were whispering. She'd walked out of the diner feeling love, and in her absence two sides had begun to form in this town—those who supported the Monroes and those who supported Tanner. Even with love in her heart, Cassie was reluctant to choose a team. She started to leave.

"Cassie, stay. Please," Shane called to her. He patted the envelope. "Bentley and I are done here. Why let two perfectly good milk shakes go to waste?"

Cassie hesitated. The temptation of a sweet man and a sweet drink were compelling. But Bentley wasn't asking her to stay. He wasn't even meeting her gaze. Where had her beloved Monroe gone?

Shane stood, taking the envelope with him. "Come on, Gabby. Share a booth with me. I'll buy you a shake and you can tell me all about those cute little stepsisters of yours."

"They have colic." Gabby slid into Shane's usual booth. "I can't get any homework done. Or sleep. Can I come spend the night with you guys?"

"Will you babysit?" Shane countered. "Franny and I haven't had a night out in ages."

Gabby lowered her chin to the table, setting it on her hands. "That's a hard pass."

"Cassie?" Bentley held up Quinn's milk shake. "There's an empty seat next to me and a milk shake with your name on it."

There was her Monroe. Warm feelings toward Bentley and a future filled with steamy kisses had Cassie finally agreeing.

They slurped their shakes without speaking for a few minutes. Gabby and Shane laughed and continued to negotiate some sort of babysitting bargain. A few diners came in. A few left.

"You know that conversation we had during the ride into town?" Cassie asked, stirring her milk shake remains with a straw.

"The one where I pointed out that horse trainers have no career advancement?" Bentley grimaced. "I apologize for that. It was out of line."

"No. It's fair. I was thinking about my grandfather on the drive in this afternoon. He's pushing eighty and scrambling to make ends meet. It's not smart to spend my whole life struggling to make do. I just wish *cowgirl* could be my job description forever." She wished she wasn't being forced to be practical, working to keep the lights on and the stock fed.

"You're wondering what other jobs you might be qualified for? Or what jobs you could do here in town? Other than carnival ride ticket taker." His empathetic gaze seemed to see her every thought, her every concern.

Cassie slid the milk shake glass toward the service end of the lunch counter. "Ride operator is still on the table." As was a relationship with him. If only she could work up the courage to talk about kisses and dating and…and *love*. He was her idea of perfect. "But yes, I'd like to know what my options are."

"What about working at the Bucking Bull? They offer weekend trail rides to Mike Moody's hideout." He touched the brim of her hat. "You could still be a cowgirl."

"I don't know if that's a good fit for me." The idea unsettled her. She was sure the trails were clearly marked and that she wouldn't get lost, but she didn't think she could swallow her pride and work for Franny. It would give the impression that the Bar D couldn't support three people. Which was true, but still…

"I can tell that idea's a bust," Bentley said gently. "Why don't you take a couple of online courses? That's what Gabby does."

"I'm too old for school." She was practically thirty and over-the-hill, not to mention set in her ways.

Obviously, Bentley didn't agree. He sat back and gave Cassie a once-over that made her all hot and bothered. "Hang on now. You're not that old."

He says all the right things.

Nevertheless, she shook her head, wishing this conversation didn't make her feel inadequate where he was concerned. "I don't have the money."

Bentley placed a hand on hers and she didn't shy away. "If money were no object, what would you want to do with the rest of your life?"

"I don't have the luxury of—"

"Just play along, Cassie." He repeated the question.

Cassie stared at their hands while she chose her words. "I enjoy waking up with a purpose, with things needing to be done and… and long-term goals ahead of me. Other than that, I don't know."

Bentley nodded.

"What does that mean?" Her question was barely a whisper.

He shrugged. "That you're really no different than the hundreds of thousands of college freshmen out there." He pointed at the large plate glass window and what was beyond. "That's the whole point of college, you know. To explore different subjects until you find something that fits."

"College is not under discussion." Cassie tried to pull her hand free.

Bentley kept hold of her. "Change is a scary thing if it's thrust upon you. I loved my old job and my hometown. It's why I'm looking locally and not rushing into something new."

"If horse training paid the bills, we wouldn't be having this conversation. I love horse training." *And I could love you*, she added silently. *If you didn't love your hometown and your logic so much.*

"It's okay to stick with what brings you joy." He squeezed her hand. "And we both know that's not operating carnival rides."

He wanted her to tell him not to work on the rides. Cassie didn't fall into his trap. He didn't believe they could be together forever. Perhaps that was true. But what was wrong with being together a few more days?

"YES, I'VE NEGLECTED YOU, ROMEO." Cassie entered the large palomino's stall carrying a currycomb with a few bite-size apple nuggets stuffed in the pocket of her jeans. Bentley had told her to do things she enjoyed. It was time to do just that.

The gelding nudged her shoulder and then

nuzzled her pockets, looking for a treat, which she obligingly gave him.

"I don't suppose you know what I should be doing with the rest of my life?" Cassie began brushing Romeo. Then she put his halter on, gave him another treat and led him out of his stall. "Or how to draw a quiet man out of his shell?"

Ajax sat in the sunshine just inside the barn door. He didn't move as they clopped past. Clearly, the dog had a preference for Monroes with pied piper abilities. Millie was playing with a beetle at the corner of the barn, also choosing to let Cassie go about her business without so much as a friendly meow.

Cassie put Romeo through his paces in Liberty Training, round and round the paddock without a lunge line. Romeo was a well-behaved gentleman and eager to please. He was quick to obey her commands to stop and turn. The gelding gave her confidence. He made her wish that she could earn a living wage as a horse trainer. But it was a juvenile wish, similar to romantic notions about East Coast engineers. She might get excited by wishes and notions, but she needed to keep her boots and her expectations firmly planted on the ground.

When Romeo had worked the edge of energy off, she called him to her in the center of the paddock and gave him another treat. "Okay, buddy. Now you need to show me that you haven't forgotten how to perform."

They ran through his repertoire. First, the crowd-pleasing stunts—he took the brim of her hat in his teeth and trotted off with it; he brought the hat back and extended his nose until she kissed it; and then she stood at his shoulder and he gave her a hug, curling his head and neck around her. None of which caused her any back pain. It was her heart that was aching.

Before they moved on to the harder stuff, a familiar truck pulled into the ranch yard.

It was Rhett and Grandpa Diaz.

"Hey, Cassie! We were a success!" Her grandfather headed to the house, Ajax at his heels. "I'm pooped."

Rhett came over to the paddock and hooked his arms over the top rail. "I remember when you taught Whistler how to hug you. Our horses and our dog would be uncivilized if you weren't around."

"Is that a backhanded compliment?" Cassie led Romeo over to the railing. "Or deflection because you forgot to move hay before you left?"

"Ouch. Umm. I'm going to go with the first

option. And that's about as much as a brother compliments a sister." But Rhett smiled cheerfully when he said it. "Sorry about the hay."

"And the coffee." She couldn't let that one slide.

"And the coffee." Rhett nodded.

"You're home a day early." Just like Tanner.

"There are only so many places we could stop to put up flyers and talk to folks about rodeo school." Rhett heaved a sigh. "It's good to be home. Did you realize Grandpa is old now? He requires taking care of." He raised a hand. "No, don't answer that question. Of course, you knew. You've been managing his meds and medical care for a year. How are things?"

"I can't complain. The ranch is still standing, and so are Tanner's kids. But you should know that Tanner wasn't happy when he found us in town having milk shakes with Bentley and Shane."

Rhett shook his head. "There are so many Monroes around town lately, you can't spit without hitting one."

"Speaking of Monroes..." Cassie gave Rhett a sly look. "Olivia Monroe stopped by and asked for you. Just so you know."

Romeo licked her back pocket in the hopes of getting another treat.

"Really?" Rhett was unfazed by her news of his late-night caller. "And just so you know, Tanner is determined to have you teach trick riding at rodeo school."

Cassie shook her head.

"I told him as much." Rhett reached over the rail to scratch underneath Romeo's forelock. "You look better, sis."

"Rhett, don't think you can sweet-talk me into teaching." Cassie told him that Dr. Carlisle had wanted her to limit herself physically.

He leaned on the rail. "You don't have to teach kids to gallop while standing on a saddle. You could teach horse tricks."

Cassie rolled her eyes. "You mean Liberty." The command of a horse without a lead rope, lunge line, or reins. "Give horsemanship the respect it deserves by using the proper name."

Rhett shuffled his feet a little. "You know, you're good at making animals behave. People pay me to help them become better ropers. Maybe you can earn money training people to train their horses."

"Nobody around here would be interested in that. I'd have to move. Or travel. I'd be better off running the carnival rides." At least then, she'd be with family at the Bar D.

"What century are you living in? You don't have to leave this paddock to teach nowadays.

You create videos, some free and some folks pay for. And if enough people watch them, you'll get advertisers on your channel who pay to run an ad before your content."

"That's not a thing." And honestly, she wasn't sure she'd understood everything he'd said. She was like Grandpa when it came to technology. She had little use for the internet and only watched shows on TV or in the movie theater.

"Video learning is a thing. I'm considering it myself." Rhett tugged his phone from his back pocket. "You could do videos about training horses. Maybe even do some featuring stunts you train horses to do for a movie that's going to star two of the biggest names in Hollywood—power couple Wyatt Halford and Ashley Monroe." He pulled up a video on his phone of what looked like a young woman training her horse to paw the ground. "If you recorded behind-the-scenes sessions of how you trained horses for certain movie scenes, you'd be more interesting than cute cowgirls teaching horses how to take a bow."

"Cute cowgirls?" she teased.

"Focus, Cassie. Look at the views." Rhett moved his phone closer to her.

She peered at the small number and nearly fainted. "Ten thousand views? Ten thousand? You think I could do something like this here?"

"You could do this anywhere."

Anywhere? Like Pennsylvania, where Bentley was from?

CHAPTER FIFTEEN

"Look at me. I hardly wobble. Right, Uncle Bentley?" Gabby danced past.

The morning after Tanner returned to town, Bentley sat drinking his tea in the lobby of the Lodgepole Inn. Next to him on the couch, Laurel sat holding one of the twins, whose little foot was pushing against Bentley's arm.

"Uncle Bentley?"

"No wobble. Right." Bentley would agree to anything as long as Gabby didn't stumble into the stone fireplace and hurt herself.

"Why the long face?" Laurel nudged his shoulder with her own.

Oh, I don't know. My sister doesn't want my help or the support of anyone in the family other than Shane. I can't stop thinking about an injured cowgirl I have no future with. And Shane gave me a DNA test to swab a child.

"I'm thinking," Bentley said, which was the best answer he could come up with. "You know how I am."

"Yes, I do. You're probably rebuilding those

carnival ride engines in your head." Laurel spared him a fond glance. "Or tackling some weighty issue, like world peace."

"Not likely." Gabby came to a stop in front of Bentley. She began to plié. Her dips weren't smooth, and her arms were stiff and angular.

And because Bentley was a fixer, he wanted to tell her to make adjustments. But he hadn't forgotten Shane's advice a few days prior, so he kept silent.

"Uncle Bentley's got a crush on Cassie Diaz," Gabby said with a knowing smile.

That earned a quick glance from Laurel, and then a soft chuckle. "Uncle Bentley got bit by the love bug," she crooned to the baby, who pressed her foot harder against Bentley's arm. "It's about time."

"We're just two ships," Bentley said matter-of-factly.

"You say that as if you're the *Titanic* and your relationship is doomed." Laurel gave him a searching look. "That's why you've had such a long, sad face. Don't get discouraged. True love, the kind that weathers icebergs and snowstorms, is worth figuring out."

He sighed. "And if the figures don't add up?"

"Love doesn't offer right or wrong answers. The solution is unique for every couple." Lau-

rel spoke as if she'd had great experience over-
coming hurdles to true love. And considering
she'd married a man who wasn't the father of
her twins, maybe she had.

"You should listen to Laurel." Gabby swept
her leg forward, toward Bentley, and back, toward the large stone fireplace with its raised
hearth. "She's incredibly wise."

Laurel chuckled. "I am wise, but Gabby's
only singing my praises because she wants a
new laptop, and she believes I can convince
her father to give her one."

"If there's an issue with her laptop, I can
look at it." Fearing Gabby would hurt herself, Bentley got to his feet and repositioned
her so she faced the check-in desk and could
kick forward and backward as much as she
pleased without making contact with anyone
or anything. He sat back down, hoping they'd
come to an end of the discussion into his personal life.

"I don't know Cassie that well. Is she nice?"
Laurel made funny faces at the baby.

"Gosh, yes," Gabby said.

"She's fantastic," Bentley agreed. "Bright.
Down-to-earth. She has a big heart and a good
sense of humor." Plus she made a wickedly
good peach cobbler.

"Why do I sense a but in there?" Laurel glanced at Bentley once more.

"Isn't it obvious?" Bentley shrugged. "Because her life is here."

"Star-crossed lovers. Never meant to be." Gabby began to swing her other leg. "It's exactly like the *Titanic*."

"I agree with you there." Bentley heaved a demoralized sigh. "Cassie and I... We... It's impossible."

"Gosh, Uncle Bentley. Didn't you tell me once that *impossible* is just a state of mind? You have to look at a problem from a different direction to solve it." Gabby leaped toward the check-in desk, throwing her arms out, presumably for balance. She gathered herself and leaped again. "A new perspective. Fresh eyes. That sort of thing."

"Wise words," Laurel murmured with a proud smile.

"I'm not taking advice from a twelve-year-old." Bentley got to his feet but was suddenly unsure where he was going to go. He had a few hours to kill before a group of volunteers was going to attempt to clear out the barn at the Bar D. The diner held no appeal without Cassie. His room upstairs held no appeal. The front porch. The back porch. The rest of his life.

The baby began to fuss.

Bentley picked her up and walked around to the other side of the room, away from leaping ballerinas-in-training. The infant had a small, round head and big blue eyes. She sighed contentedly and without meaning to, Bentley thought of Cassie and her desire to have kids. "Which twin is this?" They were identical.

"Hope." Laurel sank back against the couch cushions. "She'll be hungry in another few minutes. And then you can walk Hazel while I feed her. You've always been such a good helper, always willing to chip in where needed."

Bentley might have agreed if not for the request Shane had made to collect Mia's or Quinn's DNA. Had he done the right thing yesterday at the diner?

At the check-in counter, Gabby opened her laptop. "Oh, look. A new ballet lesson is live." She sat on a stool and started the video, filling the air with classical musical and a lyrical French voice.

"Her instructor is in France," Laurel told Bentley. "The world is getting smaller every day."

"It is, isn't it?" Bentley stared out the window at a passing car. Second Chance was remote. Although the internet made it possible for people to work and have relationships over long distances.

But everyone knew long distance didn't work out long-term.

It was just… When he thought of Cassie, a part of him was willing to try.

"TELL ME AGAIN what's going on this morning." Grandpa Diaz sat at the kitchen table drinking his coffee and sorting his monthly pills. His black checked shirt hung open over his once-white T-shirt. He held up a pill bottle. "Is this one new?"

Cassie dutifully read the label. "It's the same diabetes medicine you've been taking for a few weeks now."

"Huh."

Cassie recognized that tone of voice. It meant her grandfather was considering not taking the pill. "You need to put one in the morning slot and one in the evening slot. And if you want to argue, I'll call Dr. Carlisle for you to argue with."

"Huh. I guess I'll put one in the morning slot." He dropped a pill in. "And one in the evening slot." He dropped in another. "You never answered me about today's activities. You invited Monroes over?"

"A bunch of our friends are coming over

to help us clean out the second barn." Cassie braced herself for an argument. "Not just Monroes."

Her grandfather scowled. "That barn doesn't need cleaning."

"We need to make room for the restoration team to do their work." Cassie tried not to sound impatient, but she was afraid she failed.

"Is that so?" Grandpa continued sorting his pills. "Huh."

Ajax got up from his dog bed, slowly chewing his bunny squeaker. *Squeak-squeak.* He faced the direction of the hallway.

Rhett entered the kitchen and gave Ajax a pat on the head. He was fresh from the shower, dark hair slicked back. He did a double take upon seeing Cassie. "You did your hair for a dump run?"

Grandpa spilled his pill bottle. "Hey! I didn't agree to throw anything away!"

"Nobody's going to the dump." *Today*, Cassie silently added as she hurried to gather up his blood pressure medicine. So what if she'd straightened her hair and put on a little makeup?

"You did your hair for a clean out?" In true brotherly form, Rhett refused to let the hair thing go. Grinning, he poured himself a cup of coffee.

"Clean out, shmean out. That's all good stuff in there." Grandpa continued sorting his pills, peering into the compartments.

"We're cleaning and organizing, making room for the workers to work." Cassie smoothed her hair over her shoulder, wondering if Bentley would notice her hair or her eyes… The men in her family were staring at her. "Why is that so hard to understand?"

Rhett gave Cassie's shoulder a significant stare. "I get it now. You did your hair for Tanner."

"That's the first thing anyone's said today that I approve of." Grandpa snapped all the pill compartments closed and returned his pill bottles to the zippered plastic bag he kept them in.

"Please." Cassie rolled her eyes.

"He's making a life here," Grandpa said. "Fish where the fish are. He's a good catch."

"For someone else," Cassie murmured.

The back door opened. Tanner and his kids entered.

"Good morning, everybody. I have a favor to ask." Tanner didn't look up from removing Quinn's and Mia's boots. "My kids wanted to come today. Something about the Clark boys being here to help out. Did you arrange a play-date, Cassie?" There may not have been suspicion in his tone, but when he looked up there was suspicion in his eyes.

"No playdate. But she did her hair," Rhett said, earning an elbow to the ribs from Cassie. *"Ow."*

"The Clarks are one of the families coming over today to help *organize* the second barn," Cassie said, catching her grandfather's eye.

He nodded in apparent agreement. *Organize* was definitely preferable to *clean* in his book.

"We promise to be good," Quinn said, although based on his track record when Adam was around, Cassie didn't believe him.

"I'm always good," Mia said, twirling a dark brown curl and blessing the room with her angelic smile.

Tanner stepped forward. "Look, I know it's asking a lot to have you watch my kids, but they really want to help out today."

"It's no trouble." Rhett scoffed. "Cassie will keep an eye on them."

Cassie pinched her brother's arm. *"We'll* all watch them, just like we all do chores around the ranch, like stocking the hayloft when it's our turn."

Rhett rubbed his arm and nodded.

"Thanks." Tanner turned to go.

"But, Tanner…" Cassie waited until he faced her. "Your kids are a good judge of character. It might benefit all of us if you stay around today, too." The fate of the Bar D was in Monroe hands. Should she remind him of that?

"Oh, Daddy. Would you stay?" Quinn grabbed his father's hand and swung it from side to side. "You'll like Adam. He's a good rider. And Charlie is, too. And Davey." Basically all the Clark boys.

"No, son. I've got a meeting in Boise with a company that might sponsor our rodeo school." Tanner patted Quinn's cowboy hat. "Next time, for sure. And I'll help when I return. Promise."

CHAPTER SIXTEEN

"THE BOYS ARE COMING! The boys are coming!" Quinn was beaming, practically beside himself with joy. He held on to the kitchen counter and kicked up his heels. "Adam, Charlie, Davey and Adam."

Cassie shared some of the boy's enthusiasm, smiling as she took out the last batch of cookies from the oven. She was eager to see Bentley again. "Quinn, you said Adam twice."

"'Cause he's my favorite." Quinn collapsed onto the linoleum and shook his limbs as if he needed to burn off some of his excitement.

Honking heralded the arrival of the troops who'd volunteered to help clear out a working space in the second barn. Mia and Quinn ran for their boots. Grandpa buttoned his shirt and tucked it into his jeans.

Honk-honk!

Cassie smoothed her hair over her shoulder, and waited for the mudroom to clear, when what she really wanted to do was run outside along with Quinn and Mia.

Rhett rinsed his coffee cup in the sink. "Your hair looks nice, but you didn't do that for Tanner."

Brothers! "Can we let the hair thing go?"

Rhett grinned. "I'll let the hair thing go if you let the Olivia thing go."

"What are you two doing just standing there?" Grandpa huffed like an angry stallion as he stuffed his feet in his old boots. The kids had already run out the door. "Do you trust your friends to know what you want done? I store my treasures in there." By treasures, he meant junk that only he found value in.

"We'll be careful when we *organize* things," Cassie promised him, knowing she couldn't truly promise anything.

Grandpa stopped at the door. "You know, I've been thinking. Maybe we shouldn't move anything."

Oh, no.

"If we don't move anything, we can't fix the rides." Cassie tried very hard to hang on to her patience. It was tough when in her heart she was so anxious to see Bentley. "You can't have it both ways." She should maybe listen to her own advice. "Shane has very graciously lined up volunteers to give us a hand to organize things."

"You should have called me before plan-

ning this. We could have done this ourselves."
Grandpa stomped his foot. "But I can see that
horse has left the pasture. You just go ahead
and run the place without me. Invite everyone over to rifle through my things as if I'm
dead and gone."

"I'm sorry. I didn't go into detail on this earlier because…" There was no avoiding it now.
"Because Dr. Carlisle put me on bed rest for
a few days and then told me to refrain from
any heavy lifting for a week. After my accident, the doctor in Boise told me I might need
surgery and…" She stopped herself from revealing her worries about being able to have
children.

Rhett and Grandpa stared at her, waiting
for her to say more.

Her hand flopped helplessly midair. "Asking permission to do something that needed to
be done to keep us afloat seemed unnecessary
while I was on bed rest and worried about the
future…I guess."

Outside, someone honked a horn again.

"But…you're fine now?" Concern lined
Rhett's normally carefree features.

She nodded. "Well, I'm on the road to recovery." She had a plan. More rest. MRI. Another exam and consult.

Grandpa cleared his throat. "Cassie, the

Diaz family always perseveres. But you and I... We've got a tough road ahead." He hurried out the door.

"That threw him for a loop that he wasn't expecting." Rhett carefully hugged her. "If you want, I can send the troops home for the day because I can tell there's more you aren't telling me about your condition."

"We can't put this off. Let it go."

"Okay." He tugged a lock of her hair. "I wouldn't want you to waste a good hair day on me and Grandpa."

In the ranch yard, a crowd of people awaited them. Reality sank in. It was a gathering of people who'd be going through her grandfather's stuff, a collection that had no rhyme or reason and was years in the making.

Grandpa was mingling with the crowd, putting on a good front, as if he wasn't unsettled. Bentley's head rose above the rest. His gaze found hers.

Cassie's heart beat faster.

"The reason for good hair becomes clearer." Rhett frowned. "And you wore your best hat."

The gray felt. Cassie put on a brave face and looped her arm through Rhett's. "I can tell you're just being an overly protective brother. Don't be."

Rhett narrowed his eyes as he stared in Bentley's direction.

"Stop glowering. He thinks I'm brave."

That narrow-eyed gaze turned to her. "He's a Monroe, Cassie. They have a life outside of town, in a big city."

"I know." For a moment, the trepidation about leaving town returned, making her tense her shoulders. But giving up ranching and leaving Second Chance with Bentley was truly a long shot. She rolled her shoulders back, tamping down romantic notions. "Whatever feelings we have toward each other, we both know it's short-term."

"I don't like you getting hurt."

"But you're not me." She clasped his arm. "And Tornado Tom taught me that I can take a little pain."

Rhett made a sound of disapproval as they approached the ranch yard proper.

Whistler was making friends at the pasture gate, boys were chasing each other in the paddock and Ajax was happily circling them all slowly, presumably having rid himself of the zoomies already. It was good to have so many people at the ranch. All that bustle of energy and activity made it feel as if the Bar D was thriving once more.

"Nice of you guys to finally join us." Shane

had his arm slung across the shoulders of Franny Clark, his fiancée.

"The brains of the outfit have arrived," Bentley said warmly, nodding to Cassie.

And yet, it was Shane who mobilized the volunteers. In no time, he'd divided the group into work crews. Most folks would haul things outside of the barn in teams where Cassie and Grandpa would then sort through the items for storage or—she shuddered to acknowledge— the trash.

Mia ran up to Cassie. "I need a cookie."

"Me, too." Cassie escorted her to the house, followed by a cavalcade of young cowboys.

"Is that all the cowhands?" Bentley was sending off the last of the young cowboys from the mudroom when Cassie wiped crumbs from Mia's mouth and hands. "If it is, I can tell you how gorgeous you look."

Cassie blushed. Her hair fell smoothly over her shoulders, like black silk. Her brown eyes glowed with warmth and ease. "That's what rest will do for someone, I guess."

"You've always been beautiful." To keep from reaching for her, Bentley helped Mia into her boots, careful to keep her dress hem out of the way. And then he had no reason not to

touch Cassie, except for the obvious excuse
that they had no future ahead of them. "Go
on, Mia. Catch up to the boys." He held the
door for the little cowgirl, closed it after her
and then turned to face Cassie. "I was thinking about long-distance relationships and—"

She was in his arms before he could complete his sentence, kissing him before he could
slow things down.

After she'd thoroughly kissed him and he'd
thoroughly enjoyed it, he drew back enough
to stare into her eyes. "Good morning."

"It is such a good morning." Her arms were
wrapped around his waist as if she wouldn't
mind another round of kissfesting.

"Hip feel okay?" His hands roamed gently
across that part of her. "Hurting anywhere?"

"If you're asking if kissing you taxed my
injuries, the answer is no." She grinned up at
him, brown eyes twinkling with mischief. "If
you're thinking about asking me if you can
kiss me again, the answer is yes."

He appreciated that she understood how
much thinking needed to be done, about everything, but especially about her. They could
discuss the possibilities of a long-distance relationship later. But for now, Bentley didn't
waste more time thinking. He kissed her. And

kissed her. And would have kept on kissing her, except someone called his name. And then hers.

"THE CHAIRS ARE where they put the bosses," Grandpa told Cassie as they took their seats in dusty folding chairs.

Unaccustomed to sitting by and watching others work, Cassie felt about as useless as a glass of water at a bonfire. But that didn't stop her from smoothing her hair and setting her cowboy hat just so. Bentley had mentioned something about long-distance relationships before she'd kissed him. Long-distance. It felt like a theme. If she acquainted herself with Bentley and with technology, maybe everything would turn around—her horse training business, her bank account and her love life.

The first boxes to come out fell apart from exposure to the elements. It was just as well. Their contents belonged in the trash—an old toaster, a length of rope, a pile of clothes that were stiff from layers of rain, snow and dust. Car parts came out next—spark plugs, rusted tire lugs, a flimsy jack and short jumper cables. Ranch tools comprised another layer—a hay hook, wire cutters, a small coil of barbed wire, a metal fence post, hoof picks and clippers. All ruined by exposure to the elements.

Surprisingly, Grandpa put on a brave front. "You know, that was the first toaster me and the missus ever owned. Toward the end, I grew fond of burnt toast because the missus wanted a fancy television instead."

Franny slung her arm around Shane's waist. "Love means never complaining when someone burns a meal."

"I never said I was good in the kitchen." Shane swung Franny around until he held her bent backward as if they were doing the tango. "I make up for it in other ways."

"You do indeed." Franny grinned. "Are you going to kiss me or test those strong arms of yours awhile longer?"

"Hmm." Shane pretended to consider his options for a moment. And then he brought Franny to her feet and kissed her.

Adam made a strangled noise. "Mom! Papa Shane! You promised no kisses until after bedtime."

The couple's kiss dissolved into laughter.

Bentley captured Cassie's gaze with a tender smile that made her long for another excuse to run an errand with him.

Grandpa held up the extremely short jumper cables. "I ordered these from one of those high-end catalogues that used to come in the mail. I thought I threw those away long ago."

He dropped them to the ground. "Funny how I thought there were treasures stored in here, isn't it?"

"Funny," Cassie murmured, heaving a sigh of relief.

When several spiders and spider nests were discovered, Cassie shamelessly retreated under the excuse of needing something to put the mounting pile of trash in. She backed Grandpa's ancient truck, which had the longest truck bed, into the pasture so that the trash could be more easily transported.

When she returned to her seat, Mia came to sit in her lap. "Are you tired, sweetie?"

Mia shook her head.

Bentley emerged from the barn. He stood near her, drinking water and shifting his feet as if he wanted to say something.

I make Bentley speechless.

Cassie grinned up at him. "How's it going?" *And what do you have in mind for a long-distance romance?*

"There's light at the end of the tunnel." He returned her grin, reaching out to ruffle Mia's curls. "With this hard work, we'll all sleep good tonight, even you, Princess Mia."

It was then that they were joined by some unexpected guests—the occupants of the homestead, and a Monroe whom Cassie had never seen before, a woman who wasn't dressed for the mountains, much less a ranch pasture. Those heels…

"Captain Olivia! Santa Claus!" Quinn and Mia ran to greet Olivia and the old man, who did, indeed, resemble Old Saint Nick.

The Clark boys ran over to join them. The old man dished out pats on top of cowboy hats and then bent down to say something to Mia that made her smile.

The woman in elegant high heels greeted Bentley, picking her way carefully over the pasture. "I'm looking for Shane." She glanced back toward Olivia and the old man.

"He should be out any second," Bentley told her, pointing toward the barn. "He was wrestling with an old refrigerator. I think the fridge is going to win." Bentley introduced them to his cousin Kendall.

Turning on the charm, Cassie's grandfather found another chair for her. "Honey, you're going to fall into a prairie dog hole and hurt yourself in those city shoes."

Olivia bravely dived into the barn, so to speak, followed by Bentley.

"Is this a barn raising?" Kendall's cool gaze cataloged everything. "Are you going to build a fourth wall?"

"It's a barn cleaning." Cassie explained about the carnival rides.

"They're real moneymakers," Grandpa assured Kendall, who looked politely dubious, if there was such a thing.

Mia returned to Cassie's lap. She pointed at Kendall's feet. "I like your boots."

"They're all the rage in New York." Kendall turned her feet to and fro. "I didn't think I'd be visiting a ranch today or I would have worn something with a little less...*something.*" Her smile changed her entire demeanor from intimidating to approachable.

That smile allowed Cassie to ask, "I'm not very good at Monroe family trees. Which branch are you from?"

Kendall's smile didn't waver, an indication that she didn't consider the question intrusive. "I'm a cousin to everyone I see here. My oldest brother, Holden, is engaged to Bernadette Carlisle."

"She's my doctor. I had an accident recently or I'd be helping in the barn." Cassie felt like that was necessary to explain. She wasn't a slacker.

"We have a brother Bo, who's currently in Texas." Her gaze took on a faraway look, as if she were worried about Bo.

"I met him once at the diner," Cassie said.

"Is he coming back to Second Chance anytime soon?"

"I hope so." Kendall seemed surprised at her answer. "I handle public relations for our family. It helps if I don't have to track them down, like I did with Olivia, and like I'm going to have to do with Bo."

"Make way!" Rhett shouted before Cassie could ask why the family needed a public relations person.

Rhett and Shane brought the troublesome refrigerator out. Bentley helped them load it into Grandpa's truck, displaying a strong back that Cassie both admired and envied.

"I suppose the old girl had to go sometime." Grandpa moseyed over to the truck. "That fridge ran for twenty-five years. Felt like part of the family when the missus wanted to replace it with one that made ice cubes."

"I've seen scavengers pick up appliances at the dump to refurbish." Rhett hopped down from the tailgate. "But something's growing in there. The smell is lethal."

Bentley and Shane backed him up, leaving Grandpa shaking his head and muttering about "the poor thing."

"Shane, a word." Kendall drew him away from everyone. Cassie couldn't hear what she told him, but she could tell by the gestures she was making that she was upset.

"It's a sad day, Cassie, sayin' goodbye to those things." Grandpa sat back down. "A sad, sad day."

"But we'll get through it," she reassured him, realizing Mia had fallen asleep in her arms. She cradled her closer.

"You were made for that, Cassie." Bentley's smile was full of kindness. He dusted himself off before returning to the barn.

"My word, but that boy's sweet on you," Grandpa said in wonder.

Cassie refrained from telling him that she was sweet on Bentley. But she hugged that sweetness to her heart with the same care that she held Mia in her arms.

The next layer removed seemed to be comprised of furniture taken from the house. Her great-grandmother's sewing machine. Her great-grandfather's rocking chair. Her mother's bureau and her father's chest of drawers.

Sophie Monroe circled the pieces as they came out. "If you want to get rid of some of these, I can sell them in my shop in town."

Grandpa readily agreed that this was what should be done. He wanted them to go to someone who'd cherish them.

Pieces of the rides began appearing. The

rocket ship for the merry-go-round. A few metal cars for the train. The boys swarmed each new component, tugging, sitting and doing everything but kick the tires, of which there were none or they would have. When the first of the Ferris wheel cages came out, they were excited to climb inside.

Their efforts woke Mia, who stretched and yawned.

"You're not getting in those," Cassie told the boys firmly.

The cages were oval with a seat across, meant to adjust to the circular movement of the Ferris wheel while keeping whoever was inside…well, inside. They had no flat bottom and with every push by the boys, they rocked like eggs on a countertop.

"I think it's time for a horseback ride." Franny wiped her hands on the legs of her blue jeans. "That is, if Cassie is open to letting the boys ride her stock."

Four boys and one little girl turned pleading eyes Cassie's way.

"I'm sure the horses would love some exercise." Cassie set Mia down and led them toward the main barn.

In the ranch yard, they found Cam preparing lunch, manning her grandfather's barbecue. Whatever he was cooking smelled delicious. Two long tables had been placed in the shade near the barn's longest wall. Bowls and platters of food were spread across them.

"You've got about an hour until lunch," Cam told them.

"That'll work." Cassie's mouth watered as she led the group into the barn. The horses were curious to hear young voices and eager for some attention, poking their heads over stalls and nickering greetings.

"Cassie, if you tell us which horses to saddle and what tack to use, we can do all the work." Franny stopped in the breezeway and peered at a photo of Cassie hanging upside down from a galloping horse. "I envied you back then. You had nerves of steel."

"Did I?" Cassie couldn't remember.

"You did. Don't you lift a finger today though, Cassie." Emily, Franny's sister-in-law, studied the photo wall. The three women had gone to school and been on the rodeo circuit around the same time. "Shane told us you're on the mend."

Cassie was simultaneously grateful for the gossip and embarrassed to admit a weakness to these women. They were her peers, and successful ranchers. "There's a picture of us over here." Cassie pointed to a photo of five cowgirls on their horses. "That was the only year I tried for the rodeo queen crown."

"You would have won if they awarded points for trick riding." Franny shook her head. "Look at my hair. It's so…so…"

"Big." Emily laughed, a rich sound that filled the barn and warmed Cassie's heart. "But you know what hasn't changed, Franny? That warm smile of yours."

"It took Shane to help me find it again," Franny murmured, running her finger down the edge of the picture frame. "Now, if he just resolves this thing with Tanner, maybe he can rediscover his smile."

Emily turned to Cassie. "Do you know him well? Tanner, I mean. He's scarce around town."

Cassie glanced toward Tanner's kids, who clustered with the rest of the children at Poppy's stall. "He's…he's a good dad. And a good man." She kept her voice low. "I hope things turn out for him, for all of them." She hoped they had a guardian angel, someone who'd help pave the way with the Monroes.

"Ride! Ride! Ride! Ride!" Adam and Quinn marched in a circle in the breezeway.

"Adam," Franny said. Even Cassie recognized that as the do-not-disobey Mommy voice. "You're lucky you get to ride after the stunt you pulled here the other day."

Cassie assumed that was the unauthorized pony ride, but with Adam, you never knew. "No harm, no foul."

Franny made a noncommittal noise.

"Can I ride Poppy?" Mia asked, running over to grab and swing Cassie's hand. As usual, she was wearing a dress, but she also had on her favorite cowboy boots. "With a saddle this time?"

"Okay," Cassie allowed, even more proud of the little girl.

Cassie bustled about, indicating which horses could be ridden by the boys and where their tack could be found. Finally, the horses were led to the pasture that served as their arena, and the kids mounted up.

"Clark boys. You know the drill." Franny was a real taskmaster with the kids. Experienced at training riders. "Ride in a circle and practice your form. Quinn, you can't ride unless you hold the reins all the time."

"Yes, ma'am," Quinn promptly replied.

"Quinn, heels down." Franny studied every little rider, including Mia, who rode Poppy as if she'd ridden her a hundred times already. "Mia, sit tall in that saddle. A horse respects a good rider."

Mia's feet didn't reach the stirrups and her dark curls were covered by an old bicycle helmet Cassie had remembered was in the barn's storage closet. At Franny's direction, she stuck her calves out and her heels down.

"Future cowgirl in the making." Emily hung her arms over the top railing of the gate. "Look how well she rides in a dress."

"She's plucky." Cassie smiled. "Like the Clarks and the Monroes."

"Agreed," Emily said with an infectious grin. "We Clarks are a stubborn lot. I hear you're sweet on Bentley. He's the genius in the family, right?"

"Subtle, Em." Franny had moved closer to the two. She rolled her eyes. "You don't have to answer, Cassie. Your love life is your business."

"Which is something you never, ever said to me," Emily shot back but she was still grinning. And then she turned her attention to Cassie. "The Monroes are placing bets on how much longer Bentley's going to stay. Has he told you anything?"

"That's cheating, Em." Franny shook her head.

"It's not cheating." Emily stuck her nose in the air. "I'm researching. They say he's a genius and practically lives in a workshop with all his high-tech equipment. They say he doesn't last long away from his work. That implies he won't last much longer out here."

Cassie glanced toward the second barn, but she couldn't see it from the pasture gate, which meant she couldn't see Bentley. She couldn't reassure herself that he was busy and present and happy, content with the small challenge of fixing antiquated engines.

Content being with me.

Earlier, Bentley had mentioned the possibility of a long-distance relationship. Did that mean he was leaving soon?

Cassie bit her lip.

"Seems odd then, that Bentley's still here," Emily continued. "What does a genius find to occupy his mind in the remote mountains of Idaho?"

Cassie bit her lip harder. What could she, a cowgirl who spent all her time outdoors, offer a reclusive engineer? What in the world did he see in her?

"Well, I'm betting Bentley stays." Franny marched forward, tossing over her shoulder, "That others are speculating he could leave any day is just that. Speculation."

Any day? It was too soon. Cassie didn't even know if she could have kids. They'd never discussed personal dreams, like family size or what style house they preferred. How could they work long-distance when they knew so little about each other? In spite of that, she admitted, she was falling in love with the pied piper.

Cassie clutched the gate rail.

"Hey." Emily came to stand next to Cassie. "Are you okay?"

Cassie didn't know. "I'm fine," she said anyway.

"Adam, a horse is not a drum," Franny went on giving instruction, unaware that Cassie was breaking apart inside. "Stop tapping Roxie's withers like that. Good job, Davey. See if she'll canter for you. Charlie, that's too much slack in your reins. You're the driver, not a passenger." She glanced over her shoulder at Cassie and Emily. "In my experience, Monroes put family first. Then business. Bentley will stay as long as he feels Shane needs his help with Tanner."

Would he stay if I needed him? If he believed I loved him?

Cassie couldn't ask Bentley to stay, to give their relationship real time before it became part-time. But more importantly, she couldn't ask Bentley to be anything other than true to himself.

CHAPTER SEVENTEEN

"I DIDN'T EXPECT to see you here."

Olivia turned at the sound of the deep voice.

Rhett tipped his hat. He was dusty and dirty, hands covered in tan leather work gloves, and overall, a sight for sore eyes.

They stood inside the large barn near a stack of miniature metal boats and what looked like sections of a narrow railroad track.

"Honestly? I joined in to avoid more arguments with my cousin Kendall," Olivia admitted. She liked the way Rhett's dark eyes were fringed with thick lashes. Those lashes were probably the only thing about him that were delicate. The rest of him was chiseled to masculine perfection. "And since my brother Bentley talks less than most, I figured helping out here would be like a reprieve."

"Olivia, I found a canoe!" Sonny called from a corner.

Rhett frowned. "That would be my old canoe, dubbed *Unlucky*. Boat captains aren't the only people to name watercraft, you know."

"*Unlucky* is the same canoe that dumped you into the lake?" Olivia studied the lines of the old wooden canoe. "She's no longer seaworthy. There's a hole in the bow."

"The size of my boot, yes." Rhett nodded, grinning roguishly. "It would be unlucky to try to put her back in the water, don't you think?"

Olivia nodded, chest constricting and forcing out all air. It was the image of a boat sinking that had done it. A roaring built in her ears. She needed a change in focus. "What of these boats?" She pointed to the small metal ones and struggled to draw a breath.

"Those aren't seaworthy either." Rhett patted the metal hull, which echoed like an empty steel drum. "They go on that track there. Kids are supposed to imagine they're on a boat ride."

"Sometimes using one's imagination is the safest course," Olivia heard herself say, as if from a far-off distance. It felt like her ears were stuffed with cotton and a train was rumbling past on those scattered tracks.

"Look." Sonny wove his way through the stacks of boxes toward Olivia. "I found some oars." He brandished two paddles. "One for you and one for me."

Olivia wanted nothing to do with the oars. Or boats. Or water.

A bead of sweat trickled down her spine.

"Those paddles came with the unlucky canoe." Rhett chuckled, not realizing Olivia was in the midst of a panic attack. "I'd toss them out. Bad luck."

"Hey, Olivia." Bentley appeared behind her. Without asking, and with a gentle touch, he steered her in a new direction. "I could use your help over here."

One step. Two. They passed things that weren't boat related. Breathing came easier.

"What do you need?" Rhett sounded like he was right behind Olivia, bless his handsome and somewhat clueless self. He wasn't as attuned to Olivia's moods as her brother. "I can help, Bentley."

"No. This…uh…requires a boat captain's perspective. Can you give Sonny a hand, Rhett? He seems to be stuck." Bentley stared directly into Olivia's eyes, and it was as if they were teenagers again and he was trying to build an alibi for Olivia after she'd been caught sneaking out at night. "Come on." He smiled slightly as Rhett obligingly changed course.

That smile of Bentley's was slight because he was probably afraid that she might snap at him. That's how she'd dealt with her reticent older brother. Talk over him. Challenge him. Make him feel that she was so much more successful than he was. She was the captain, after all. The face of the team. Bentley only made the boats. Watercraft that allowed her to win races if she sailed them the way they should be. Her success fueled the Monroe line of boat sales, but it was Bentley that assured their quality. Or at least, it had been. Nothing was as it was a year ago.

Her annoyance with Bentley gave way to an odd form of nostalgia mixed with guilt. She wanted to hug him, apologize for being a heartless prima donna and hug him some more. Instead, she simply said, "Thanks."

He smiled at her, perhaps a little easier, a little quicker than he had before. "I thought you needed a save back there."

"All that talk about boats sinking." Olivia shivered. "It's bad luck."

They both knew that wasn't all it was. But that was the thing about family and people who loved you.

They let you lie to yourself.

CHAPTER EIGHTEEN

"MORE SELF-AWARENESS WOULD help you achieve greater things, cowboy."

Bentley glanced up to see Sonny talking to Rhett.

Rhett tipped back his cowboy hat and said in a slow voice, "What makes you think I haven't achieved great things already?"

Bentley smiled. Sonny probably didn't notice Rhett's champion belt buckle.

Holding two paddles, Sonny made an encompassing gesture that included the now-depleted stacks of stuff in the barn. "Clutter detracts from purpose."

"I'd say that's subjective." A muscle in Rhett's jaw ticked, an indication that Sonny may have been sharing helpful hints with Cassie's brother for longer than was welcome.

Rhett left the therapist and joined Bentley in a twelve by twelve space in another section of the barn. Bentley's workspace was carpeted with a canvas drop cloth covered in Ferris wheel engine parts.

"You got to work fast," Rhett noted.

"I'd say I'm on track to achieving great things." Bentley gave the cowboy a sly look.

Rhett resettled his hat, half glancing over his shoulder at a retreating Sonny. "There's some folk hanging about that would say you've made a greater mess than you started with. I heard tell that clutter detracts from purpose."

Bentley chuckled.

The cowboy's gaze returned to the engine pieces. "I thought you got this engine going the other day."

"That was luck more than skill." Bentley picked up a thin engine belt that was so badly worn it was a surprise that it hadn't snapped. "You know, the goal of every sports psychologist is increased performance."

"Is that what that fella is?" Rhett shook his head. "He asked me about the canoe I broke and then about my five-year plan, whatever that is, and pretty soon, he was challenging everything I said."

"All with good intentions, I'm sure." Bentley carefully set the belt back down. He was placing all the pieces in order to make the rebuild more efficient. He could enjoy his time here if he fulfilled his purpose and conquered the challenge of restoring the old engines. And if he clicked enough with Cassie that a long-distance relationship made sense. "Sonny's here to help Olivia." A statement which only reminded him that Olivia had asked for Rhett the other night when she'd knocked on the back door of the ranch house. He considered the cowboy next to him.

With that black cowboy hat, big attitude and ready smile, Rhett was probably used to charming the ladies. Bentley wasn't sure he wanted him working that charisma on his sister.

He glanced around what he could see of the barn's interior and then out across the pasture. He spotted Olivia walking with Sonny toward the main ranch. "Speaking of Olivia… She's in a fragile state. Nowhere near ready for dating. And when she is ready, she won't be here. She's a citizen of the world."

"Are you warning me off your sister?" Rhett tipped his hat back once more.

"For both your sakes." Bentley nodded.

The cowboy's stare hardened. "I might give you the same advice. Cassie isn't right for a Monroe."

Not appreciating the comment, Bentley gave the cowboy what Gabby would no-doubt call the stink eye.

"You Monroes are… What did you call it?

Citizens of the world? While Cassie is a resident of Second Chance."

Bentley gave him the barest of nods, unable to deny it. Cassie may talk about hanging up that cowboy hat of hers and going elsewhere, but even he could tell she belonged here. She was a part of this place.

"And Cassie's needed here to help care for our grandfather."

Bentley's chin reversed direction, coming up.

"It's why she needs to find someone who wants to be here. Put down roots and maintain the ones already planted."

"Someone like Tanner, you mean?" Bentley's heart squeezed. *Someone who already had kids she could love in case things didn't work out for her medically.* "A different kind of Monroe."

Rhett stood tall. "Someone who already calls Second Chance home."

The day was warm, but Bentley felt chilled inside, because logically, Rhett was right. He wished he'd never started this conversation.

Shouts arose about lunch being ready.

"You seem like the kind of man who'd do the right thing." Rhett extended his hand.

"You, too." Bentley clasped it, giving it a decisive shake, hoping that he could live up to the cowboy's expectations, at least, for Cassie's sake.

Because he'd already broken the moral standards that he set for himself, the ones his grandfather had respected him for.

It wasn't fair to think of Cassie, who meant so much to her family, as someone who could fill the emptiness inside of him. He needed to be fair. He prided himself on being fair.

But a part of him still wanted to find a way they could be together, even if logic was telling him that wouldn't make sense for either of them.

"COME ON. LET'S EAT." Frowning, Rhett opened the pasture gate for Cassie. He sounded like his nose had been bent out of shape.

"Thanks, but..." Cassie glanced at Bentley, who was making his way toward her with Whistler at his side. "I'll wait for all our volunteers to gather before I eat."

Rhett clasped her wrist. "Cassie, leave it."

"Leave *him*. Is that what you're saying?" It was Cassie's turn to frown. "What's wrong with you?" All day, he'd taken little opportunities to express his disapproval. Her wrist came free with a gentle tug, but that didn't mean her brother was giving up.

"Nothing about you and him makes sense,"

he said, cutting right to the chase. "You think that Monroe is going to want to live in town full-time the way Shane has? He builds boats, Cassie. He won't hang around watching you train horses."

"We're adults." She tossed her hair. "Adults have long-distance relationships all the time."

Rhett tsked, sending a hard stare in Bentley's direction.

"And you told him what you think." Cassie didn't ask. She was sure of it. Dang it. Bentley was the type of man who wouldn't want to cause a rift in anyone's family. "Butt out of my life, Rhett."

He swore. "I told you not to ride that bull and—"

"Stop. I don't want to hear any more about how you think I should live my life."

Rhett looked at her long and hard before shaking his head. "Don't get lost in this, Cassie. Just... Don't get lost." He turned on his heel.

And Cassie turned on hers, facing Bentley and struggling to put a smile on her face. "It's just like you to be the last one to take a break." She inserted herself between Whistler and Bentley so that the mare would stay in the pasture. "Such a hard worker." She closed the gate behind them.

Bentley dropped a gentle kiss to her forehead and then stepped back. His arms were streaked with dirt and grease. His T-shirt was smudged, too, and draped with a remnant of a cobweb. A lock of his hair stuck up in the back.

Cassie didn't care about his physical state of disarray. She cared about changing the resolved look in his eyes, especially if it meant it hastened his leaving.

"I take it Rhett let you know that we talked," he said flatly.

"My brother doesn't speak for me." Cassie leaned against the metal gate, putting an invitation in her eyes she didn't want Bentley to ignore. They were alone. Not even Ajax or Millie were near.

Kiss me and everything will work out. They'd find a way.

Bentley didn't take her up on that invitation. Instead, he traced the line of her jaw. "You know, I could argue all day long that the odds are against us."

"I hope that isn't what you had planned." She captured his hand, pressing his palm to her cheek. "I would have straightened my hair for nothing."

"We don't have to argue," he said softly.

"Because our conversations have revealed the truth all along."

He's going to kiss me and everything will work out.

"I realize we haven't known each other that long, but I feel like I understand you." His attempt at a smile was weak, but she chalked it up to Rhett's interference. "You love horses, Cassie. You've enjoyed performing and competing in the rodeo, but lately you've found a niche in horse training. You love the history and heritage of the Bar D. You feel safe here. And comfortable emotionally." He brushed a thumb over her cheek. "And when we met, there was something safe and comfortable about me. We share some values and a fondness for kissing…" He cradled her face in his hands, staring deep into her eyes. "But the things you love are here. And so are the people who need you. No one needs me here, and I think that means I should move on before we get entangled and things get even harder."

"No." She curled her fingers around his wrists. "I need you. And we don't have to stay. I could leave. We can—"

"You need familiar ground to rebound financially. You need a safe place to heal, surrounded by the people that love you. I live in the heart of a city. There are no pastures for horses. No backyards for big dogs."

"Don't say we're that different." Whispering, she clung tighter to his wrists.

"What happens if you don't heal the way you want to? I know how badly you want kids and I... You'll want family around you if that happens."

There it was—her ability to have children. She'd suspected it could be a dealbreaker.

But Bentley wasn't done severing what they had. "My future is just as uncertain as yours is. As Olivia's is. As is the town's." He took her hands in his, gently, not possessively. He was reverting to logic when she wanted him to trust something that had no equation for him to solve—his heart.

But she had no defense, no retort. Not when the question of having children was unresolved. She had nothing left to argue with. Nothing to fall back on but her pride.

Cassie slipped her hands free and let them fall to her sides, where they might catch pieces of her heart as it shattered. "Everyone says you're the smartest man they know. And look at that. You've convinced me, too. Goodbye, Bentley. Please tell Shane to find someone else to fix the ride engines. You're free to go."

UNABLE TO FACE anyone working at the second barn, Cassie got Romeo out to do a little training.

The alternative was shutting herself in her room and crying her eyes out while the volunteers speculated that she was doing just that.

Pride. It gave her a headache.

If she could, she'd gladly trade in her pride for thicker skin. Then what little courage she had could go toward running away with Bentley.

That's not what he wants.

She'd never imagined running away with him and leaving her horses and family behind. He'd been right about that.

She started Romeo running around the paddock. He circled her and circled her, mirroring the direction of her thoughts.

Soon, Cassie had an audience of young cowboys and one little cowgirl. They sat on the top rail of the paddock.

"Do you speak horse?" Quinn asked.

"There's no such thing as horse speak," Adam said derisively.

"How else do you explain this?" Quinn pointed at Romeo. "Either Cassie speaks horse or that horse is smarter than you and me."

Cassie smiled and kept her thoughts to herself.

"I want to do it." Mia climbed down from the rail, skirt fluttering in the breeze. "I *can* do it. I can do it with Poppy."

Cassie doubted that. Poppy had behaved well with Mia in the saddle, but the pony had essentially followed whichever horse was in front of her around the pasture. Cassie had no idea how well a pony would take to Liberty Training.

"How about we try it with Romeo first?" Cassie took her gray felt cowboy hat and put it on Mia's head. So what if horse saliva stained the brim of her best hat? Her entire life was in tatters. "You stand over here and tell Romeo to take your hat."

Mia stomped her boots, setting them wide. And then she put her little fists on her hips. "Romeo, take my hat." She stomped a heel again, much the same way Grandpa did.

Cassie moved behind Mia. "Romeo—"

"No." Mia turned, shaking her finger at Cassie. "I do it."

"Okay." Cassie held both her hands up. "You're the boss."

Mia turned around, pulling the hat lower over her ears. "You heard that. I'm the boss, Romeo."

The boys on the rail began to giggle and guffaw.

"Romeo!" Mia stomped both feet, creating a little dust cloud. "Take my hat."

Romeo had already anticipated the command. He ambled over to Mia, took Cassie's hat and then placed it on Cassie's head without waiting for permission.

We've practiced this stunt too much.

Mia craned her neck up at the tall horse. "Hey. Give me that back, Romeo."

And surprisingly, Romeo did. And then he extended his nose to Mia's.

"He wants a kiss," Cassie told her.

The young cowboys were disgusted.

Without hesitation, Mia planted a kiss on the gelding's nose. "I can make Poppy give kisses, too." She tugged on Cassie's shirt. "You can teach me."

Quinn climbed down from the railing. "Can you teach me, too? Other things. Not horse kisses." He made a face.

Rhett was walking past the paddock, a twinkle in his eye. "Imagine that. Teaching without doing acrobatics or straining your back."

Very funny.

Though, he had a point. It was new. And perhaps only a side step outside of her comfort zone. But it opened the door to teaching online, as Rhett had suggested. And once she started to try new things, maybe she'd build up her confidence and try others.

But first, baby steps.

CHAPTER NINETEEN

"I'M ONLY HERE because I have a strong sense of responsibility to the Diazes," Bentley told Shane after a lunch he hadn't eaten. "I'll finish out today, but you need to find another mechanic."

Shane scoffed, trying to tug a coil of barbed wire free of a Ferris wheel cage at the back of the barn. "You're here because you rejected the best thing that's happened to you in the past decade—Cassie—for heaven only knows why." He glanced up at Bentley. "Do you want to tell me why?"

"No." He'd done what was right. And now there was a hole where his heart was supposed to be. "Hey, Shane…"

His cousin was no longer kneeling a few feet away. Bentley glanced around. Most of the volunteers had left.

"I'm going to find wire cutters," Shane called from behind a stack of old barrels. "I know I saw some earlier."

It was just as well that Bentley kept his heartache to himself.

Quinn ran into the barn and came to sit at Bentley's feet. "I'm bored."

"I thought you were playing with the Clark boys." And therefore occupied.

Adam skipped into the barn. "Cassie said we laugh too much to be horse trainers." He sat next to Quinn and stared at Bentley. "Now the horses got put up and we still don't know horse speak."

"Cowgirls are smarter than cowboys when it comes to horse speak," Quinn said cryptically.

Bentley didn't even try to decipher what that meant. "What do your parents tell you to do when you're bored?" He wasn't here to entertain them, nor was he in the mood to entertain them.

"My mom tells me to go outside," Adam admitted. "My Auntie Em tells me to do chores."

Quinn grabbed a handful of dirt, letting it fall through his fingers. "My dad tells me to watch my sister."

That was easy. Bentley didn't have to think twice. "Go outside. Watch your sister."

Adam's two older brothers shuffled in. They spotted a big cardboard dishwasher box on its side and sat on it before Bentley could tell them not to. The cardboard promptly gave way, and they went tumbling inside it, booted feet the only thing showing. Their hoots of laughter let Bentley know they were unhurt.

"I want to try." Adam danced around the box, undoubtedly trying to find a way on it or in it.

"That box is trash." Bentley pulled the older Clark boys free. Both were grinning and looked at the box as if ready to try its bench worthiness again. "You boys haul it out to the trash truck. Go on."

The two older boys tugged it dutifully, banging into stuff on their way out and having a good time of it.

"We're still bored," Quinn said dejectedly.

"I thought you boys were going to throw a rope or something." There had been talk of that at lunch.

The older boys returned.

"We roped with Rhett already. I roped Adam," Charlie admitted with a huge grin.

"We lost privileges," Davey added, his grin unrepentant. "For roping each other."

"You knocked my hat to the ground," Adam said in an angry little voice. "And didn't say you were sorry."

Davey and Charlie exchanged glances and unapologetic grins.

"Shane!" Bentley looked for his cousin. Was he the only adult in the barn? "Why don't you boys move on out of here?"

"Why?" Quinn asked. "We aren't doin' nothing."

Exactly. "You might get hurt." That's what inquisitive, bored kids did, at least in Bentley's experience.

"Can we go to the other pasture?" Davey asked.

"No."

"Why not?" Charlie took up where his older brother left off.

"Because you might get hurt," he repeated. Who knew what animals were kept in the other pasture?

Quinn keeled over.

"Quinn! Hey." Bentley bit back a curse and bent down at his side. "Are you all right?"

"No. I just dropped dead from boredom." Quinn dissolved into a fit of giggles.

Bentley fell over, which wasn't an easy feat considering the space was cramped and there were boys surrounding him.

"Uncle Bentley." Quinn got to his knees and shook Bentley's shoulder. "What happened?"

"It was…" Bentley gasped dramatically. "It was questions. Questions killed me." He went limp.

Quinn scrambled to his feet. "That's not funny."

But all the other boys were laughing.

Bentley stood, dusting himself off. Not that it was any use. He was covered in dirt from head to toe. It was just so annoying now that he wasn't lost in the complexities of rebuilding the engine. "Why don't you boys play a good old-fashioned game of tag?"

"I love tag," Quinn said.

"Not it! Not it!" Davey and Charlie clambered to their feet and ran out to the pasture.

"Not it," Adam cried, following close at their heels.

Bentley glanced down at Quinn, whose cheeks were turning as red as his father's did when he got upset. "I think this means you're it, buddy."

Quinn stomped after them, body rigid. "I hate being *it*."

Shane squeezed his way between a Ferris wheel cage and a wooden wire spool that was large enough to be a table. "I found the wire cutters. What's up? Why do you look so annoyed?"

"Your kids needed you." Bentley tugged at the tangled coil of wire wrapped around a Ferris wheel cage door, but his heart wasn't in the task. "Correction. All the kids needed you."

Shane began snipping sections of the barbed wire free. "They don't need me. They needed a new direction, and you gave it to them."

"I'm covered in filth and who knows what else, and the last thing I need right now is the old pied piper label. All I wanted to do was work on something in peace."

Shane tsked. "You'll never have uninterrupted time when you have kids."

"Well, that's just it, isn't it? These aren't my kids. Where's Tanner?"

"Tanner won't come near this place while we're here." Shane waved off Bentley's sputtered objections. "By the way, I sent that DNA test overnight and paid a rush fee. We should have the results in just a few days."

Something soured in Bentley's gut. He couldn't leave until the results came back. He'd set things in motion and had to be here to face the consequences. But that didn't mean he was going to work at the ranch while he waited. It would just make his separation from Cassie that much worse. "Today is my last day at the Bar D."

"Why? Did you overthink your relationship with Cassie?" Shane struggled to snap another barbed section free. "I have so been there. I never wanted to stay in Second Chance, but it took me forever to admit that I can create the life I want wherever I want, which is exactly wherever Franny is."

"I hate you right now," Bentley bit out, steadying the cage.

"Why? Because I've told you where you have to land if you and Cassie have a future? Or because you aren't ready to accept that's the commitment you need to make to have a future with her?"

"Both."

"Hatred understood."

Bentley stood back and let Shane clip the wire free, because apparently his cousin knew what he was doing.

CASSIE DREW A deep breath and knocked on the door to the old homestead.

Something Bentley had said earlier—the parts that hadn't broken her heart—had her seeking out Olivia. The boat captain's future was as uncertain as Cassie's.

The door swung open. "Yes?" It was the old man. Sonny. He gave her a polite smile.

"You left before dessert. There was plenty, so I made you a care package." Cassie extended a container and tried to peer around the man, hoping to catch sight of Olivia. All she saw were the outdated furnishings that her grandparents had used. Grandpa had left them here when he'd moved into the main house after her parents left.

"Dessert? That was very thoughtful of you." Sonny opened the lid to the container and examined its contents, poking things around with his finger and sniffing. "Carrot cake. Brownies. Peanut butter cookies. It's a good thing my body isn't a temple." He grinned, and it was just like looking into the face of Santa Claus.

Could he grant wishes? She'd been very good this year and needed one.

"It's small thanks for your help today." Cassie continued to sneak glances inside. Olivia wasn't in the living room and the homestead was otherwise quiet. It was time to be blunt. "Is Olivia here?"

Sonny snapped the plastic container's lid closed. "This is her meditation hour." At the volume Sonny was speaking, Olivia probably wasn't meditating. "You should come back another time." He gave her another polite smile and closed the door.

Cassie took a few steps back, being careful not to fall off the small stoop. "It was a stupid idea anyway."

"Hey. Cowgirl," a female voice whispered. Olivia stood at the corner of the homestead, curling her finger as she beckoned Cassie to join her.

Cassie hightailed it over.

Olivia led her around to the back porch. Two brown plastic Adirondack chairs sat facing the west. It was where her grandparents had sat in good weather and watched the sun set.

Olivia plunked down in one chair, stretching out her short legs. "I'm sure Sonny's grateful for the dessert. A couple months with me and he's getting tired of his own cooking."

For all her current doubts and worries, Olivia had a real presence, like Franny and Emily. Every move, every word reinforced that whatever this woman did, she was in charge and would persevere no matter what.

Cassie wasn't sure she could live up to those standards. "Am I interrupting your meditation? I can come back." Or forget about her question completely. She was losing her nerve fast.

Olivia stared at her over the top of her mirrored sunglasses. "Have you ever tried meditation? You close your eyes and focus on your breath and how your body feels. Or at least, that's what you're supposed to do. I close my eyes, take a breath and then get distracted by a million little things tacking and jibbing about in my mind."

"I'm not much for things like meditation," Cassie blurted.

Olivia didn't miss a beat. "Is that because you're a closed-minded type or are you just afraid to try things you don't understand?"

"The latter." Cassie lowered herself into the other chair, hands twining nervously. "I have a habit of getting lost and maybe not fighting past the obstacles life puts in my way." She shrugged. "Who knows? Maybe I'd like meditation. Or yoga. Maybe if I was more adventurous and stubborn, I'd know what I wanted to do with the rest of my life. I'd know how to do it without letting the Bar D fold. I came to ask for your advice because female boat captains have probably faced adversity and come out ahead. Except now, looking at you, I've just realized that you were this mighty adventurer who was afraid of nothing and now you've…"

Think of your words, Cassie.

She pressed her lips together.

"I've what?" Olivia crossed her arms over her chest and gave Cassie a dark look.

"I meant no disrespect." Cassie tipped her cowboy hat back, wondering if it was better to leave now with her pride intact, or hang in there to see if she could learn anything from

Olivia, anything that might help her convince Bentley that they had something worth figuring out an equation for. "I just…"

"Spit it out," Olivia snapped. "I hope you wouldn't fumble with your words if there was a mountain lion behind me about to attack."

"No. Of course not. I was just wondering…" Cassie swallowed the nerves that were making a lump in her throat. "What are you going to do next? How do you come back from losing so much?" Not to mention suffering a broken heart. She frowned. "No, that's not it. My question is, how do you reach for your dreams, knowing that you can't have it all?"

Olivia said nothing. She looked like she could hardly dare to take a breath.

Cassie nodded. "That's okay. The world… people…can send such mixed messages. I was just wondering if you had any advice to give me." She ran a hand behind her neck. It felt dirty and gritty, making it apparent that nothing in her life was smooth, not even her skin. "I shouldn't have expected you to have the answers."

"Oh, yes, you should have," Olivia whispered. "Women who blaze a trail are supposed to be full of words of wisdom." She gave a little half shrug. "But not if you're the world's biggest failure." Her eyes were wide and full of unshed tears. "I'm more like you than you think. Uncertain of what I should do with the rest of my life. Scared to go back to what I used to do. Scared not to. This place… This backwoods, simple little place. I can hold on to what's left of my pride here." Olivia wiped at a tear. "But I'm smart enough to know that there's more left for me to do. I can't stay here forever. I wouldn't be happy. And you wouldn't either. Both of us need to be brave and make decisions about our lives, no matter how scary those decisions are."

"Really?" This was what Cassie had come for. She felt like hugging her. "How do you know that?"

"Because you wouldn't have come looking for advice if you were content with your life. You need to choose a different path." She tsked. "The only mistake you made was not stopping a moment to realize that I am *not* a role model or the right person to be giving advice."

"But you are." Sonny stepped out of the back door.

Olivia launched herself to her feet. "Holy moly, Sonny. You can't just eavesdrop like that. It's creepy. We could have been talking about something personal, like guys and sex."

Cassie shook her head. There was a line even she wouldn't cross.

"This is a breakthrough. Half the struggle to reclaim your life is acknowledging you want more out of it." Sonny hugged Olivia. And then he drew Cassie to her feet and hugged her, as well.

It felt good, that hug.

"That's it." Olivia shoved her sunglasses higher on her nose. "I'm staying in Second Chance until Christmas."

"There are kids in town who'd like to see him play Santa," Cassie murmured.

"Ha!" Sonny shouted. "You won't stay that long, Olivia. Let's go for a boat ride. I have two paddles and won't take no for an answer." He headed toward the lake. "You'll be back on the ocean in no time."

Olivia didn't move. "Can you believe him?"

"I can." Cassie shrugged. "Everyone likes a good comeback story. No matter how long it takes you to return, it's bound to be epic." More than a cowgirl risking her heart to stand by a man she'd just met.

"I see what you're doing." Olivia tapped her temple. "You're creating a picture of me succeeding in your head. And in the very next picture, you're creating an image of you getting lost in the mall. Big failure. Boo-hoo."

She was practically spot-on. "How did you guess?"

"Because I created a picture of you walking through the mall with a big goofy smile on your face and my brother carrying all your shopping bags. And then the next image in my head was of me falling overboard." Olivia sighed and picked her way toward the water. "I have a lot of work to do on myself." She paused at the corner of the house, glancing back. "If my brother shares his feelings with you, it's the real deal and worth risking it all for. He overthinks everything, but he's a knight in shining armor. And if you hurt him, I'm going to take you sailing and toss you overboard."

"Really?" Cassie mashed her hat firmly on her head and squared her shoulders, finding a stray perseverance gene. "Well, if you break my brother's heart I'll… I'll…" She had no good retort.

Olivia's laughter filled the air, twining with Sonny's hearty guffaws.

To avoid them, Cassie walked behind the house to reach the dirt road.

"Holy smokes, you look mad." Tanner joined her, having come from the direction of the cabin he was staying in. "Did that Monroe spitfire light a spark under you, too? That Kendall is a piece of work."

"It was Olivia." Cassie set off toward the ranch proper. "What set Kendall off at you?"

"My entire existence." Tanner chuckled. "You and Olivia?"

"No comment."

"Hey, uh, I got a text today from Rhett. He thought I should ask you out to dinner?"

Cassie practically growled in frustration. "I'm going to dunk his phone in the water trough."

Tanner laughed. "Yeah, I didn't think you and I had that kind of chemistry either."

BENTLEY STUDIED THE main pieces of the Ferris wheel's engine on the drop cloth. He'd disconnected and removed the motor, gear box and control panel. And now he was assembling his tools like a surgeon about to perform delicate surgery to remove the rusted parts in each.

Mia was asleep nearby on a covered bale of hay, snuggled against Ajax.

He knew he'd worn out his welcome at the Bar D, but the barn was quiet. No boys vied for his attention. The working conditions were perfect to sink into the zone. If only Cassie's stricken face at the pasture gate didn't keep surfacing in his head.

I did the right thing. That wasn't always the case.

He didn't want to believe it, but he suspected that Cassie had doubts and fears, too. If they were meant to be a couple, she would have fought for him. Wasn't that the way love worked?

Movement at the front of the barn had Bentley looking up. Sadly, it wasn't Cassie.

Tanner frowned, hands on his hips. "I'm looking for my kids."

"Mia's here," Bentley said softly. "Quinn went with the boys to the Bucking Bull."

"I didn't want them to—"

"Before you get mad, consider the friendships Quinn is forming." Bentley got to his feet, which sparked a chain reaction.

Ajax got up and shook himself. Mia stretched, eyes fluttering.

Tanner moved to kneel next to her. "Hey, baby girl. Time to head home."

Mia murmured something unintelligible.

"She had a good time today," Bentley said, because the little girl had, and he wanted Tanner to know the Monroes weren't trolls.

Mia climbed into Tanner's lap, blinking sleepy eyes Bentley's way. "Uncle Bentley is the best."

Bentley let that statement sit for a while.

"You've got yourself a project here," Tanner said in a voice that was conspicuously absent of sarcasm or disdain. He gestured toward the engine parts.

"Yeah." Bentley ran a hand back and forth over his hair, which generated a cloud of dust. "I thought there were three ride engines that needed care or refurbishment. But it looks like there are four. You wouldn't have any mechanical skill, would you? As it turns out, I'll be leaving town in a few days."

"I'm not the right man for this job. Or for Cassie, if you were wondering." Tanner waited for Bentley's response.

"I didn't wonder." Bentley passed a hand across his body like a windshield wiper. "It's probably for the best they find someone else for both projects." Did he sound like a sad sack? He hoped not. "I'm used to making engines more efficient and faster. Somehow, I don't think faster kiddie rides is a good thing."

"Not unless you're a ten-year-old boy, I reckon." Grinning, Tanner stood, lifting Mia to his hip.

"I'm hungry." Mia rubbed her eyes. "And thirsty."

Tanner brushed her curls from her eyes. "We'll take care of that right soon."

The soft tone coming from a gruff cowboy made Bentley smile.

That smile made Tanner frown. "Don't be such a...a..." It seemed like he was searching for a word that wouldn't offend his daughter. "A Monroe!"

"Would it be so bad?" Bentley asked seriously. "To be a Monroe?"

Tanner's frown deepened to a scowl.

"I'm just wondering why we're the enemy. I mean, I understand why Shane rubs people the wrong way. But me? Everybody loves me."

"My Grandma Ruth has scraped by her entire life." Tanner measured his words, flavoring them with equal measure of resentment and love. "All I have to do is look at the things that you Monroes have... Your grandfather and Ruth's first husband found a treasure chest full of gold. And you want me to believe that Harlan put it all back?" Tanner scoffed. "After Hobart died, Harlan used that money to finance his start in the oil fields. And he didn't give his former sister-in-law a dime."

"Hang on." Bentley stepped clear of the engine pieces. "I think Grandpa Harlan got his start by marrying an oil heiress in Texas."

"You can believe that if you want, but I

know different." Tanner marched off. Mia waved.

Bentley waved back. He'd done his best, come what may.

CHAPTER TWENTY

"DON'T LET THE dog in!"

Too late, Ajax trotted past Cassie on the lookout for his squeaker toy.

A summer storm had just passed through. Ajax tracked mud through the house. He paused in the middle of the living room to shake all the water off.

"Sorry, Cassie." Rhett hung his hat and removed his boots in the mudroom.

It had been three days since Cassie had kissed Bentley and then been given the kiss-off. Three days since Bentley had begun taking apart the engines and then stopped. Three days since Olivia had tossed down a challenge to Cassie to decide what she wanted. And what had Cassie done since? Fallen back into her safe, comforting routine. Maybe she needed to hire Sonny.

"Come on, Rhett." Cassie and her brother had agreed to disagree when it came to Bentley and were still snappy around each other. "You know Shane is coming over to talk about how we operate the carnival rides as a business."

"Is that today?" Rhett grimaced. "I think I need to ride fence or something."

"You don't need to ride fence when we've only got forty heifers and they stay in one pasture." She grabbed the damp mop from a closet. "I've told you and I've told Grandpa—over and over. I am not running these rides by myself. Now, move along so I can mop. *Again*." She had no time to fill a bucket or do a complete mop job. She ran the mop back and forth over the kitchen floor. Something in her hip twinged, but not with the veracity of the week before. "Grandpa, nap time is over. Shane will be here soon."

Her grandfather may or may not have stirred from his spot on the couch.

"All right. Okay." Rhett took the mop from her and completed the job. "But I really wish you could figure out your love life. You're cranky without Bentley and he's cranky without you."

Cassie sidled up next to Rhett. "How do you know Bentley's cranky? Have you seen him? Did he mention me?"

"I saw him at the Bent Nickel." Rhett put the mop away. "And no, I didn't talk to him.

His cousin Cam told him to stop being crabby. He's not your perfect man, Cassie."

"Nobody's perfect." But Bentley had seemed perfect enough for her.

"There's Cowboy Campbell." Rhett had the gall to say that straight-faced.

"You want me to hold out for Cowboy Campbell? He's a fictional character in books that were written when Grandpa was little." She was fond of the books, but Cassie would have laughed if Rhett hadn't looked so serious.

The corner of Rhett's mouth twitched. "You love him. You said so yourself. Many times."

"When I was six!"

"Don't ever say I don't listen to you." Grinning, Rhett locked his gaze on Cassie's. "Repeat after me. I'll be fine without Bentley Monroe."

"Cowboy Campbell," Cassie muttered, refusing to play along.

Squeak-squeak-squeak. Ajax returned, trotting up to Cassie but just out of reach. He gave a playful growl and shook the stuffed rabbit. *Squeak-squeak-pop!* The dog's eyes widened. He worked the toy around his jaws, chewing, chewing, chewing—all without any squeaks.

"You popped your squeaker, buddy?" Rhett tsked. "Life's hard."

Cassie could relate. The bottom of her socks

were now wet and their big dog was droop-ing. Great. "How about a frozen carrot, Ajax?" She found one in the freezer. "This should lift your spirits."

Ajax dropped his toy, stared at the carrot, stared at Cassie and then stared at the vege-table again. Fixated.

Cassie waved the carrot in front of the dog, not that he seemed to notice. "I know it's sad, but I can't fix your bunny." That required a trip to the store to buy a new one. She cupped his head in one hand and offered him the fro-zen carrot once more. He loved frozen carrots.

Ajax slid down to the floor, propping his head on his deceased bunny toy.

Apparently, he loved the squeaker more than carrots.

Rhett looked sad and hummed the first few bars of Taps.

"Stop it." Cassie put the carrot back in the freezer. "Grandpa, time to rise and shine. Shane will be here any minute." She thought she heard a truck pull into the ranch yard. She glanced around, going through her clean-ing checklist. Toilets. *Check*. Dusting. *Check*. Floors. *Check*. Kitchen surfaces. *Check*. "I'm ready. We're ready."

"What, exactly, is Shane coming here for?"

Rhett walked around Ajax, went to the refrigerator and got himself a bottle of beer.

Cassie snatched it from him and put it back. "Stay focused." *Grrr.* Didn't Rhett get it? This wasn't a social occasion. "Shane's going to tell us how to operate the rides. Keep track of payroll. How to advertise or put up signs or something so people will stop. You want to save the Bar D, don't you?"

"Yes." Rhett leaned against the kitchen counter and frowned. "But I never wanted to run the rides."

"Neither do I, but don't tell him that. He's paying to fix them up. Once we get that income, we can focus on our dreams, right?" Cassie hurried into the living room. "Grandpa, wake up." She shook his shoulder, suddenly concerned. Was he breathing? When was the last time she'd seen him move? *"Grandpa?"*

The old man sat bolt upright. "What? Where's the fire?"

"Grandpa, you scared me half to death." Cassie rushed back into the kitchen, nerves frayed enough to snap. She reached in the fridge for Rhett's beer.

"Oh, no you don't." Rhett put the beer back. He took her by the shoulders once more. "You need to breathe. It's just Shane."

"I'm not a businessperson," Cassie confessed. "I deal with handshakes and take people at their word. I don't know how to manage people or promote a business. I don't even promote myself!"

Rhett looked her in the eye. "Maybe that should change. Promoting yourself, I mean. It'd give you something to focus on besides Bentley."

"You're not allowed to mention his name." Cassie shrugged free of his hold. "Things would have been fine if you hadn't interfered."

"They would have been *false* if I hadn't interfered. You'll thank me when you're older."

"I'm older and I'm tired of this bickering!" Grandpa said.

Someone knocked on the front door.

Ajax stood but didn't run to the door or bark, seemingly reluctant to leave his beloved toy.

Grandpa opened the door. "Well, looky here. Not one Monroe, but two." He stepped aside and let the men in.

Bentley? For a moment, Cassie's heart pounded hopefully.

"Hey, everybody. I brought my cousin Holden." Shane introduced him around while Cassie tried to contain her disappointment and suppress another round of feeling less than adequate. Everyone knew Holden was the successful moneyman in the Monroe family.

Cassie never balanced her checkbook on the first try. Still, she gave them a smile, invited them to sit at the kitchen table and offered them water or coffee, lingering at the kitchen sink, prepared to deliver whatever they needed.

The dog sank back down to the floor, so distraught over the death of his toy that he hadn't succumbed to a case of the zoomies when Holden came in.

Grandpa and Rhett sat at the kitchen table. No one spoke. In fact, the men looked around at each other as if waiting for someone else to start talking.

Shane held out two envelopes. "Mackenzie received mail packets for you." The general store was the town's official post office. "One for you and one for Rhett."

"Who are these from?" Rhett tore into his. A check fell to the floor. "Money! I must have won the lottery, Grandpa." He opened the accompanying letter.

Meanwhile, Cassie had read the return address on the label. "It's from Ashley Monroe." The actress turned film producer. She opened hers more carefully. There was also a check and a letter. "It's a retainer for the movie she's producing here next year. And a list of stunts she wants horses to do." The list was daunting, but the check would tide her over for several months.

"Mine's a signing bonus to do some background roping in the film." Rhett looked pleased as punch.

"I'd forgotten we signed paperwork when she was here in June." There was a sticky note inside Cassie's envelope.

Bentley reminded me that people were waiting on their checks. Ashley.

Bentley had reminded his cousin to pay them.

What would you do with your life if money was no object?

That's what he'd asked her. She'd brushed the question aside, since money had always been an issue.

The kitchen was quiet once more. Cassie glanced at each of the Monroes in turn, waiting for one of them to take the lead.

"Do you know what I could really use?" Holden asked with a wry chuckle.

Cassie shook her head.

"A beer. My fiancée is pregnant. I haven't had a beer in months. And with the day's heat and that muggy rain shower, I could use a brew." Holden glanced around the table. "Am I right?"

"You're spot-on." Rhett was out of his seat, leaping over a mournful Ajax and handing out bottles of beer like he was a waiter in need of a good tip.

"None for Grandpa." Cassie headed off that spot of trouble at the pass. "Or me."

"I guess I'm now a man of a certain age," Grandpa said, but didn't put up a fuss. Alcohol didn't interact well with some of his medications.

Rhett and the Monroes happily settled in with their beer. Other than Ajax, the mood was lightening.

Cassie poured two glasses of water and took a seat next to her grandfather, giving him a glass.

"I brought Holden with me today because he came up with an interesting proposition." Shane was the beer label ripping kind of drinker. He peeled a strip of the label off, rolling the damp paper in his fingers. "I suspect…or I should say that it's come to my attention that none of you want to operate the rides we're restoring."

Cassie, Rhett and Grandpa all made mild noises of dissent.

"You don't have to pretend," Shane said gently. "We have a proposition to make." He turned to Holden.

"There's an Old West mining attraction about an hour north of here," Holden began. "The Standing Bear Silver Mine. They offer a fun tour through a historic town and the mine, plus horseback riding. They're good people— you'd like them. We were thinking that your rides might get more use there."

"That's a long drive to make every day." Grandpa said what Cassie had been thinking.

"That wasn't quite what we'd envisioned. In this scenario, you could sell the rides to the mine operators," Holden said with just the right note of compassion, as if he knew how much Grandpa cherished those rides. "A lease-to-own deal that would provide you with income over the next three to five years."

Yes. Yes-yes-yes-yes! Cassie held her breath.

Rhett was nodding his head.

That left Grandpa. His brow furrowed. "Sell them? What made you come up with that idea? These attractions have been in our family for sixty years."

"And once they're restored," Shane said, just as gently as his cousin, "they deserve an environment where they'll be cared for and loved for sixty more. Let's hear from Rhett and Cassie."

Rhett deferred to Cassie by taking a long draft of his beer.

"Do you think the mine owners will take care of the rides?" she asked.

Holden nodded. "They're excited about the prospect of adding something new. It gives tourists one more reason to come by."

"Then I vote sell." Cassie took her grandfather's hand and gave him a look that she hoped said he should agree with her.

"I'm with Cassie," Rhett said, staring at his beer. "No disrespect, Grandpa. But if I was going to run a business, you know I'd open an adventure tour operation, maybe in town where the old river rafting company used to be."

Holden and Shane exchanged glances.

Grandpa looked like he was considering the deal. But his head moved back and forth, as if he was going to refuse the offer. He turned toward Cassie. "I guess…I guess I should listen to those who'd be inheriting them one day if we kept them."

Cassie squeezed his hand. "I love you, Grandpa."

"I appreciate you letting them go," Rhett seconded.

While Holden haggled with Grandpa—because the old man couldn't just take what was offered—Cassie put on her boots and dragged Rhett out to the barn.

"Now, since that's settled, I need to be proactive about making training videos."

"Now?" Rhett still carried his beer.

"Yes, now. When you realize things can be different if you get up and do something, you need to get up and make them different by doing something." Starting with the videos was a step in the right direction. And the direction she wanted to head was toward Bentley.

"You sound like a greeting card." Rhett paused to drink some beer.

Cassie took his bottle away. "Listen to me. If I'm going to prove I won't get lost spreading my wings and taking chances, I need to do it now."

"Okay." Rhett dug his cell phone out of his pocket. "Strike while the iron is hot."

And while Bentley was still in town.

"SHE'S LATE." KENDALL paced the lobby of the Lodgepole Inn.

"She likes to make an entrance." Bentley sat drinking his tea in peace. Other than Kendall there was no one to disturb him. Nary a ballerina-in-training in sight.

Laurel, Gabby, Dr. Carlisle and the twins had gone to Ketchum for a checkup with a pediatrician who specialized in premature baby development.

There would have been silence and it would have been golden, if Kendall hadn't been stomping across the lobby in Gabby's place.

"She's late," Kendall said again. She had an expensive camera hanging on a strap around her neck. She'd scheduled a photo session with the siblings so she'd have something to say to the press and post on social media about Olivia, other than no comment. "Olivia is never late."

"It might just be nerves." Bentley knew a lot about nerves. He kept expecting to see Cassie in town. He kept wondering what he'd say if he did.

Logically, he knew he'd made the right decision. But while he had to bide his time in town until the DNA results came in, Bentley kept wanting to drive out to the Bar D, sit down with Cassie and work through all the possible scenarios of them being together until they found one they both agreed upon.

"Here she is." Kendall threw the front door open wide. "Here she is."

"You wanted a family picture." Olivia entered the lobby in shorts and a wrinkled T-shirt, flip-flops snapping. Her nose was pink from too much sun and her curls were twisting every which way. "Here I am."

Sonny came in behind her. His T-shirt today was seafoam green and proclaimed: Love And Believe in Thyself.

"I can't take your picture like that." Kendall dragged Olivia toward the stairs. "Your hair is out of control. You've got no makeup on. And that shirt makes you look like a lifeguard at the public shores."

"This is who I am now," Olivia protested, but she went upstairs anyway.

Sonny sat down on the opposite end of the couch from Bentley. "So this is town." He glanced around the lobby. "I thought there'd be more to it."

"I guess that depends on how deep you look." Bentley sipped his tea. It was getting cold.

"Have you seen Cassie lately? She's been trying to sort things out." Sonny fluffed his white beard.

"Did she talk to you?" That seemed unlikely. "And if she did, shouldn't you honor client confidentiality?"

"She and Olivia chatted. It was a good talk,

full of female empowerment and support. I could feel the love." He leaned forward, a conspiratorial look on his face and a twinkle in his eyes. "Granted, I was eavesdropping, but sometimes that's what you have to do to get results."

"I don't approve of eavesdropping by health care professionals." Yet Bentley wondered how Cassie was doing all the same.

Sonny sat back, folding his hands over his chest and smiling.

Time passed. Cars went by. Upstairs, feminine voices murmured.

And still, Bentley thought about Cassie.

He turned to face Sonny. "Okay, I'll bite. How's she doing?"

The old man's smile broadened, making his cheeks round and red. "Your sister is making progress. We talked about moving her treatments closer to the ocean today, but she wouldn't hear of it. At least, for now."

"Great." Bentley nodded, before clarifying, "I meant, how is *Cassie* doing?"

"Now that I don't exactly know, other than she sought out advice from Olivia regarding reaching for one's dreams. And then Tanner walked her home."

Bentley drew a measured breath as unexpected jealousy shuddered through his veins.

"Here we are." Kendall skipped down the stairs. "Doesn't she look fabulous?"

Olivia came down the stairs at a much slower pace. Kendall had brushed her curls and put a headband in her hair. Olivia wore an off-the-shoulder blouse that was more suited to a nightclub than a picture in a mountain meadow. Her face looked like an overly painted doll.

"Breathtaking," Sonny said, clapping.

"This won't do." Bentley got to his feet and grabbed Olivia's hand. "Come with me." He led her upstairs to his room, ignoring her protests.

"Bentley, stop. I just want to get this picture over with. It doesn't matter what I look like. Haven't you ever heard of Photoshop?"

Bentley opened the door to his room and ushered his sister inside. "Kendall made you in her image. She's not going to touch up or tone down anything." He dug through his suitcase until he found a pale blue T-shirt. He tossed it to her. "Put this on."

Olivia held it up. "Monroe Marine Racing. Pit Crew. Very clever humor. But I can't wear this. It'll be huge on me."

"We'll tie it in the back with that hideous headband. I see women do that all the time." Bentley rooted around in the corner of his bag until he found a baseball cap. He tossed that to his sister.

"Monroe Marine Racing." She sighed. "This is starting to feel like one big lie."

"Is it?" He guided her into the bathroom. "The racing team doesn't exist without you."

Olivia caught sight of herself in the mirror. "OMG! I had no idea she had done this to me. She wouldn't let me look in the mirror."

"I guess that means you're changing clothes."

"I guess that means I'm changing clothes."

After she closed the bathroom door, Bentley sat on the bed to wait.

"Hey, brother dear. You need to go see Cassie before it's too late."

"Nice try, but I'm doing the right thing." And he wasn't happy that Olivia had brought it up. He flopped back on the bed and stared at the ceiling. "Can you imagine what would happen to a cowgirl who traded in her horses for a relationship with me? Not to mention a relationship thousands of miles away from their family and friends? I can. The relationship would never last."

"They have horse farms outside Philly. But isn't that presumptuous of you? What's to keep you from moving your operation here? Whatever your next operation is."

"Oh, I don't know. The lack of materials? Or a pool of local expertise? You think I haven't tried thinking this through?"

"You're the only person who thinks logically when it comes to love. That isn't how it works, you know."

"Have you ever tried planting a flower in the garden in December?" he asked.

"Uh, no." She sounded like she thought he'd fallen overboard on purpose during a race. "December isn't the right time for planting."

"Exactly." He pulled himself together and sat back up.

"Oh. I get it. Right cowgirl, wrong season."

Bentley didn't add that there might never be a right time for them. It was enough that Olivia stopped talking about Cassie.

His sister emerged, looking more like herself preaccident. A cap on her head. A T-shirt with sleeves rolled up and the excess material twisted in back. She'd even removed most of that makeup. "Well?"

"You look seaworthy. Or at least good enough that I'll have my picture taken with you." That earned him a smile. This was new territory for himself and his sister. And it was all because she was working through her personal baggage.

They traipsed back downstairs.

Kendall wasn't thrilled. "I know better than

to complain, but I wish your branch of the family would embrace wearing something other than T-shirts."

"We've decided the fireplace is a better backdrop than an open field," Bentley said, sitting on the hearth. "We know who we are."

Olivia sat next to him. "And we know who we aren't."

"It's good to hear positive affirmations." Sonny smiled approvingly.

Kendall snapped a picture, and then another, muttering something under her breath.

It wasn't positive. And it wasn't an affirmation.

THE MRI RESULTS were in. And Dr. Killjoy Simon had forwarded Cassie's file to Dr. Carlisle.

Cassie sat in an exam bay at the town clinic, trying to be patient as the doctor flipped through the information.

"I feel really good," Cassie told her. "There's still some stiffness in the morning and some twinges if I move too quickly, but I'm good." Good enough to avoid the need for surgery? Good enough to be cleared to have children?

"Ah, I get the picture now." Dr. Carlisle closed her file. "So, the biggest injury you suffered was a fracture to your posterior sacroiliac." She laid a gentle palm on Cassie's hip. "But you had another fracture down low in your ischiopubic ramus."

"I'm afraid to ask where that is."

"It's basically your pelvic floor. That's why Dr. Simon cautioned you about pregnancy. During delivery, the ischiopubic ramus will sometimes fracture. If you didn't allow both fractures to heal, it would be a problem if you were to get pregnant. Your hips carry and stabilize your weight and your baby's weight." Dr. Carlisle rubbed Cassie's back. "But you're not going to get pregnant until both fractures are healed. Are you?"

"If you're asking me to abstain, don't waste your breath. I'm not seeing Bentley anymore." Her heart still protested the very idea that they weren't together.

"That's too bad. Everybody said you two were sweet together." The doctor made a note in Cassie's chart. "No ranch work for you for another three weeks. And then we get an X-ray to see if you've healed properly to decide if you need three more. I saw Bentley head over to the diner earlier. You know he plans to leave soon, right?"

We were sweet together.

Cassie's heart panged and her mouth started running. "We don't want the same things," she blurted. That wasn't quite true. "I mean, we both want kids and we're attracted to each other, but we don't know what comes next."

Dr. Carlisle blinked. "After what?"

"After it's decided what's going to happen to Second Chance and I finish work on Ashley's movie. I don't know if I'll have a job here. And Bentley? Bentley doesn't know or never shared with me what he wants to do next, other than he wants to stay in Philadelphia. Clearly, we're a mess. People don't embark upon a future when they have no idea what direction their future lies in." Cassie drew a deep breath, somewhat relieved to get all that off her chest.

Dr. Carlisle smiled. "Can I tell you a secret?"

"Sure." Cassie slid carefully off the exam table and leaned toward the doctor.

"Holden and I don't know what we're going to do either." She shrugged. "We're just playing it by ear."

"But…what if you don't want the same things when it comes time to decide?"

"That won't happen. We're both opinionated and a bit pigheaded, but despite and in spite of our jobs and family obligations, we find a way to compromise. And do you know why? Because we love each other." And then she laughed, as if love was enough.

Cassie realized she was right. Love should be enough.

She thanked the doctor and went to find Bentley to falsify all those clever theories of his.

CHAPTER TWENTY-ONE

BENTLEY WAS SITTING in the Bent Nickel Diner drinking tea and watching the occasional car drive past when Shane ran in carrying a mail pouch.

"It came!" he cried. "The DNA results." He slid into the seat across from Bentley. "Overnight mail. I could barely sleep for not knowing."

"Open it." Bentley didn't share Shane's excitement.

"No. I want Tanner to witness me opening it."

"That's not necessary."

"I think it is. Tanner won't be able to argue the results if he's here when the seal is broken."

Bentley disagreed. The way he saw it, Shane and Tanner would argue no matter what the results said. Especially once Tanner understood there were results to argue about.

"I'm going to call every Monroe in town—

and Tanner—and prove once and for all that he's only out to scam us."

"Shane—"

But his cousin cut him off with a wave of his hand. "Let me just send a text."

Bentley drank his tea. On the bright side, he'd be free to go in less than an hour.

The thought should have brought him some relief. He missed Cassie. But he missed her open heart and talkative nature. He missed her love of family and honor toward responsibility. He missed looking at her sweet face while she slept. He missed holding her in his arms when she stumbled. And the only conclusion all that missing led to was that he… he…he loved her.

As if drawn by his thoughts, Cassie entered the Bent Nickel and approached his table.

He loved her but she'd come at the worst possible moment. Those DNA results…

She stopped in front of Bentley and drummed her fingers on the tabletop. "I need to talk to you."

"He can't talk now," Shane cut in. "We're about to have a very important family meeting."

"Oh." Cassie looked crestfallen.

"If you could, you can wait for me at the inn." Or the general store or any of the other shops in town. Any place where she wouldn't hear what happened next.

Cassie perked up. "I'll wait here." And then she walked over to a booth on the other side of his, without giving him an opportunity to argue.

Most of the Monroes in Second Chance came in. Laurel entered with Gabby. Sophie came from her shop across the street. Holden ambled over from the medical clinic. Cam kept everyone fed and caffeinated and Shane kept checking the time.

Five minutes after Cassie arrived, Tanner walked in.

Shane wasted no time taking advantage of his moment. "I want to thank everyone for coming, including Tanner. In this envelope…" He waved it in the air like a circus ringmaster. "I hold the results of a DNA test that will prove whether or not Tanner is a Monroe."

Tanner scowled. "I didn't submit to a DNA test."

"No, you didn't." Shane ripped open the outer envelope. "But Bentley figured out a way to collect a sample that will prove…without a doubt—" he grabbed the smaller envelope inside "—that you are not a Monroe."

Tanner's scowl deepened and he directed it at Bentley. "How did you collect this sample? I don't recall eating or drinking when you were around. Did you break into our cabin and swab my coffee cup?"

"No." And that was as much as Bentley would admit to.

Cassie gasped. "He must have swabbed one of the kids."

Bentley stared at his tea mug. He couldn't look at her. He couldn't bear to see her disgust and disappointment.

A few Monroe cousins shifted uneasily. And why wouldn't they? Grandpa Harlan would never have stolen a DNA sample.

"Bentley, how could you?" Cassie asked in a broken voice.

Bentley stared at his tea mug, sick to his stomach. He'd known Cassie wouldn't approve.

Shane tore open the smaller envelope. "Ow. Paper cut." He mangled the letter as he tried to get it out. "And the results are in." He paused, peering at the letter. "Hang on."

"Just read the results," Bentley sputtered. So he could see this to the end and leave town.

Shane drooped. "He's a Monroe."

"Yes, he is," Bentley said with relief, having known the whole time. Only then did he dare look toward Cassie.

"Don't say it like it's something to be proud

of," Cassie ground out, looking everywhere but at him. Blinking back tears, she headed toward the door. "Come on, Tanner. You're better than this."

Tanner stared at Bentley for a long moment. And then he walked out with her.

"He's a Monroe…" Shane dropped into the booth across from Bentley. "I was so sure he wasn't."

"DNA doesn't lie." Bentley paid his bill and made the rounds, saying farewell to everyone, biding his time until Cassie drove out of his life forever.

"You'll come back for Christmas," Laurel said as if it was a done deal.

And risk seeing Cassie again? She hated him.

She was outside right now, having a heated discussion with Tanner.

Bentley shook his head.

"You'll come for my wedding though." Shane also spoke with certainty. "For New Year's weekend."

Bentley shook his head.

"You're not going to your parents' house, are you?" Cam seemed upset at the thought. "They cut you off."

Finally, Cassie drove away.

Bentley sucked in a deep breath and told

Cam, "I haven't made any plans." Other than to find a dark cave where he could lick his wounds and tell himself he'd done the right thing—with Cassie and with Tanner.

Gabby followed him out the door. "I have a recital coming up. It's virtual. Can I send you a link?"

"Sure." At least he wouldn't have to show his face during those online gatherings.

Tanner stepped in his way. "We need to talk."

Gabby plastered herself next to Bentley. "I know what Uncle Bentley did was wrong, but he did it for the right reasons. You got what you wanted. You're a Monroe."

"Gabby. Honey." Bentley gently steered her in the direction of the inn. "Please go home. Tanner has every right to be mad about the idea that someone would take his kid's DNA without asking."

Tanner grunted. Gabby glanced at Bentley with an equal mixture of grief and disappointment.

"Go on, Gabby. I'll be fine."

Instead of obeying, Gabby doubled back around to the diner.

"WHAT ARE YOU DOING?" Olivia stood in Sonny's bedroom doorway. They'd barely returned from Kendall's organized photoshoot with Bentley.

Sonny barely spared her a glance. "What does it look like I'm doing? I'm packing."

Anxiety gripped Olivia's gut. "You can't leave. I'm not fixed." Far from it.

Sonny straightened, gave her a sad smile and then crossed the room to give her one of his big bear hugs. "But you're at a point where you don't need me anymore. The sooner you acknowledge that we're all imperfect and forgive yourself for making mistakes, the sooner you'll get on with your not-so-perfect life."

She drew back, staring at the words on his yellow T-shirt and the symbol for yin and yang. "You changed your T-shirt." She read the message. "We All Have Light And Dark Parts."

"Yes." He went back to his suitcase. "Congratulations. You pass."

"Pass what? I was just reading your shirt." How could he leave her? "Who's going to feed me?"

"That's your inner child speaking in your fraidy-cat voice." He pressed a hand over his chest, frowning. "What do we do when we're afraid?"

"We ask ourselves if there is real danger." Olivia hugged herself. "The danger in my head is real."

He glanced at her. He'd gotten a lot of sun

yesterday. His face looked sunburned, especially his cheeks. "Are you thinking of self-harm?"

"No! I'm thinking if I can't return to sailing that I've just wasted half my life with nothing to show for it."

"Fear is raising its ugly head again. Or should I say Stan?" Sonny shrugged his shoulders back, reminding Olivia of the name he had given her fear, and swallowed thickly. "I don't feel well." He plopped down on the bed, as if his legs had suddenly given out.

Olivia looked at him closely. The skin she'd thought was burned was hot and sweaty. His eyes were dilated. She was trained in first aid and CPR. Here was a man in distress. She ran into the other room to grab her phone and dialed 911. It wasn't until she got a recorded message that she began to panic.

CASSIE DROVE TOO fast over the potholes, making her truck shake in a way that was far too familiar and would have drawn Bentley's ire.

Bentley. She couldn't believe he'd been so underhanded.

She pulled into the ranch yard, skidding to a stop in the gravel. She gripped the steering wheel as the dust she'd kicked up settled around the truck and drifted in the open window.

Bentley. She felt as if he'd betrayed her. First by listening to logic, and then by listening to Rhett. And now this.

Rhett came out of the barn and stared her way. He and Grandpa were watching Tanner's kids this morning.

I can't stay here.

Cassie shoved the truck into Reverse, drove out of the ranch yard and headed farther down the road, toward the lake and the old homestead, seeking solitude. She came over the rise to find Olivia running toward the road, waving her arms.

Cassie skidded to a stop once more, covering the truck and Olivia with a thick layer of dust.

Olivia didn't care. She ran right up to Cassie's window. "Help me. Sonny's collapsed. I can't get through to 911. I heard your truck and—"

"The nearest EMT is Ketchum, over an hour away." Cassie shoved the truck into Park, forgetting for a moment about Bentley and disappointment. "Dr. Carlisle is in town. Let's get Sonny there."

Together, the two women helped Sonny

into the truck. His face was red and his skin clammy.

"There's an ICE contact in my phone," Sonny gasped. "In case I don't make it."

"You're going to be fine, Sonny," Olivia snapped. "Stop talking about the Big D." She leaned over the center console toward Cassie. "Make him stop talking about the Big D."

"What is the Big D? And fasten your seat belt. We're in for a bumpy ride." Cassie drove the truck in a tight circle, heading back the way she'd come.

"Smart. People. Don't. Fear. Stan." Sonny wheezed.

"Yes, yes. I've heard that before." Olivia clicked her seat belt in place. "Smart people know we're all born with an expiration date. Smart people can articulate the fact that they love someone. Smart people compromise. Smart people—"

"Please. Breathe." Cassie took her cell phone from the center console and called Dr. Carlisle to tell her they were coming. And then Cassie spared Olivia a dark look. "I've had about enough of Monroes saying something moral and behaving completely different."

"Don't tell me you've seen Shane this morn-

ing." Olivia's laugh was high-pitched and bor-
derline hysterical.

"No. It's Bentley," Cassie said angrily. And
then she explained what Bentley had done.

"That can't be true." Olivia sounded so certain. "Bentley never cut a class as a student.
Bentley leaves a note on someone's car if he
accidentally causes a ding by opening his
door. Bentley dots every *i* and crosses every
t. He'd never collect a DNA sample without
permission, especially from a child."

Could Olivia be right?

They reached the main highway. Cassie hit
speed dial to call Rhett and tell him where
she was going.

On a gut level, she wanted to reject what
Olivia was saying.

But in her heart…

In her heart, she knew what Olivia said was
true. Bentley would never have swabbed little Mia.

But if he hadn't, who had?

CHAPTER TWENTY-TWO

"I'M NOT REALLY a Monroe," Tanner told Bentley. "Grandma Ruth didn't have Hobart Monroe's child. According to her, when she left town, she wasn't pregnant. Something isn't right here."

"Oh?" Bentley glanced around to make sure they were alone. Inside the diner, Monroes were drifting toward Gabby, who was talking excitedly and waving her arms. Bentley began walking toward the old church on the other side of the stop sign. "Now that you know, you don't have to go telling everyone."

"But…" Tanner tipped his cowboy hat back and still managed to keep up with Bentley. "I'm not a Monroe. Shane is in the diner right now calculating how much money is in my cut of the town."

Bentley waved a hand dismissively. "He's already done that."

"Stop this." Tanner took hold of Bentley's arm. "You didn't swab Mia."

"I didn't," Bentley admitted.

Tanner frowned. "But that means you swabbed...*yourself*?"

Bentley nodded and resumed walking to the church. "And don't think I didn't have a moment of doubt, because despite the fact that no one's ever questioned if *I'm* a Monroe or not, there are skeletons in everyone's past."

"You've got to go back and tell Shane the truth." Tanner caught up to him.

"No. This way, Mia and Quinn will be taken care of. Winter is on the horizon. You'll be able to open a line of credit at the general store and buy the kids good coats. Next spring, you'll be able to afford a pony for Mia and a horse for Quinn. Isn't that why you're here?"

"No. I'm here because Grandma Ruth was married to Harlan's brother when they found the gold. She deserves to be taken care of in her old age. That's why I'm in Second Chance. I can make my own way in the world." His words rang out like a preacher at the pulpit.

There was no traffic. Bentley crossed the highway, thinking about Tanner's reasons for showing up in Second Chance, his reasons for wanting to reject a full share, testing the words for the weight of truth. Testing them against his own moral compass and that of Grandpa Harlan's.

He climbed up to the meadow, breathing

in the sweet scent of grass and wildflowers with the musky scent of fertile earth. It was so different from the salt tang of the ocean. But there was still the wind and the sun on his face. Those things were similar. Not bad. Similar.

If I could build ships here, I would, if it meant I could be with Cassie.

But his actions in protecting Mia and Quinn had ruined his chances with her. He could assess his mistakes at a later date. It was time to sort through the issues Tanner presented. His misplaced sense of honor was at risk of undoing everything Bentley had put in place.

Bentley reached the church and sat down on the slope. After a moment, Tanner took a seat nearby. From here, they had a good view of most of the valley, the Salmon River and the gray Sawtooth Mountains. The sky was blue and the meadow was the faded, colorful shade of late summer. It didn't feel like a day when everything would fall apart. But then again, the day he'd let Cassie go had also been one of beauty.

Tanner cleared his throat. "Gertie Clark called my Grandma Ruth back in June, telling her all about the found gold. We were there visiting, and since Ruth is hard of hearing, she had Gertie on the speakerphone. And after the call was over, Ruth told me about being married to Hobart Monroe, a preacher from Idaho. That part, I knew. And then she wove a tale about him being Harlan's brother. That part I didn't know. We never made a connection between Mr. Moneybags Harlan Monroe and her long-dead first husband, Hobart Monroe. It still blows my mind." Tanner looked wearily up at the sky. "And then she told us about how Harlan, Hobart and Gertie's husband searched for lost gold. She made it sound so real. So… so…believable."

"It is. Those three men searched all over these mountains for that gold. And then when they found it, someone tried to take it from them and killed Hobart." There was more to the tale than that, but Bentley didn't think now was the time to review the details. Tanner was about to make a big mistake, letting go of the funds that would secure his future and that of his children.

"I came here because I knew a wealthy family like the Monroes would respond to my claim by trying to buy my silence." Tanner hooked his elbows around his knees. "We camped out the first couple of nights we were here. And then Laurel offered us a room at the inn." He sounded surprised. "And then Sophie gave us a key to that cabin. I thought there'd be a sheriff showing us the way out of town and instead…"

"You were shown kindness." Bentley was rather proud of his family for that.

"I didn't come for charity or kindness." A little of the familiar resentment had crept back into Tanner's voice. He mashed his cowboy hat firmly on his head. "Frankly, I was mad at all of you for being so gullible."

Bentley chuckled. "All of us?"

"Okay, Shane had the right idea about me being here, and I don't begrudge him any-thing…except thinking that it was right to take a DNA sample from one of my kids." Tanner clenched and reclenched his hands. "I should slug him for that."

"All our lives would be easier if you didn't. He had his reasons and a breaking point, same as you." *Same as me, too.*

"Holden came to see me about a week after we arrived and he…" Tanner frowned. "He took a good look at me and the kids, and left without offering me anything."

Bentley imagined that Holden had come to the same conclusion he had. If those kids were Monroes, they deserved better than a discounted buyout. They deserved a full share. But he'd ask his cousin about that later.

"And then Rhett rode by one morning and

invited us over." Tanner shook his head. "One talk about hard times led to another. And suddenly we were putting on a rodeo school together. I'd really like to see that through. My name is on those flyers, along with Rhett's and Raymond's."

"Why wouldn't you go through with the rodeo school?"

Tanner scoffed as if Bentley was thick-headed. "Because someone is going to figure out that I'm *not* a Monroe. Not by blood. And then Shane is going to have me arrested for fraud."

"Being accused of fraud doesn't necessarily mean you can't hold your rodeo school."

Tanner removed his hat and rubbed a hand through his hair. "It does. I'm not that kind of man."

"No. You're the kind of man who shows up with two kids and claims to be a Monroe and then loses his nerve. You should have walked in and told Shane the truth."

Tanner shook his head. "You didn't see him. He didn't extend a welcome."

Bentley nodded. "And now it's come to this. You need to think of your kids. They're the reason you did this."

"No. Now there, you're all wrong. Grandma Ruth's short-term memory is failing," Tanner said quietly. "The doc said she might develop Alzheimer's. If she were still a Monroe, my dad and I wouldn't have to worry about how to pay for her care."

Bentley searched Tanner's features, again testing for the feel of truth. "That's all you came here for? Money for Ruth?"

Tanner nodded. "I know my kids deserve better. But I'm a hard worker. We'll be fine." He gestured toward the town proper. "We don't need to be a Monroe."

"But now you are." Bentley got to his feet. "And to me, Ruth is a Monroe, too."

"Why are you being so stubborn?" Tanner stood and swatted Bentley's shoulder with his cowboy hat as if he was an annoying fly. "I'm not going to risk going to jail because you decided I needed charity."

"You don't get it, do you?" Bentley brushed at the shoulder where Tanner had hit him, as if it was of no consequence, because it wasn't. "You didn't know Grandpa Harlan—your great-step-uncle Harlan. Family was the most important thing to him. I had dinner recently with the Clarks, including Gertie. I think she knows you aren't a Monroe. But she believes as Ruth's grandchild, blood relation or not, that you're family to us. And I believe that's what my grandfather would have wanted, too, had he known about Ruth's situation." Bentley wasn't entirely sure why his grandfather hadn't kept tabs on Ruth. "Grandpa Harlan would have said there was enough room in the spotlight for every Monroe."

"I won't lie." Chin thrust out, Tanner stared back toward town. "I'm not dishonest." He shifted his feet. "Much more than this one time, that is."

"I'm not asking you to lie any more than you already have. To me, your situation hasn't changed." Bentley was growing weary of making this man see. "You own a small fraction of a town. So what? Shane's managed to postpone a vote on what to do about that until the new year. If any money's to be made, it'll be from the sale of real estate. Again, if that happens, it won't happen until next year. You also own a share of some gold, along with the Clarks. But we decided to wait and sell the gold as part of the promotion of Ashley's movie. I'm sure you've heard my cousin is producing and starring in the tale of Mike Moody. Shane's hoping the tie-in will drive up the gold's value. The DNA test does nothing for you financially except opening the door to credit in town."

Tanner's mouth had dropped open.

"You're already living in a place rent free

under the hospitality of the Monroes. So, you see, Tanner." Bentley clapped him on the shoulder. "All I've done is remove the stigma that you're trying to cheat the Monroes, which should make it that much easier for you to build those family relationships with the Monroes in town. Real relationships. And that also gives you time to introduce the state of Ruth's health and the care you anticipate needing for her." Bentley paused. "Unless she needs money immediately."

Tanner shook his head. "She's living with my dad and his wife right now. It's the future we worry about."

"Understood." Bentley made his way back down the hill. "Do you agree to go along with the DNA results for now?"

"I suppose, but I don't like it." Tanner matched him stride for stride. And then he smiled. "I don't like it, except for the fact that I can rub it in Shane's face."

"Just a little." Bentley was kind of looking forward to that, too.

"Just a little," Tanner agreed. "You'll let me know if I step over the line, I'm sure."

"Oh, I won't be here. I'm leaving town."

"When?"

"Today. Now."

A truck squealed to a stop in front of the medical clinic. Cassie's truck.

"Dr. Carlisle!" she shouted, climbing from behind the wheel. "He's struggling to breathe!"

Bentley's heart dropped to his toes and he started running.

CHAPTER TWENTY-THREE

"IT'S SONNY," OLIVIA cried in a panicked voice when Dr. Carlisle reached Cassie's truck. She'd been waiting at the bottom of the path. "I think he's having a heart attack."

"Yes, Cassie told me." In a blink, the doctor had the passenger door open and her stethoscope pressed to Sonny's chest. "I'm going to take care of you, Sonny. Deep breath now. That's it. And another. Good. When you can, talk to me about your chest pains. When did they start? What do they feel like?"

"They feel like a heart attack," Olivia sobbed.

"Tell. Stan. To go. Away," Sonny gasped.

"Stan!" Olivia wailed.

Cassie didn't pretend to know who Stan was. Dr. Carlisle's gaze connected with Cassie's, and then it slanted quickly toward Olivia.

"Olivia," Cassie said sharply, as she opened the rear door on the other side of the truck from Sonny. "I need you over here. Now."

The former sailboat captain made her way

slowly to a door on Cassie's side of the truck, barely taking her eyes off Sonny.

"Wow. You're good, Cassie. My sister doesn't usually obey other people's commands." It was Bentley, a tall and comforting presence.

"Shush. She's had a shock." Cassie opened the rear door and helped Olivia down. "Honey, I know you're worried about Sonny, but you have to take a breath and let the doctor do her thing."

"It's Stan. And the Big D." Olivia was crying. Tears rolled down her face. "But she's a doctor and she knows CPR." Olivia poked her head in the driver's-side door. "Don't worry, Sonny. She knows CPR if you flatline."

"Okay. All right." Cassie steered Olivia away from the truck. "You are one calm captain in a crisis." Not.

Olivia wrapped her arms around herself. "I know what it's like to die. And to…to…get a second chance."

"Tanner! Bentley! Come around to this side, please." Dr. Carlisle shouted, but she shouted calmer than anyone Cassie had ever heard.

Kendall joined Cassie, slinging her arm around Olivia's shaking shoulders. "Your comfort companion will be fine, honey. We'll take him back East. They have the best doctors. And we'll find you a nice, quiet resort where you can continue to get your head on straight."

Olivia cried harder.

Across the highway, the crowd from the Bent Nickel filled the parking lot. There were a lot of Monroes. Rhett mingled among them, easily visible by his black cowboy hat. He'd followed them into town, leaving Grandpa in charge of Tanner's kids. Her brother waited for a passing car and then jogged across the road to join them.

Dr. Carlisle had Tanner and Bentley create a chair by holding each other's forearms, and then they carried Sonny up the hill to the medical clinic.

"I'll send Sonny back East," Olivia was saying. "He deserves the best care. But I'm not going anywhere."

"Honey, in your current state, you shouldn't be alone." Kendall was right, of course. Once Sonny was stabilized, Olivia would see that.

"I won't be alone." Olivia wiped her nose with her forearm. "I'll have my boyfriend with me."

"What boyfriend, honey? You broke up with Dean after the accident." Kendall rubbed Olivia's back.

"Him." Olivia threw herself into Rhett's arms, leaving everyone, including Rhett, speechless.

RELYING ON RHETT to sort out his unexpected love life, Cassie climbed the stairs to the medical clinic to reach Bentley.

He and Tanner came out the front door.

"Take care, man," Bentley said, offering Tanner his hand.

Instead, Tanner threw his arms around Bentley and hugged him. "We're family, no matter how others define family, remember? Drive carefully."

Bentley was going? Cassie was heartbroken. She waited for Tanner to pass her before asking, "Bentley, can I talk to you?"

"I'm leaving in a few minutes," Bentley said in an even voice she envied, because she was shaking inside and out.

"Please. I just spent the last twenty minutes in a panic. I need you to hear me out." She led him over to the porch edge and sat down, swinging her legs under the rail and resting her arms on top of the rail.

After a moment, Bentley joined her, folding that big body between the rails.

"I overreacted about the DNA." Cassie risked a glance in his direction. "I don't blame you if you're mad at me about assuming you would swab Mia or Quinn. After the shock wore off, I realized you couldn't have done it. You *wouldn't* have done it. It was Shane or Kendall or…" Anyone but Bentley.

"Don't blame anyone else," he said gruffly, but he wouldn't look at her when he said it. "Tanner is family to me."

"Okay." She took his hand. It was warm and strong, and she no longer had a right to hold it. "I'll believe whatever you tell me. But that won't change the way I feel. Whatever your involvement was, you had the best of intentions."

The fracas Olivia had caused moved across the street toward the Bent Nickel, leaving things quieter on this side of the highway. Now, she could almost make out Dr. Carlisle's calm voice as she treated Sonny inside the clinic.

This was Cassie's chance to make things right with Bentley, to silence his logical arguments and make him listen to his heart. "After the bull stomped on me, I only agreed to a minimum of pain treatment in the hospital. But apparently it was enough to make me… Well, you know the effect painkillers have on me. I didn't understand everything the doctor told me."

"About not being able to have kids?"

She nodded. "My hip fractured in two places and Dr. Simon didn't think I should have kids until the breaks healed properly. I translated that into me being unable to have kids unless he performed surgery. I kind of feel sorry for Dr. Simon having to navigate that conversation."

"I'm sure he understood." Trust Bentley to try to ease her mind. He was focused on her so intently, she couldn't take her eyes off him. Those strong cheekbones. That straight nose. They accented his intelligent, compassionate eyes.

She found and squeezed his hand. "I'm still on the mend. Three more weeks of no ranch work." She bet Rhett would roll his eyes when she told him. "But that means my outlook for motherhood is brighter."

And this was where she expected the birds to sing and Bentley to enthusiastically proclaim that he was willing to pick up where they'd left off.

"I'm happy for you, Cassie," he said gently.

No-no-no. This was all wrong. Cassie fumbled for a clearer explanation. "That day at the gate…I let you go. I didn't want to. But I didn't want to have you fall in love with me if I couldn't be a mom. You are so great with kids, and I couldn't stand in your way of having a family of your own."

"You thought…" Bentley shook his head. "While you were handling a life-and-death emergency just now, I was explaining to Tanner that family isn't made by shared DNA."

Cassie tried to decipher what he was saying. When she'd left town, Tanner had been intent upon pounding Bentley with his fist. It was surprising that they'd sorted it out.

"Don't you see?" His smile was as gentle as his hold on her hand. "Family is made by blood and love, but one could form a family without the other. Steprelatives. Adoption. Your ability to have kids wasn't why I backed away from our relationship."

"But…"

"And you couldn't stop me from falling in love with you, Cassie." Bentley paused, as if he was waiting…

The meaning of his words sank in. "You love me?"

He chuckled. "Looking back, I started to tumble head over heels the day you fed me peach cobbler. And by the time Mia and Quinn dogpiled me, I was certain you were the only woman for me."

"But…" Cassie felt as if she'd fallen into a deep pothole and lost her footing. He loved her and she loved him, so she should be ecstatic. "Then why let Rhett scare you off?"

"He didn't scare me away." Bentley linked their fingers. "Everything around us is complete and utter chaos. You have so much on your plate that I wanted you to find your path without thinking about me."

Oh, this man. Cassie wanted to give him a good shake and then kiss him into his senses. Instead, she stared at their joined hands while he kept on spouting his logical nonsense about why they couldn't be together.

"If this was an experiment, Cassie, I'd have to call it a failure. There isn't just one reason we couldn't move forward. There's fifty." He pointed to the group of Monroes arguing in the Bent Nickel's parking lot. Olivia still clung to Rhett.

"Fifty. Wow. That's a lot." She kissed the back of his hand. "Let's clear away one thing. I'm not hanging up my cowboy hat. Ashley sent my retainer, and Rhett had an unusually bright idea about how to expand the reach of my horse training business."

"I'm happy for you." His attention seemed riveted on the back of his hand. "But I'm not sure that solves every obstacle we face."

Of all the hardheaded things to spout… "If I told you that Rhett found a way for me to train horses and people from anywhere, would that remove another obstacle?"

"It might," he allowed.

"Then let's talk about that thing you said to me the other day…" Cassie kissed his knuckles, smiling when his gaze turned to hers. There was love there. She felt it, knew it deep down in her bones. "You seemed to think that no one in Second Chance needs you. But I present Exhibit A, Olivia Monroe." It was her turn to point across the street to the Monroes.

He seemed reluctant to take his eyes off Cassie, but he dutifully looked where she directed. "I haven't seen Olivia melt down like that since she was two."

"She needs you. And I need you. Absolutely. Wholly. Forever. I know that's only two things out of fifty, but if you give us a chance, I can come up with forty-eight more reasons we need to listen to our hearts, not the logic in your brain."

He didn't say anything. But that was the thing about Bentley—he needed time to think.

Cassie gave him another minute because she couldn't wait any longer to take Olivia's advice and say, "Love isn't a science experiment. But if it were, I'd consider this one a success. I love you, Bentley. I know it came at us hard and fast—"

"Like Tornado Tom." She could swear he almost smiled.

"And although I feel it deep in my fractured bones that we're destined to be together forever, I'm okay saying this is our happily-right-now. I'll give you time to think about our future in between hand-holding and kisses, but please, don't leave."

He was truly smiling now. "What am I going to do with you?"

"Well, there's several months until you Monroes decide what to do with Second Chance. You can spend all that time with me figuring it out and—"

He kissed her. And it was such a tender kiss that Cassie lost her train of thought.

Bentley drew back, only a little, which seemed to be his style—not that she was complaining. "Let's get one thing straight. We love each other."

Cassie nodded.

"And people who love each other work through the hard stuff."

Cassie nodded again, so happy she whooped, which only made Bentley's smile grow and the group of Monroes in the Bent Nickel's parking lot turn their heads.

"So, our happily-in-love today is just the beginning of our happily-ever-after forever."

He nodded. "Got it. I'll have to buy a journal to record my observations and hypotheses."

If there was logic in there, Cassie was far too happy to argue. The important thing was that Bentley was kissing her again, and as far as she could tell, she had many more kisses in her future.

EPILOGUE

"DID YOU EVER IMAGINE?" Smiling, Cassie bumped Rhett's shoulder with her own.

"Nope." Rhett chuckled, bumping her back. "Look at them, smiling like this is the best day ever."

"Yep. And the kids are having a good time, too." Cassie used her phone to snap a photo of Grandpa riding in the engine car, as the train went around the large circular track at the Standing Bear Silver Mine. Her grandfather's gap-toothed smile was infectious.

All the restored train cars were hooked up and painted with colorful scenes, including a bear and its cubs walking through a meadow, a stagecoach racing down a country road, and a woman riding a bucking bull. In total, there were seven cars, including the engine and caboose. Tanner's kids and the Clark boys each rode in a car. Mia waved as she went past. Bentley sat behind her in the caboose, long legs tucked nearly up to his chin. He smiled and waved, too. And then he gave Cassie a contented look, the one that told her he was glad she'd convinced him to listen to his heart.

She snapped a picture of him.

It was mid-October and the first of the restored rides had been delivered. When the snow melted in spring, Bentley promised to have the rest of the carnival rides in good working order.

"I was wrong," Rhett admitted.

"How so?" Cassie looked at him.

"You would have been unhappy with Cowboy Campbell. Bentley's practically perfect for you." Her brother grinned.

"I'd make fun of how bad that joke is, if I wasn't happily in love." She snapped a few more pictures. She wanted to remember this day.

She'd been telling herself that ever since Sonny's heart attack. The kind, caring man was fine and had only recently left town. And Olivia...

Cassie gave her brother a speculative look.

"Next stop, Standing Bear Silver Mine!" Grandpa brought the train to a slow stop. The engine turned off with a well-behaved purr.

"Whoo-whoo!" Bentley stood in the red caboose and held up both arms as if signaling a touchdown. "We forgot to add a train whistle." He climbed down and then lifted Mia out.

She scampered off to cluster about the boys, who alternated between offering great praise for the ride and dismissing it as tame.

Grandpa climbed out of the engine with nary a wobble. "We can always transport the train back to the ranch until we find one. Doesn't seem right to deliver a product that's incomplete."

"No," Cassie said quickly. "The train stays here." The carnival rides had been sold with payment contingent upon delivery. Partial delivery. Partial payment.

"But…" Bentley wrapped his arms around Cassie and drew her close. "I'm going to miss the train. It was my favorite."

"You'd say the same thing if you'd succeeded in fixing the Ferris wheel's rotation mechanism," Cassie teased him, pleased to be in his arms. They'd been together for months now. Cassie had never been happier. And yet, she was waiting to hear what Bentley wanted to do after all the rides were fixed.

"You might be right." Bentley turned, keeping one arm across her shoulders. He led her to the train. "But then again, you might not be. Sit here." He positioned her on the front of the train engine and then stepped back as if considering his work. "Do you trust me?"

"Yes." Cassie didn't hesitate to answer. "I love you."

"I've been thinking…" Bentley began. And then he stopped.

And because Cassie knew him so well, she waited for him to collect his thoughts.

He ran a hand over his thick dark hair, staring at his feet. "I've been trying to figure out how I can build a mechanical shop in town, so we can stay in Second Chance."

Cassie knew this. They'd talked about it plenty of times. The equipment he used to make engines and boats was too large and required a consistent environment in terms of heat and cold.

"But I was thinking about it all wrong." Bentley stepped closer. "I was looking at my future the way you were in the summer, using the parameters of what I used to do for a living." He took her hands. "And what I think I want to do is different, requiring a different kind of shop."

"Tell me more." Cassie used their joined hands to draw him closer and press a quick kiss to his lips.

"I think I want to make toys. There's a lot of innovation in the field," he went on quickly, staring deep into her eyes as if expecting her to laugh.

She'd never laugh at anyone's dream, especially his.

"I'm inspired by children." He glanced over at the five kids running around the mine's porch steps. "And frankly, these last few months with Sonny around. Well, it's practically like hanging out with Jolly Old Saint Nick."

She laughed. "Are you sure that'll make you happy?"

He nodded. "And if it doesn't, I might try my hand at robotics. Although once we're married, I have an excellent idea for a maternity swing, one that helps with back pain and—"

"Hang on." Cassie could barely force the words out because somewhere in that sentence there'd been a mention of marriage that had sucked the air right out of her lungs. *"Once we're married?"*

He dropped to one knee, still holding her hands. "You will marry me, won't you, Cassie? I love you so much, more every day."

"I—"

"Is he proposing?" Rhett called from the porch, where he stood next to their grinning grandfather. "Kids, go ask Uncle Bentley if he's proposing!"

Four precocious boys and one adorable girl rushed over, surrounding them.

Which would have been an unwelcome interruption if they each hadn't been holding a single, long-stemmed red rose, and if they each hadn't extended those roses to her.

"Have you said yes yet?" Mia asked, batting her pretty eyes.

"Of course, she said yes." Quinn thrust his rose toward Cassie's face. "They are in looo-ve."

"That'll do, kids." Standing, Bentley shooed them off, and then faced Cassie and her bouquet of roses. "Too much?"

"Just right." Cassie beamed, clutching the roses to her chest like a beauty queen. "And the answer is yes, love."

"Cassie, that's the best answer I've ever heard. Oh, and about the ring." He cleared his throat. "I was thinking about making us a set. I've always wanted to work with soft metals and—"

She pressed her fingers to his lips, bursting with joy that her life was going to be filled with companionable silences and well-considered words from this man. "You know, you were right about one thing." She removed her hand from his lips and curled it around his neck, drawing him closer as her voice dropped to an intimate whisper. "The train is my favorite ride now, because when I think of you proposing, I'm going to remember this engine and how thoughtful you were and how much—"

He cut off her reply with a kiss, one that promised to love, honor and cherish. All the things Bentley was so very good at.

* * * * *

*For more romances in
The Mountain Monroes miniseries
by Melinda Curtis,
visit www.Harlequin.com today!*

Get 4 FREE REWARDS!

We'll send you 2 FREE Books plus 2 FREE Mystery Gifts.

Love Inspired books feature uplifting stories where faith helps guide you through life's challenges and discover the promise of a new beginning.

FREE Value Over **$20**

YES! Please send me 2 FREE Love Inspired Romance novels and my 2 FREE mystery gifts (gifts are worth about $10 retail). After receiving them, if I don't wish to receive any more books, I can return the shipping statement marked "cancel." If I don't cancel, I will receive 6 brand-new novels every month and be billed just $5.24 each for the regular-print edition or $5.99 each for the larger-print edition in the U.S., or $5.74 each for the regular-print edition or $6.24 each for the larger-print edition in Canada. That's a savings of at least 13% off the cover price. It's quite a bargain! Shipping and handling is just 50¢ per book in the U.S. and $1.25 per book in Canada.* I understand that accepting the 2 free books and gifts places me under no obligation to buy anything. I can always return a shipment and cancel at any time. The free books and gifts are mine to keep no matter what I decide.

Choose one: ☐ **Love Inspired Romance**
Regular-Print
(105/305 IDN GNWC)

☐ **Love Inspired Romance**
Larger-Print
(122/322 IDN GNWC)

Name (please print)

Address   Apt. #

City   State/Province   Zip/Postal Code

Email: Please check this box ☐ if you would like to receive newsletters and promotional emails from Harlequin Enterprises ULC and its affiliates. You can unsubscribe anytime.

Mail to the **Harlequin Reader Service:**
IN U.S.A.: P.O. Box 1341, Buffalo, NY 14240-8531
IN CANADA: P.O. Box 603, Fort Erie, Ontario L2A 5X3

Want to try 2 free books from another series? Call 1-800-873-8635 or visit www.ReaderService.com.

*Terms and prices subject to change without notice. Prices do not include sales taxes, which will be charged (if applicable) based on your state or country of residence. Canadian residents will be charged applicable taxes. Offer not valid in Quebec. This offer is limited to one order per household. Books received may not be as shown. Not valid for current subscribers to Love Inspired Romance books. All orders subject to approval. Credit or debit balances in a customer's account(s) may be offset by any other outstanding balance owed by or to the customer. Please allow 4 to 6 weeks for delivery. Offer available while quantities last.

Your Privacy—Your information is being collected by Harlequin Enterprises ULC, operating as Harlequin Reader Service. For a complete summary of the information we collect, how we use this information and to whom it is disclosed, please visit our privacy notice located at corporate.harlequin.com/privacy-notice. From time to time we may also exchange your personal information with reputable third parties. If you wish to opt out of this sharing of your personal information, please visit readerservice.com/consumerschoice or call 1-800-873-8635. **Notice to California Residents**—Under California law, you have specific rights to control and access your data. For more information on these rights and how to exercise them, visit corporate.harlequin.com/california-privacy.   LIR21R2

Get 4 FREE REWARDS!

We'll send you 2 FREE Books plus 2 FREE Mystery Gifts.

Love Inspired Suspense books showcase how courage and optimism unite in stories of faith and love in the face of danger.

FREE
Value Over
$20

HARLEQUIN SELECTS COLLECTION

19 FREE BOOKS IN ALL!

From Robyn Carr to RaeAnne Thayne to Linda Lael Miller and Sherryl Woods we promise (actually, GUARANTEE!) each author in the Harlequin Selects collection has seen their name on the *New York Times* or *USA TODAY* bestseller lists!

YES! Please send me the **Harlequin Selects Collection**. This collection begins with 3 FREE books and 2 FREE gifts in the first shipment. Along with my 3 free books, I'll also get 4 more books from the Harlequin Selects Collection, which I may either return and owe nothing or keep for the low price of $24.14 U.S./$28.82 CAN. each plus $2.99 U.S./$7.49 CAN. for shipping and handling per shipment*.If I decide to continue, I will get 6 or 7 more books (about once a month for 7 months) but will only need to pay for 4. That means 2 or 3 books in every shipment will be FREE! If I decide to keep the entire collection, I'll have paid for only 32 books because 19 were FREE! I understand that accepting the 3 free books and gifts places me under no obligation to buy anything. I can always return a shipment and cancel at any time. My free books and gifts are mine to keep no matter what I decide.

☐ 262 HCN 5576   ☐ 462 HCN 5576

Name (please print)

Address   Apt. #

City   State/Province   Zip/Postal Code

Mail to the **Harlequin Reader Service:**
IN U.S.A.: P.O. Box 1341, Buffalo, NY 14240-8531
IN CANADA: P.O. Box 603, Fort Erie, Ontario L2A 5X3

Get 4 FREE REWARDS!

We'll send you 2 FREE Books plus <u>plus</u> 2 FREE Mystery Gifts.

FREE Value Over **$20**

Both the **Romance** and **Suspense** collections feature compelling novels written by many of today's bestselling authors.

YES! Please send me 2 FREE novels from the Essential Romance or Essential Suspense Collection and my 2 FREE gifts (gifts are worth about $10 retail). After receiving them, if I don't wish to receive any more books, I can return the shipping statement marked "cancel." If I don't cancel, I will receive 4 brand-new novels every month and be billed just $7.24 each in the U.S. or $7.49 each in Canada. That's a savings of up to 28% off the cover price. It's quite a bargain! Shipping and handling is just 50¢ per book in the U.S. and $1.25 per book in Canada.* I understand that accepting the 2 free books and gifts places me under no obligation to buy anything. I can always return a shipment and cancel at any time. The free books and gifts are mine to keep no matter what I decide.

Choose one: ☐ **Essential Romance**
(194/394 MDN GQ6M)

☐ **Essential Suspense**
(191/391 MDN GQ6M)

Name (please print)

Address   Apt. #

City   State/Province†   Zip/Postal Code

Email: Please check this box ☐ if you would like to receive newsletters and promotional emails from Harlequin Enterprises ULC and its affiliates. You can unsubscribe anytime.

Mail to the **Harlequin Reader Service:**
IN U.S.A.: P.O. Box 1341, Buffalo, NY 14240-8531
IN CANADA: P.O. Box 603, Fort Erie, Ontario L2A 5X3

Want to try 2 free books from another series! Call 1-800-873-8635 or visit www.ReaderService.com.

---

*Terms and prices subject to change without notice. Prices do not include sales taxes, which will be charged (if applicable) based on your state or country of residence. Canadian residents will be charged applicable taxes. Offer not valid in Quebec. This offer is limited to one order per household. Books received may not be as shown. Not valid for current subscribers to the Essential Romance or Essential Suspense Collection. All orders subject to approval. Credit or debit balances in a customer's account(s) may be offset by any other outstanding balance owed by or to the customer. Please allow 4 to 6 weeks for delivery. Offer available while quantities last.

Your Privacy—Your information is being collected by Harlequin Enterprises ULC, operating as Harlequin Reader Service. For a complete summary of the information we collect, how we use this information and to whom it is disclosed, please visit our privacy notice located at corporate.harlequin.com/privacy-notice. From time to time we may also exchange your personal information with reputable third parties. If you wish to opt out of this sharing of your personal information, please visit readerservice.com/consumerschoice or call 1-800-873-8635. **Notice to California Residents**—Under California law, you have specific rights to control and access your data. For more information on these rights and how to exercise them, visit corporate.harlequin.com/california-privacy.

STRS21R2

COMING NEXT MONTH FROM

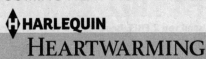

HARLEQUIN
HEARTWARMING

#395 A TEXAN'S CHRISTMAS BABY
Texas Rebels • by Linda Warren

Chase Rebel and Jody Carson wed secretly after high school—then life and bitter hurts forced them apart. Now they're back in Horseshoe, Texas, still married, but no longer sweethearts. Can past secrets leave room for second chances?

#396 A SECRET CHRISTMAS WISH
Wishing Well Springs • by Cathy McDavid

Cowboy Brent Hayes and single mom Maia MacKenzie are perfect for each other. Too bad they work together at the dating service Your Perfect Plus One and aren't allowed to date! Can Christmas and some wedding magic help them take a chance on love?

#397 HER HOLIDAY REUNION
Veterans' Road • by Cheryl Harper

Like her time in the air force, Mira Peters's marriage is over. When she requests signed divorce papers, her husband makes a final request, too. Will a Merry Christmas together in Key West change all of Mira's plans?

#398 TRUSTING THE RANCHER WITH CHRISTMAS
Three Springs, Texas • by Cari Lynn Webb

Veterinarian Paige Palmer learns the ropes of ranch life fast while helping widowed cowboy Evan Bishop. But making a perfect Christmas for his daughter isn't a request she can grant...unless some special holiday time can make a happily-ever-after for three.

Visit
ReaderService.com
Today!

As a valued member of the Harlequin Reader Service, you'll find these benefits and more at ReaderService.com:

- Try 2 free books from any series
- Access risk-free special offers
- View your account history & manage payments
- Browse the latest Bonus Bucks catalog

Don't miss out!

If you want to stay up-to-date on the latest at the Harlequin Reader Service and enjoy more content, make sure you've signed up for our monthly News & Notes email newsletter. Sign up online at ReaderService.com or by calling Customer Service at 1-800-873-8635.

RS20